M000073448

# The Captain's Heiress

## Amy Jarecki

OLIVER HEBER BOOKS

*All rights reserved.*

No part of this publication may be sold, copied, distributed, reproduced or transmitted in any form or by any means, mechanical or digital, including photocopying and recording or by any information storage and retrieval system without the prior written permission of both the publisher, Oliver Heber Books and the author, Amy Jarecki, except in the case of brief quotations embodied in critical articles and reviews.

PUBLISHER'S NOTE: This is a work of fiction. Names, characters, places, and incidents either are the product of the author's imagination or are used fictitiously. Any resemblance to actual persons, living or dead, business establishments, events, or locales is entirely coincidental.

Copyright © 2022 Amy Jarecki

Book Cover Design by: Dar Albert, Wicked Smart Designs

Published by Oliver-Heber Books

0 9 8 7 6 5 4 3 2 1

# 1

## EARLY SUMMER, 1813

When laboring to piece together ancient, brittle fragments, a single error could render an entire tablet untranslatable. Which was why Isabella Harcourt had resituated her writing table in the window embrasure and covered it with white linen. Not only was she making the best use of the sunlight, day after day, she toiled alone in her quest to uncover the story from the tablets she had unearthed among the Roman ruins in the southeast corner of her father's estate.

With her quizzing glass in hand, she curled forward as she searched for a piece about the size and shape of her little fingernail. "*Aha*, have I found you?"

After selecting a pair of surgeon's tweezers from their place at the side of the table, she held the quizzing glass steady while carefully plucking the fragment from the white cloth peppered with many of the same bits and pieces. Isabella gripped her elbows against her sides to hold her hands as steady as possible while she moved the tiny piece above the ancient wooden tablet and carefully placed it into the gap.

"Not quite..." she mumbled, lightly tapping the piece with the point of the tweezers until it slipped into place, or at least it seemed as if it had done. To verify, she leaned nearer with her glass and examined the fragment's edges. "Very close fit, indeed."

She sat back and examined the Latin word the sliver had completed: *nudus*.

Though Isabella was a very sensible woman, her face warmed considerably as she stared at the word that, translated into English, meant nude or naked. Moreover, her words came out a bit breathless as she interpreted the sentence: "*When I close my eyes, I see you naked before sleep comes to me.*"

Isabella flicked open her fan and cooled her cheeks. "My goodness, sir, you weren't shy about expressing the depth of your love for your wife, were you?"

Behind her, soft knock resounded from her bedchamber door before it clicked open.

Jolting upright, she shifted a bit of paper over the tablet—not that anyone at the manor would care overmuch about the ancient Roman's love letter to his wife, but being discovered translating the word *nudus* was disconcerting all the same.

"There you are," said Papa, which was rather odd. At breakfast this morning, Isabella had mentioned that she planned to work on translating the tablets today. She worked on them most days, really, as they had become somewhat of an obsession.

Carefully, she placed her tools on the right edge of her writing table, side by side, their handles perfectly parallel, at least as perfect as one could possibly manage. Then, after pushing her chair away, over her shoulder she regarded her father, who had moved in front of the hearth, standing with his hands clasped atop his waistcoat. "I thought I'd find you here, my dear."

"Yes, I suppose it was hardly a guess, given that we discussed today's agenda over coddled eggs and toast."

"Indeed," Papa said, then cleared his throat and consulted his pocket watch. "Well...*ah*...you are aware that I have always wanted what is best for you, are you not, my dearest?"

Isabella's first hint that something was off was his mention of finding her, but now that Papa had referred to her as dearest, an endearment he rarely used, not to mention he failed to look her in the eye, Isabella feared the worst—had someone died? One of the servants? A close relation?

She pushed to her feet and gave her father her full attention. Kingston Harcourt was a former officer in the army and always looked everyone in the eye, to the point where he frequently rendered newcomers most uncomfortable.

"I can concur with that," she said rather uncommittedly as her mind riffled through her childhood, much of which was spent alone, or at least without her father in residence at the West Sussex manor, during which time she often wondered if he cared about her at all. Regrettably, she'd never known her mother, who had died in childbirth. Though Isabella wasn't exactly sure if it was in her best interests to be raised by nursemaids, tutors, and governesses while Papa was executing his duty for king and country, or if her upbringing was more aptly in Britain's best interests, arguing such a point would be senseless. The fact of the matter was her father believed he had always acted with her welfare in mind, and there was never any use debating otherwise.

"Good, good." Papa turned and stared up at the portrait of Isabella's paternal grandmother above the mantel, loudly clearing his throat. "I have decided it is time for you to marry."

Suddenly rendered speechless and dry-mouthed, Isabella gaped at her father's back, her skin growing hot and clammy.

*Surely he misspoke.*

Had Papa just taken a few nips from his flask? It was a bit early for imbibing in liquor—even for him. When her father neither turned nor expounded upon his declaration, she snorted with a sardonic laugh. "Marry? Good heavens, it has been years since we broached *that* subject."

Still, she hadn't imagined he'd just blurted out that he *had decided* she needed to marry. Isabella crossed her arms over her midriff and paced several steps before collapsing onto the settee. At the ripe age of five and twenty, she was well and truly a spinster. Yes, she'd endured a London Season, but had fallen quite short of the *ton*'s expectations for the daughter of a knight. She wasn't a particularly graceful dancer, she was positively abominable at flirting, and more than once she'd found herself at a complete loss for words when addressed by a courtier. Oh, and yes, she had learned that when attending a ball, one did not exactly encourage a gentleman's affections when one turned and fled to the women's withdrawing room.

"It is time to seriously consider it again, my dear." Papa pulled a letter from inside his doublet and ran his fingers over the creased parchment. "I have been exchanging correspondence with a gentleman in America for some time."

A stone the size of a cannonball lodged in the pit of Isabella's stomach—or was it her throat? "About me?" she squeaked, realizing the cannonball was truly gagging her, and praying Papa had been writing to the

American about the breeding of bantam chickens or any topic that did not include her.

"Indeed. His name is Mr. Arent Schuyler. He has amassed quite a fortune...and..."

"And...?" Isabella's palms grew moist. Perhaps it was best if her father didn't continue this discourse. "Has Mr. Schuyler come to England?"

Papa tapped the missive against his palm. "No. He is in Georgia."

"The state of Georgia? In America?" No, her blathering didn't exactly sound intelligent, but her father had just come into her bedchamber and told her he had decided she would marry and then mentioned corresponding with possibly a complete stranger, across the Atlantic Ocean.

"That's what I've been trying to say. Mr. Schuyler is a well-respected *older* gentleman who is seeking a well-mannered English wife with whom he can start a family. Did I mention he is well-to-do?"

"Yes, you did say that he had amassed a fortune. How, may I ask?" If Papa uttered a single word about the slave trade, she would explode.

"Silver."

"Oh." Isabella folded her shaking, sweaty hands. "Oh my."

"Quite." Papa finally met her gaze. "He has offered a very generous finder's fee, one that will enable me to live out the rest of my days in comfort."

This was new. They'd always lived comfortably, if not frugally, at the manor, and never once had her father mentioned the coffers might be a bit sparse. "But do you not have a pension from your time in the army?"

"I do—however, it is hardly enough to keep this estate afloat. Also, I must add that once I am gone, your cousin will inherit, and though he's a decent man, you will be best served by marrying Mr. Schuyler."

*For the love of daisies, Papa is as sober as a stone and as sane as he had seemed to be at breakfast.*

Isabella placed a hand over her mouth, her mind darting through a number of plausible arguments, and quickly settled on the most sensible. "Surely the gentleman will want to meet me first. One doesn't usually exchange a few letters with a woman's father and decide he's in love."

"Love has nothing to do with it. The man was quite taken with my descriptions of you—he was even impressed by your fanatical obsession with those ridiculous tablets."

"Ridiculous? Papa, you helped me excavate the site, and you did not think they were ridiculous when we found them."

"Yes, well, that was before you cast every other interest aside and shut yourself away in this chamber. Those tablets have become your ruin."

She pulled a pillow embroidered with roses onto her lap and hugged it. "So, Mr. Schuyler believes me ruined?"

"Of course not. He has made an offer of marriage, which I have accepted on your behalf. Furthermore, I have had the good fortune of corresponding with the Duke of Dunscaby—as you are aware, his father was one of my closest friends."

Unable to respond, Isabella gave a cautious nod.

"As it turns out, His Grace has established quite an enterprising venture for his brothers, the second eldest captaining his own ship." Obviously oblivious to the expression of horror Isabella had fixed upon her face, Papa rocked back on his heels and grinned. "Fortunately, Lord Gibb will soon be taking a shipment of whisky to America, and I have reserved a berth for you on his ship, the *Prosperity*."

Holy help, the gentleman from Georgia was not intending to travel to England. This state of affairs could not grow worse. "You're sending me to America?" she squeaked, clutching the pillow so tightly the seams were surely about to burst.

"Yes. Have you heard nothing I've said? Come, Issy, this is a good match with a mature man who I am quite confident will treat you well."

"What if after I arrive we discover we are not suited?"

"How can you be so negative at a time when you ought to be over the moon? Good heavens, my dear, I have put forth a great deal of effort to secure this betrothal on your behalf. The least you can do is express your appreciation. Moreover, I expect you to apply yourself to this marriage with the same fervor you have applied to your tablets."

Isabella looked to her pillow while a tear dripped onto the black velvet. This was the most flabbergasting news of her life. Not only were hundreds of questions whirling around in her mind, she was nauseated, and quite possibly about to regurgitate her breakfast, and Papa wanted her to fling all caution out the window and shout for joy?

She was about to be ferried across the Atlantic Ocean on a ship laden with whisky, where, after suffering the perilous crossing, she would meet a stranger who, with a stroke of his pen, had convinced her father that he owned a silver mine and would treat her like a queen.

*What if he owns a tar pit and only claims to be a silver*

*miner? I'll be sailing on the* Prosperity? *The* Deprivation *is more apt.*

She glanced up, regarding her father out of the corner of her eye. "How much time do I have before I must set to packing my things?"

"I'm glad you asked, my dear." Papa headed for the door. "We shall be taking the carriage to Dunscaby's estate in Musselburgh—it abuts the Firth of Forth, where Lord Gibb's ship will meet us." He rested his hand on the latch and glanced over his shoulder. "We leave at dawn."

"Dawn?" she asked, her gaze darting to her tablets. "That's not enough time."

The door closed, only to be reopened by Maribel, Isabella's lady's maid, who slipped inside, her expression bereft.

Casting the pillow aside, Isabella pushed to her feet. "How long have you known?"

"Your father informed the serving staff moments before he came up here. 'Tis pure insanity below stairs. The coachman is already preparing the carriage and a wagon. The footmen will be bringing your trunks shortly."

Isabella clapped a hand over her mouth, tears splashing into her cheeks as she closed her eyes. "I cannot believe Papa would do this to me."

"It is a shock to us all, miss." Maribel, who had been Isabella's ever-present companion since they were children, wrapped her in an embrace. "I'll be with you—never fear. We shall face this together."

Unable to hold in her sobs, Isabella buried her face in the maid's shoulder. "Thank you."

"There, there. We must make haste." Maribel smoothed her palm up and down Isabella's back. "You do intend to take your tablets, yes?"

"Oh, a-a-absolutely. Before anything else, they must go," Isabella managed between sobs. Gathering her wits, she pushed away and headed for her secretary. "My notes, journals, and books must all be packed. The finished tablets need to be crated with utmost care to ensure the glass does not break, no matter h-how rough the seas."

She ran her finger along the frame of the first tablet she had translated. "We shan't be leaving these here."

"Of course not."

Maribel removed the frame, but Isabella immediately took it from her. "I want to pack the tablets myself. Please tend to my clothing and effects."

# 2

"Drop anchor!" Captain Gibb MacGalloway shouted, pleased with his chosen mooring in the Firth of Forth off the Musselburgh coast. He'd strategically nestled his sizable barque between a schooner and a larger brig where his ship ought not be immediately recognized.

He opened his spyglass and panned it across the scene occurring in the private park behind Newhailes, not the largest, but his brother's favorite of the ducal estates. Martin, the patriarch of the family and Duke of Dunscaby, had sent word that Gibb was to sail into the firth after delivering the shipment of American sharecropper cotton to the MacGalloway mill and loading scores of barrels of MacGalloway whisky into the *Prosperity's* hull.

"It appears there's quite a gathering," said Archie MacLean, quartermaster, and best mate a captain ever had.

"Aye, a gathering of giggling imps." Still peering through his spyglass, Gibb spotted his two youngest sisters Modesty and Grace. They babbled among a plethora of young ladies, whom he would definitely avoid. The wee chits all wore their hair down or in pigtails with ringlets, which meant every last female was far too young to be trifled with.

A bit farther to the left, Gibb also recognized Miss Hay, the lassie's governess, who was doling out slips of paper, after which the girls dispersed in dozens of directions.

In the distance, ample quantities of white muslin moved among the columns of the Summerhouse, a Romanesque Palladian bridge built across the curling pond—used for the sport of curling during winter but now being transformed to a watery refuge by a flock of swans. Inside the Summerhouse, Gibb easily picked out his mother, holding court in the center of a party of women who, he guessed, might be the mothers of the gaggle—and yet another gathering of females to be avoided at all costs.

Spotting a flicker of white, he shifted the glass off the port bow, where he found the view a great deal more interesting.

*Hmm. Who might this be?*

Though the woman's face was hidden by a bonnet, judging by her posture and lithe movements, she was not a child. The fact that she was sitting off alone beneath the great sycamore was a good indication that she was not one of the mothers in the Summerhouse.

Perhaps he might have a bit of fun before Martin got hold of him. The duke was forever concocting new ventures of which Gibb was expected to approve instantly and exuberantly. Often, said ventures required a monumental effort of rearranging and posed a royal pain in Gibb's backside. Nonetheless, such endeavors usually fattened his coffers, and for that he was eternally grateful.

He closed his spyglass and looked to Archie. "Lower my skiff, then give the men a day's leave."

"Your skiff is already waiting and manned, Cap'n. And I'll grant leave to all except those on watch."

"Excellent, and tell the crew not to step beyond Fisherrow Harbour, else we might end up sailing without them. I dunna intend on remaining here any longer than necessary."

"Aye, sir."

Gibb had the crew pull his skiff ashore in the northeast corner of the estate—behind the tree line, where he wouldn't be seen. After letting the men know they could find a schooner of ale by walking five minutes along the shore, he skirted down the line of trees until he spotted the sycamore he used to climb with his brothers when he was a lad—the same tree now providing shade to the recluse who, quite obviously, was avoiding the celebrations.

From behind the enormous tree's trunk, he watched the woman for a time as she turned the pages of her book and looked out to sea now and again, shaking her head and sighing. But dash it if he couldn't see her face. The brim of her bonnet was akin to a trumpet, and no matter which way she turned her head, the blasted hat refused to even reveal the color of her hair.

The woman's neck was long, her shoulders femininely petite, and she wore a pink shawl lightly draped over her elbows. Well, the only way to determine if she was a beauty or nay was to introduce himself.

Shielded by the trees, he hastened up a few yards, then stepped out and approached as if he had never been right behind the lass. "Either your book is extremely riveting or you're as averse to crowds as I."

The lady startled, jolting subtly before she looked up. Black hair with tight curls framed an oval face.

With little color in her cheeks, her mien was a tad plain, but pleasant enough for Gibb to idle away the afternoon while avoiding his brother.

"I'm not terribly fond of crowds," said the lass, her eyes narrowing as if she were trying to place him. "Her Grace is hosting a house party for her daughters and their friends, and I'm afraid I'm a little too old for scavenger hunts."

Gibb slid onto the bench beside her without so much as an introduction. The mere thought made him grin. He detested polite society and the gutted rules they adhered to almost more than he detested Napoleon. *Almost.* Napoleon was a tyrant who needed to be introduced to a guillotine.

"So, Lady Modesty and Lady Grace are hunting treasure, are they?" he asked.

"Yes, in the stables, of all places. Though I daresay the stables at Newhailes are large enough to house a dozen families."

She wasn't wrong. The duke required ample space in which to store all his carriages as well as his horses. Gibb chuckled. "At least the park is quiet." Judging by the numbers of young girls he'd seen they must have sounded like a flock of laying hens before they'd been dispersed.

The lass smiled, albeit sadly. "It is."

Gibb hesitated for a heartbeat. Goodness, her eyes were dark—almost as black as her hair. And why the blazes would a woman be melancholy when visiting Newhailes? For visitors, the manse and grounds were akin to stepping into a storybook. And this woman wasn't even wearing mourning.

"Och, 'tis a fine day for reading." He leaned in and glanced at the page. "What has you entertained? A love story with a dashing hero and a wilting violet?"

She showed him the cover. "*Mythic Early History of Italy and its People*. No white knights and damsels, I'm afraid."

Perhaps the reading material was a bit too dreary for the lass—or perhaps not. Gibb crossed his legs and sat back, his kilt slipping up his thigh a bit. He didn't bother to push it down. He rarely did. Once he left the King's Navy, he'd donned a kilt and hadn't put on a pair of trousers since.

"Are you something of an antiquarian?" he asked.

"You could say that. My father and I uncovered a villa on his estate in West Sussex, and I've been captivated by Roman history ever since."

"Fascinating." He looked at the woman again, wishing he could pull the pink ribbon securing her bonnet and remove it from her head. On closer inspection, her look was remarkable—not a classical beauty, but complex, with a small chin and cheeks that needed to be broad enough to accommodate those enormous eyes.

Gibb didn't often slide onto benches with gentlewomen and engage them in conversation. In fact, since he joined the navy, he hadn't interacted with them much at all. Most of his contact with women consisted of discreet interludes, usually above a tavern not far from any given shore. A woman who enjoyed antiquity was something novel indeed.

He tapped the book. "Tell me something riveting about *Mythic Early History of Italy and its People*."

She smoothed her hand over the cover. "I do believe you are teasing me, sir."

"Not at all. As a matter of fact, as we were riding across the border into England, my brother and I once took a bit of a detour and explored some ruins near Haddington—decidedly Roman, they were."

Lovely black eyebrows disappeared under the bonnet, as if he'd just ignited a spark somewhere in the recesses of this bluestocking's mind. "What did you find?"

"A great deal of rubble atop stone walls—charred as if there had been a fire."

"How intriguing." Miss Raven Hair leaned forward. "Did you report your find to the Society of Antiquaries?"

"Nay, a sheep farmer and his dog decided we were trespassing." Gibb chuckled at the memory. Little did the scrappers know they were chasing after the eldest sons of the Duke of Dunscaby. Good Lord, had the old farmer been a bit more accurate with his musket, Gibb mightn't be here at the moment—that or he'd be the duke, God forbid.

He pointed to a pair of archery targets standing alone sporting not a single arrow. "I take it archery wasna popular among the wee lassies."

"I don't recall any of them giving it an attempt. Though there was quite a to-do with battledore and shuttlecock—at least until the scavenger hunt was announced."

Gibb spotted the quivers of arrows and bows up along the tree line. "Do you enjoy archery?"

"I do." The raven-haired lass set her book aside and sat a bit taller. "I'll have you know I was the West Sussex Fair champion of eighteen-oh-seven."

"I am duly impressed," he said. Six years ago, this woman was most likely about his sister Grace's age—or near enough. "If you're a champion, then how about a wee wager?"

"Are you an archer, sir?"

"More or less. Have I taken archery lessons? Yes. But I must admit, I havena won any awards. That puts me at a significant disadvantage," he said, giving her a wink. Gibb could expertly shoot just about any weapon invented by man, be it bow and arrow, a musket, pistols, or a slingshot. He stood and offered his hand. "Come, the day is far too fine to sit idle."

She placed her gloved fingers in his palm. "But did you not just say it was fine for reading?"

"That was before I saw the targets." He tugged her to her feet, surprised to find that she was quite petite in stature, her head not quite coming to his shoulder. "Now, how about that wager?"

"What sort of wager?" she asked as they stopped at the quivers of arrows. She picked up a bow and tested it for tautness.

"Hmm. It ought to be something verra dear." He drummed his fingers atop the MacGalloway brooch at his shoulder while a plethora of ideas rifled through his mind. It was then that he noticed her lips—pert, pink, a wee bit pouty. "I ken. If I win, you shall give me a kiss."

She released the string and let it twang. "I beg your pardon? What sort of gentleman wagers a kiss? I hardly know you."

"You ken me well enough. I like Roman history and dislike crowds. What else is there?"

"A great deal more, mark me."

He handed her an arrow, then caught her by the wrist as she took it. "What say you, lass?" he asked, gazing into those enormous black eyes. He was a sea captain first, and though he'd been raised as the "spare son" in a ducal house, he'd never completely embraced the rules of etiquette—unless he could use them to his advantage. "I've issued a challenge. Have you the courage to accept?"

Licking her lips, Miss Raven Hair cast a nervous

glance toward the house. "A-a small peck, perhaps? And no one must see."

"Verra well." Gibb liked that just fine—no meaningful kiss ought to be imparted in public. "And you, madam? What do you wager?"

The lassie's nostrils flared as she looked him from head to toe. "If *you* win, I should like to know your name, sir."

A wry grin stretched his lips. There this woman stood, completely aware that he'd sidestepped every convention of propriety, and yet she would only know his name if she won their competition. Perhaps a wee bit of mischievousness smoldered in the heart of this history-reading bluestocking?

"Why were you sitting alone?" he asked.

She loaded her bow and glanced at him over her shoulder. "I have a great deal on my mind."

Gibb smirked. She most likely had a younger sister in the group of scavenger hunters who was as much of a hellion as Grace or Modesty. Miss Raven Hair released her arrow. It fell short of the target by a good yard. She immediately turned, blushing most adorably. Ah yes, with a bit of color, there was a striking elegance to her look. "Of course, you'll allow two shots for practice."

He let his gaze dip down the length of her muslin day gown and back up. "Inventing rules as we go along?" he asked, his tongue slipping to the corner of his mouth.

"Not at all." She tossed her head, oblivious to his appreciation. "I've never used this bow before."

"I'll grant you that." Gibb bowed. "Two shots for the lady."

"You may have two as well."

Her second arrow hit the edge of the target, but

nowhere near close enough. He rubbed his hands, pleased to see his kiss might just be a certainty.

Except there seemed to be a bit of a hullaballoo in the Summerhouse. Had Mama spotted him?

"Ready?" he asked, trying to hurry the lass along.

She pulled back the string and homed in on the target. "Best of three?"

"By all means, but you must shoot all three arrows now."

"Are you suddenly in a hurry?"

*In a word, aye.*

"I think the lassies are nearing the end of their hunt in the stables," he said.

The woman fired her three arrows, one in the bull's-eye and the other two outliers. She offered him the bow, smiling as if happy with her result. "Your turn, sir."

Two footmen were now in conversation with Mama. He'd best hurry. "Three arrows," he said. He loaded one and hit the bull's-eye, then quickly dispatched the other two, much the same as the first.

"Unbelievable." The lady stood with her fists upon her hips. "I daresay you are a far better archer than you let on."

"I dunna recall saying I was *unskilled.*" But Gibb was a sailor, and he was no stranger to wagering or winning. He always wagered to win. Accepting a bet with questionable odds was fool's play. A grin played in one corner of his mouth as he grasped Miss Raven Hair by the elbow and escorted her into the thicket behind an enormous oak. "I wish I had time to dally about, but it appears my attention will soon be commanded by my brother, or my mother, and quite possibly my sisters."

Gibb placed his palms either side of her face—

silken skin, a warm thrumming beneath. "Och, ye are lovely, lass."

Dipping his chin, Gibb moved his lips toward her pert, upturned mouth. There was no time to prepare her with sweet words. Closing the distance, he took her mouth, intending a quick, gentle peck. He didn't plan for anything more than a hasty caress, long enough to ignite a spark, but short enough not to be caught.

And then Miss Raven Hair sighed—a soft, barely audible, quivering sigh.

*Holy mother*, the sound was like an arrow thrust into his heart. Gibb caught it with his mouth and pressed his lips tighter to hers—to her closed lips accompanied by her rigid posture. Did this woman truly abhor kissing, or did she have absolutely no idea what a kiss was?

Inhaling the scent of vanilla from the south seas, Gibb intended to find out. He moved his arms around her and pulled her petite, luscious body close, imparting a wealth of kissing expertise and sweeping his tongue across those lovely, pouty lips, requesting entry while he slid his fingers upward and kneaded the silken hair at her nape.

With her next sigh, she opened for him, not terribly wide, but far enough for his tongue to slip inside and stroke deeply, sampling the taste of lemonade and something sweeter—perhaps an iced tea cake?

Miss Raven Hair melted against him, kindling an odd flicker in Gibb's chest—a feeling he'd never before experienced—a feeling he'd like to explore.

"Lord Gibb?" one of the footman hollered. By the sound of his voice, the man was approximately fifteen paces away.

Damnation, Gibb had run out of time. After he

straightened, he took just a moment to gaze into those black eyes and commit them to memory. This was the last time he'd ever see this woman, and he didn't want to forget. "Do not follow me," he growled, keeping his voice low. It was a risk to be alone like this—somewhat of a risk for Gibb, a grave risk for her—which made the interlude all the more stirring. "Skirt up the tree line and do not step into sight until you reach the house."

Gibb moved from behind the tree and grinned at the footman he'd known since boyhood. "Och, Fergus, how long has it been?"

The old fellow craned his neck, trying to peer beyond the brush. "Far too long, m'lord."

Gibb grasped Fergus by the elbow and started toward the Summerhouse, buying time for Miss Raven Hair to escape. "So, tell me, how is my brother faring?"

# 3

The best thing about returning home was being the recipient of the happiness and love on his mother's face. The worst thing was being ushered toward the Summerhouse and a flock of mothers while his sisters came running from the opposite direction with their friends. "Gibb, my dear boy!" Mama exclaimed, clasping her hands over her heart. "I do not believe I'll ever grow accustomed to seeing you arrive by sea."

He enfolded her into his arms and kissed her forehead. She smelled the same as always—of lavender, sugar, and home. "Och, 'tis good to see you."

"And better to have you home." The Dowager Duchess of Dunscaby turned to her friends. "Have you met my son Lord Gibb MacGalloway, the sea captain?"

He gave a respectful bow. "Ladies, I trust you are enjoying your house party."

"'Tis a luncheon," said Modesty, the youngest and most mischievous in the family, tugging him by the elbow, then throwing her arms around him. "Mama is preparing us for when we are invited to a *real* house party."

He swept a knuckle over her freckled nose. "My

lands, ye've grown like a stalk of corn since I last saw you. How old would ye be now?"

A proud grin played upon her lips. "Thirteen."

"Thirteen? How the devil did that happen?" He looked to Grace, a classic beauty, who, much to a brother's chagrin, grew lovelier every time he saw her. He tugged Grace in as well and embraced them both. "And I'll wager you're fifteen, aye?"

"Sixteen, mind you," she said with a haughty edge. "Nearly ready to be introduced at court."

Gibb kissed her temple. "And you'll be the darling of the *ton*, when the time comes."

"Yes," Mama agreed. "Though her presentation at court cannot come fast enough for Grace, I'm quite happy to remain in Newhailes for a time."

As if on cue, Giles the butler approached and cleared his throat. "Felicitations, Lord Gibb. Forgive my interruption, but His Grace has asked to see you forthwith."

"Och aye? I've barely stepped ashore and have already been summoned by our all-powerful brother." Gibb gave Mama a wink. "If you'll please excuse me, I'll leave you to return to your guests."

As he walked toward the manse, Modesty followed and clamped on to his arm. "How long will you be staying this time?"

"I'm afraid not long—I've a hull full of whisky to take to America."

"But how are you to marry if you're always at sea?"

"Perhaps I havena any plans to marry."

"Why not?" Together they climbed the curved steps leading to the enormous double doors. "Miss Hay says it is the duty of all gently bred ladies to marry and provide their husbands with heirs. How am

I supposed to find my match if all the good men are off on adventures like you?"

"Believe me, there will always be plenty of men on the marriage mart. Besides, I'm merely a second son—not nearly as good a catch as Martin."

"I think you're a fine catch—you're in command of your own ship, and you're as handsome as Marty for certain."

While Giles opened the door, Gibb flicked one of her red curls. "Thank you for the vote of confidence. If I should ever be in port long enough to seek out a wife, I'll be sure to let everyone ken I'm as handsome as the duke."

She giggled and gave him a playful swat on his shoulder. "At least ye havena lost your sense of humor."

Gibb hoped not. Since he'd been summoned only moments after Mama sent the footman after him, his present state of humor was rather tenuous. What did Martin have in store for him now? If he considered the duke's bidding in a positive light, his brother would present him with a new, larger ship. Perhaps a fleet of merchant vessels for him to command? Now that was something dreams were made of.

Before his imagination ran away, Giles opened the door to the library and ushered him inside. "Lord Gibb, Your Grace."

"Och, there he is," said Martin, pushing up from his chair and gesturing to an older man, who stood as well. "Brother, surely you remember our father's dear friend, Sir Kingston Harcourt."

Gibb bowed respectfully. "How could I forget—as Papa put it, you spared him from the bite of a cobra in Egypt during the Second Coalition."

Sir Kingston chuckled. "To this day I am convinced

the snake was intentionally placed in your father's tent by the French."

"'Tis after two o'clock," Martin said, moving toward the sideboard. "Can I tempt you to a glass of MacGalloway's finest?"

Gibb licked his lips. "Dear brother, I'm a sailor. You can tempt me with such an offer any time of the day or night."

"I'll not argue either," said Sir Kingston.

In familial custom, the duke poured for all three men.

"How is Julia and the bairn?" asked Gibb as they sat in the wing-backed chairs at the rear of the library—the one with a low table sporting a chessboard with ivory and ebony pieces.

Martin grinned, pride gleaming in his eyes. "Both in good health and high spirits."

Gibb chuckled. His brother's wife was a spitfire for certain. "I'll wager they are."

Since they were in the company of Sir Kingston, Martin mentioned no more about family antics. "I've a favor to ask."

Of course those words came as no surprise, though the duke's favor requests were usually another taboo topic when there was a guest present. Martin wasn't in the habit of discussing family matters with anyone outside of kin. Gibb crossed his legs. "I thought you might be angling at something, else you would have let Mama and her friends regale me for a wee bit longer."

Martin held up his glass and examined the amber liquid in the beam of light streaming in through the twenty-foot window. "Ye ken I've always been one to extend an olive branch when necessary."

Gibb couldn't argue. If it weren't for the duke, he'd

still be in the King's Navy fighting Napoleon. "I'll grant you that."

His Grace glanced to their guest. "I need you to ferry Sir Kingston's daughter to Georgia."

Gibb blinked, several objections coming to mind, the first being the most important. "I beg your pardon? The *Prosperity* is not a passenger ship. She's a merchant vessel. The food is plain—comforts are few. And though my men are hardworking tars, many of them were raised in the gutter. Besides the fact that no women are allowed aboard, the fellas wouldna ken what to do with a gentlewoman if presented with one."

"Aye, I understand your concerns, but it is only for one passage...unless you're telling me that you canna handle your crew."

Wincing at his brother's jab, Gibb uncrossed his legs and leaned forward. "I dinna say that at all. I'm saying the men are bleedin' sailors—they will forever behave and speak as such."

"Isabella is a very sensible woman and keeps to herself for the most part," said Sir Kingston. "I'm quite certain you'll hardly know she's aboard your ship."

Gibb swilled his whisky. No wonder the chap was sitting in on this discussion—having him here made it impossible to argue. He'd know the female was there for certain, as would every male aboard. "I'll have no choice but to move her into one of the officers' cabins."

"Aye," Martin agreed. "And she's traveling with her lady's maid."

"Good God, another bloody female?"

Sir Kingston stretched his neck, tugging his neckcloth. "Would two not be better than one—companionship and whatnot?"

Gibb scowled—now he'd be giving two officers the boot, because there was no chance in hell he'd put a lady's maid in a hammock below decks.

"Come, I dunna oft ask for favors," said Martin. "And this one is ever so important to Papa's old friend—a decorated war hero, mind you. You must promise me to look after the lass and see that she makes it to America healthy and happy."

Och, now it was promises Gibb would be making? He took a deep breath. "Of course. I'll look after Miss Harcourt and see her safely delivered to—" Gibb tossed back the remains of his whisky and forced a smile. "I beg your pardon, but Georgia's coastline runs about a hundred miles. Where, exactly, am I to deliver the lady? Will she disembark first, or shall I offload the shipment of whisky in Virginia beforehand?"

"I'd think you ought to sail to Georgia first, then complete the remainder of your voyage as planned. I'll write to her fiancé to let him know she'll be arriving in..." Martin looked to Sir Kingston and spread his palms.

"Savannah."

"There you have it. Savannah." Martin flicked a tuft of lint from his kilt and eyed Gibb. "Approximately how long do you believe it will take you to reach Savannah?"

Of course, everyone present knew sailing across the Atlantic was nowhere as predictable as driving a coach from one end of Britain to another. "The average sail time is a month—a few weeks if a sailor is lucky; longer if he is not. The wind's as fickle as a woman."

"I do believe Mr. Schuyler maintains rooms in Savannah," said Sir Kingston.

Gibb stood and helped himself to another glass

from his brother's crystal decanter. "If that is so, perhaps it would be best if I offloaded the shipment of whisky first. That would allow me to send word from Norfolk to your daughter's fiancé ahead of our arrival."

Sir Kingston clapped his hands together. "Come to think on it, I do believe that would be best. Capital idea."

Gibb tossed back the entire glass of whisky and wiped his lips. "Well then, if you gentlemen will excuse me, I've a pair of cabins to rearrange."

"You're leaving without saying hello to Julia or James?" asked Martin.

"Are they in the next room?" Gibb asked, though he knew they were not—the next room housed Dunscaby's steward.

Martin pointed upward. "Most likely in the nursery."

"Verra well, I'll pop my head in for a moment, but I'm not about to take any chances of being mobbed by Mama's luncheon party. I'll slip out the rear door within ten minutes." Gibb looked to Sir Kingston. "Please inform Miss Harcourt that we'll be sailing at half nine in the morning. I'll send a skiff to fetch the lady and her maid."

Martin moved to his writing table and picked up his quill. "She'll need more than one."

"I beg your pardon?" asked Gibb.

The duke flicked open the silver cover on his inkwell. "Miss Harcourt is traveling with five trunks."

God's bones, this task was growing more daunting by the minute. "My ship only has one skiff. I'd be grateful if you'd engage your wherry to transport her effects to the hull of the *Prosperity*."

Dipping his quill, Martin gave a dismissive nod. "Done."

Isabella sat in the stern of the skiff, hardly able to look at the enormous ship looming in the water ahead. *He* was surely watching—either from the row of windows at the rear of the barque, or from the decks above. Most likely, the Duke of Dunscaby's brother had enjoyed a good laugh at her expense.

Yesterday she'd heard the footman clearly enough —"*Lord Gibb*," alias Captain Gibb, commander of the *Prosperity*, which had been sequestered to ferry Isabella to her doom, a voyage that would take weeks.

She, Isabella Harcourt, had never in all her days kissed a man or behaved so brazenly. The blackguard had tricked her into kissing him. Worse, she'd wanted him to do so. After all, her father had promised her hand in marriage to a miner who, it turned out, happened to be twice her age, had never married, and lived in the far reaches of Georgia.

Heaven's stars, was Mr. Schuyler so entirely hideous that he could not find a well-bred, obedient wife somewhere on the continent of North America?

To ease her trepidation, Papa had given her the letters Mr. Schuyler had written—though the contents provided little reassurance. The miner's handwriting was rather unschooled, though his prose managed to adequately describe his mine on the Savannah River and the house he had built nearby. Papa, however, had never provided a satisfactory answer as to why he replied to Mr. Schuyler's advertisement in the *Gazette*.

*I still cannot believe my father responded to the man. Had I known he was so anxious to be rid of me, I might have flirted with the vicar's son at church, or anything aside from agreeing to marry a complete stranger in a land reported to be rife with convicts and rebels.*

Now she was about to board a ship captained by a rake, a man who had tricked her into kissing him. And merciful macaroons, what a kiss it had been. Who knew kissing could be so entirely consuming? Isabella highly doubted Mr. Schuyler would kiss her thus. And she highly doubted she'd ever again be the recipient of such an erotic display of sexuality.

When she thought about it analytically, the entire encounter had been obnoxious and absurd.

From this moment onward, she decided to lock the experience away in the recesses of her mind and pretend the kiss had never happened. Isabella would forget that the roguish captain had wrapped his arms around her and drawn her flush against his extraordinarily hard chest and pressed his extraordinarily soft lips to hers. She would not think about his wayward tongue flavored with delicious spices as it swept into her mouth and performed a quadrille—a dance hypnotic enough to turn her entire body into a boneless, mindless heap of jelly.

Beside her, Maribel grasped Isabella's hand. "I know this whole ordeal is an awful muddle, but not to worry. I believe in happy endings, and one must sometimes pass through darkness to find them. At least we shall be together, and I'll wager your betrothed will be over the moon as soon as he sets eyes upon you."

Isabella gave the lady's maid a nudge. "Forever the optimist, are you not?"

"Well, being optimistic helps the days pass."

"I admire you for it. We *both* have had our lives uprooted. You every bit as much as me."

"I think not. I'll still be your lady's maid, but you will neither be at your father's manor nor in England near your Roman villa."

The skiff lightly bumped the ship's hull, and the

oarsmen secured her to the rigging. Isabella craned her neck, looking at the weave of thick hemp netting and wondering if they expected her to climb up the side of the ship. Her question was answered when a sailor pointed to a seat being lowered from a winch that had been swung out over the deck. "The captain has sent the boatswain's chair for the lassies' comfort."

She did her best to smile at the sailor, though at best it was a grimace. Was everyone on board a Scot? Was she to be referred to as a lassie throughout the duration of the cruise? The few crew members she'd met so far spoke with a thick burr, including the scandalous captain—who had been born into a dukedom, no less.

Offering his hand, the sailor helped her onto the seat, which was no larger than the swing in the walnut tree in front of her father's house.

*He* would be up there.

Would he apologize?

Would he hound her for kisses throughout the voyage?

Isabella gripped the ropes tightly as the boatswain's seat started upward, swinging precariously out over the water. She dared to glance downward, which only served to make her stomach lurch. Goodness, the ascent was rather faster than she'd imagined. There must be half a dozen sailors working the winch above.

"You're doing splendidly, miss!" called Maribel, sounding overly cheerful.

As Isabella neared the top of the ship, four hands reached out for her as the pulley continued to winch the ropes upward.

"We'll swing you over the railing now, miss," said a man who was not Lord Gibb. Nodding his way, Isabella decided that the sinking in the pit of her stomach was purely from being suspended at least thirty feet in the air and being swung over the deck.

"Good morning, Miss Harcourt. You're safely aboard now," said a lad of no more than twelve years of age as he offered his hand and helped her to her feet. Then he stepped back, removed his cap and bowed. "Duncan Lamont, cabin boy, at your service."

"That will be all, Duncan, thank you," said a very deep voice, the exact one that had lulled her in the park yesterday. By the way the sinking in the pit of her stomach turned into fluttering, Isabella evidently had not grown impervious to the sound, no matter how much she tried to convince herself to do so.

Bicorn hat tucked in the crook of his arm, Lord Gibb stepped out from behind a row of crewmen. At first his eyes widened, expressing a bit of surprise, but with a blink, his visage quickly assumed an air of confidence. He stood out among the men with a commanding mien full of purpose.

Tall and broad, His Lordship posed as the ever-so-cocksure man who had joined her in the park yesterday without so much as an introduction. No, he hadn't been an apparition. His eyes were still a shockingly deep shade of blue, with prematurely etched lines around them, which wasn't incredibly odd. After all, the man's face was tanned and his flaxen hair longer than fashionable, waving in the wind like a rogue sail, as if making a testament to his cavalier nature.

The man took her hand, bowed, and kissed it. When he straightened, he affected an unreadable expression as far away as London. "Welcome aboard the *Prosperity*, Miss Harcourt. I am Captain MacGalloway."

She curtsied. "My lord."

He tightened his grasp on her hand. "Aboard ship I am *Captain*, and never referred to as anyone's lord."

Though she was wearing gloves, it was as if the heat from his grasp had seared through the kid leather. Slipping her fingers away, she wiped them on her skirts. "As you wish."

He turned to the cabin boy. "You've already met Duncan, but allow me to introduce—"

Isabella held up her palm and stopped him. "A moment—would you mind waiting until my lady's maid arrives before you make the introductions?"

"Of course," he said, his smile replaced by a thin line as he gripped his hands behind his back.

"Cap'n says ye're marrying a miner in America," Duncan blurted, earning a clearing of the throat from the captain.

"I—ah—" Isabella glanced from the boy to Lord Gibb, who leaned forward as if he might be interested to hear her story. "Yes. That is the plan."

The lad leaned out over the rail, watching as the men began cranking the winch upward again. "I've never been to Georgia."

"But I thought the *Prosperity* had made several trips to America."

"We mostly call into ports in Virginia and North Carolina," the captain explained, his gaze shifting to the open sea. Perhaps he had already forgotten about their kiss. Perhaps he often took unsuspecting women behind trees and kissed them. "Occasionally we'll deliver a shipment of whisky to New York. It all depends on our orders."

"I see," she said, grateful to spot Maribel's bonnet as the lady's maid came into view.

The crewmen made quick work of hauling her

over the rail and onto the deck. Duncan again exercised respectful manners as he introduced himself under the watchful eye of the captain. Was Lord Gibb training the lad in chivalry, or for a more senior position? Isabella tapped her finger to her chin. Were he and Duncan related in some way?

The captain cleared his throat and bowed. "Welcome aboard, Miss—"

"Hume."

"Miss Hume." He bowed respectfully as he would to any gentlewoman. "Captain Gibb MacGalloway, at your service." He gestured toward three men, standing shoulder to shoulder, all wearing navy-blue doublets and kilts with the same tartan as His Lordship's. "Please allow me to introduce my officers, the men who oversee all the work done aboard the *Prosperity*—Mr. Archie MacLean, our quartermaster, Mr. Gowan Erskine, our boatswain, and first mate Mr. Mac Lyall."

Isabella curtsied, as did Maribel beside her. "I am pleased to make your acquaintance."

The captain gestured from bow to stern. "You are welcome above decks at all times, though I caution you not to venture below where the men have their bunks—a ship is manned around the clock. Day or night, there's always someone sleeping."

"Or at least trying to sleep," interjected the cabin boy.

The captain cleared his throat. "If you need to visit the galley, send Duncan, or any one of the crew. They have all been instructed to lend assistance whenever needed."

Isabella breathed a sigh of relief. Evidently when aboard ship, Captain MacGalloway acted the perfect gentleman.

"Damnation, this is bloody heavy!" growled a

sailor, lifting one end of the trunk containing her tablets. "We'll need a few more men in the hold to maneuver it down there."

"Absolutely not. I need that trunk in my cabin." She turned to the captain. "Please, the contents are extremely fragile."

He eyed it with an arch to a wheat-colored eyebrow. "There's not a great deal of room in the cabins. Are you certain you want that one?"

"Yes. It is an absolute necessity."

"She'll also need the large one with the pink ribbon tied around the handle," said Maribel. "That trunk contains Miss Harcourt's personal effects and clothing for the journey."

"Two trunks in Gowan's wee cabin?" asked Duncan.

Isabella cringed, looking at the forlorn expression on the boatswain's face. She should have realized she'd be putting someone out of their accommodations.

"Find a way to make them fit," said the captain.

"If they do not, I only have a valise. Miss Harcourt's clothing can be placed in my quarters—if there is enough room."

"Och aye, there ought to be," Duncan replied. "You'll be bunking next door in Mac's cabin."

Isabella smiled at the gentlemen whose cabins she and Maribel would be occupying and offered a curtsey. "Thank you so very much for the use of your quarters."

"Enough chatter. We've a ship to get underway. To the rigging!" shouted the captain before turning to the women. "If you ladies would kindly follow me, I'll show you to your cabins."

While the men started up the lattice web of ropes

leading to the sails, Captain MacGalloway led the women aft and through a door with a small corridor. At one end was a rather lavish-looking arched door, its frame carved in the shape of a serpent.

The captain stopped at the first door on the left, then unlocked and opened it. "This is your berth, Miss Hume." He dropped the key into her palm before moving along and opening the second door. "The boatswain's cabin is only slightly larger than the first. I trust it is to your satisfaction, Miss Harcourt?"

Isabella stepped inside, finding only a narrow bed and a writing table. He hadn't been wrong—if there were two trunks in this chamber, she would scarcely be able to move. He slipped the loop of twine attached to the key over his finger. "You'll break your fast and take your nooning in your cabins. Dinner is served in the captain's cabin every night promptly at seven—Miss Hume, you are welcome to dine with us."

"Oh, no," said the maid. "I couldn't. I am a servant and am not one to be served."

Isabella gave Maribel's shoulder a pat. "This is not my father's house. Are you certain you won't join us?"

"Absolutely. I'll take my suppers in my cabin, if I may."

"Verra well, suit yourself." The captain rested a hand atop the hilt of a dirk sheathed in his belt. "The ship's cook makes a palatable biscuit, but I'll admit the rest of the fare is bland and commonplace. I'm certain it goes without saying that this is not a pleasure cruise. Compared to other boats in its class, my crew is relatively small, and though we shall do our best to see to your comfort, you willna find much aboard this ship with which to while away your time—"

"Not to worry." Isabella began to tug the key off his finger, but the twine caught on his knuckle, making his fingertips brush the back of her hand. A spark ignited between them. Unable to stop her sharp intake of breath, she released her grasp and took a step away. "I-I intend to busy myself with my tablets."

The captain narrowed his eyes, removed the twine, and set the key on the foot of the bed. "The contents of the excessively heavy trunk?"

"Yes."

As if on cue, a resounding commotion came from the deck. Maribel opened the outer door, revealing six able seamen straining to haul said trunk inside. "This way, gentlemen."

While the lady's maid's attention was drawn to the task at hand, Captain MacGalloway lowered his lips to Isabella's ear. "Please accept my apologies for my wee misstep yesterday. Had I known that you would be traveling aboard my ship, I never would have—"

"Acted like a rogue and taken advantage of an unsuspecting maid?" She boldly met his gaze, raising her chin defiantly.

A shadow crossed those shocking blue eyes. "Mark me, it shall nay happen again, madam."

# 4

Gibb clenched and unclenched his fists as he left Miss Harcourt and stormed out onto the deck. God's stones, the woman was supposed to be the sister of one of Grace and Modesty's friends. He'd expected to never see her again, not spend an entire cruise crossing the Atlantic whilst catering to the woman's whims.

Worse, the temptress was engaged to be married to an American. Gibb wondered how that union had come about, given her reclusive nature. Was the gentleman in question an old family friend? Where had they met? Why hadn't Mr. Schuyler come to England and married her there?

"Damnation," he mumbled under his breath. Not a single question in his mind mattered in the slightest.

So, Miss Harcourt thought him a rogue? Well, it was a damn good thing, since her berth was about three steps away from the captain's cabin. She'd be far better off if she feared him and kept her distance.

And the lady hadn't been wrong. He *had* acted irresponsibly and taken advantage. He'd toyed with her and quite enjoyed it at the time. Except now, every time the woman came on deck, he'd have to scowl and turn away. No, he mustn't allow her to know how those black eyes made his heart thrum, or how any clever retort on that pink tongue made him want to taste her.

The sailors were singing a ditty below when Gibb stopped at the open hatch, frowning at two trunks that had not yet been lowered. "Mr. Lyall?" he called over the song, projecting into the black abyss of the hold.

"Aye, sir?" came the first mate's disembodied voice.

"Why are these trunks not stowed away?"

The man's face came into view from below. "A few boards splintered when we lowered the first. Not to worry, the carpenters will have the damages repaired in no time."

"See to it they do. These trunks need to be secure before we hit the open sea, else they'll be sliding across sea-sprayed decks, and Lord kens what damage they'll do then."

"Aye-aye, sir."

Gibb hadn't taken two steps when the next problem caught his eye. A tar balanced on the foresail's yardarm, examining an enormous, frayed hole. "Mr. Erskine, please tell me we have a spare lower fore topsail."

The boatswain hastened across the deck. "'Tis merely a wee tear. I'd rather stitch her up than swap her out with precious new canvas."

Gibb considered the options of relacing the damaged sail with a new one and mending the old to keep as a spare. "How fast can the rigging monkey sew?"

"It'll be done within a quarter of an hour."

"It had best be." Gibb checked his pocket watch. "Lads, we sail at half past ten. I want to be cruising round Berwick-upon-Tweed by dusk."

Archie MacLean stepped beside him and pointed to the pennant sitting utterly idle atop the main mast.

"Pardon me, Cap'n, but we won't be going much of anywhere unless the wind picks up."

"She'll be blowing a gale once we reach the open sea, mark me," Gibb said, saying a silent prayer that the wind indeed picked up in the next quarter of an hour. There would be nothing more humiliating than sitting like a duck decoy off the coast of his brother's estate. In Martin's eyes, Gibb felt the need to continually prove himself a competent mariner—the man responsible for selling gallons of MacGalloway whisky in a new market the family hadn't enjoyed before, as well as bringing cotton grown by free men back to his twin brothers, Andrew and Philip, who were operating a mill on the River Tay.

Gibb continued with his inspection of the upper deck and had nearly made it to the bowsprit when an unusual silence spread across the timbers—the singing stopped, discussions stopped, and other than a few gulls calling overhead, the ship was too quiet.

He didn't have to glance over his shoulder to know why, but he turned all the same. Miss Harcourt and her lady's maid had stepped out onto the decks like two swans bedecked in ribbons and lace while Duncan led the way, evidently giving a tour, waving his arms and expounding about something that was most likely trivial.

Looking to the heavens, Gibb prayed for wind, and a great deal of it. Given ideal winds, the *Prosperity* might actually make the Atlantic crossing in a fortnight. Though he hadn't managed it as yet, a fortnight had been recorded, but only after voyages with perfect conditions. He cupped his hands around his mouth and hollered at the sailor who had leaned so far out from the yardarm of the foresail that he was likely to fall. "Mr. Briggs, if you continue to gawk, the sail will never be repaired and we'll be anchored here for a week!"

The man's jolt made him slip, but he managed to keep his footing on the rigging. "Aye, Cap'n."

Gibb opened his pocket watch. "Thirteen minutes, men!"

"Cap'n," said Cookie from below, his face popping out from the hatch. "Would ye be able to spare a moment?"

Gibb gave a nod and climbed down the narrow steps to the ship's galley—not only had the ship's cook beckoned him, but he welcomed any excuse to avoid Miss Harcourt at the moment. Cookie had lost three fingers on his right hand in the wars, but he was a good sailor, and would have a position on the *Prosperity* what may come.

"Have you a problem?"

The thickset man scratched his red beard, looking a bit uneasy. "I reckon I dinna bring enough flour aboard—I wasna expecting the ladies, ye ken?"

"None of us expected them, but dinna my brother's kitchens supplement your supplies?"

"Aye—of oats, chickens, and cabbages, but no' flour."

"Verra well, half my rations of ship's biscuits, but not the men's. They've had to make enough accommodations already." Gibb patted the side of an open flour barrel. "Besides, with a good wind, I'm hoping to make it to Virginia in a fortnight—two at most."

"Och aye? Then I'll pray for wind—as long as it isna a bloody hurricane."

"Wheesht, such a word is never to be uttered aboard my ship."

"Sorry, sir, just waggin' me tongue, is all," said Cookie, rubbing his ample belly. "I could stand to lose a stone or two—I'll cut back on the biscuits as well."

Gibb clapped his shoulder. "Good man. Secure this barrel and dunna waste an ounce. We have a ship to get underway."

~

STILL UNACCUSTOMED TO Scotland's long summer days, Isabella had been surprised when it was still broad daylight and Maribel came into her cabin to help her dress for dinner. Of course, the idea of dining in Captain MacGalloway's cabin had made her a bit queasy ever since the ship weighed anchor.

After knocking on the door, she was also surprised to see it was answered by the quartermaster, Mr. MacLean. "Come in, miss. We've just been talking about you."

She smiled, the captain drawing her attention as he stood and offered a gallant bow. Regardless of her opinion of the man, his presence was commanding, from the unruly flaxen hair that dangled over one eye to the fervid blue eyes that locked with hers. "All good, I hope."

Mr. Erskine and Mr. Lyall stood as well, holding glasses. "Am I late?" she asked.

Mr. Lyall held the chair nearest the captain's seat at the head of the table. "Not at all. We were just enjoying a wee tot afore the meal is served."

She gave the first mate a nod as she sat. "Do you always dine together for the evening meal?"

"Och, nay," said Mr. Erskine. "It just depends on the sea. Some nights there's no time to sit, let alone eat—a man is lucky to grab a ship's biscuit whilst fighting a storm."

"At least the spray of water over the bulkhead softens them up a bit," Mr. Lyall added, bringing a chuckle from the men at the table.

"The meal will be served shortly," said the captain. "Would you care for a glass of wine whilst we wait?"

"Thank you," Isabella replied, taking a moment to glance about the chamber. In comparison to her cabin, it was enormous, but in comparison to her chamber at Papa's manor, it was relatively modest. The dining table was of carved cherry wood and stood in the center with five chairs, the sixth being placed by the captain's writing table—a fine piece, also of cherry wood, with a locking drawer. Along one side of the cabin was a sizeable bed shrouded by red curtains and recessed into an enormous set of shelves that took up the entire wall. On display were dozens of leather-bound volumes, from poetry and Shakespeare to historical journals. Maps were rolled and neatly contained in a lower box obviously made for the purpose.

But what caught her eye was the row of windows overlooking the stern of the ship. It wasn't difficult to imagine Captain MacGalloway standing there, broad shoulders tapering to sturdy hips, his kilt slightly askew while his hawk-eyed gaze surveyed the endless sea.

The man himself slid a glass of ruby wine in front of her and pointed toward a bit of land visible off the starboard quarter. "We're passing Dunbar now, where the warmer waters from the Firth of Forth meet the North Sea. The *Prosperity's* sails will pick up the wind, and the work of a sailing ship becomes far more interesting."

The words had barely left his lips when the ship listed with a resounding groan, nearly making the wine slosh from Isabella's goblet.

Mr. Lyall raised his glass. "There she blows, as if on cue, Cap'n."

Isabella clamped a hand over her stomach. "My, that was quite a jolt."

"'Twas just a wee roll," said Mr. MacLean. "By the end of your wee cruise, you'll hardly notice."

"Here we are," said Duncan, entering with a tray of food. He was followed by an enormous smiling man.

"Cookie, have you met our guest, Miss Harcourt?" asked the captain.

"I canna say I have." The big man placed a tray of food in the center of the table, then wiped his hands—one of which was missing three fingers—on his apron and bowed. "'Tis my pleasure, madam."

"Pleased to make your acquaintance," she said, feeling a bit green when the scent of roasted lamb wafted her way. "Cookie, is it?"

"Aye—at least, that's what the men have called me ever since I left the service of the King's Navy and followed the cap'n aboard the *Prosperity*."

"Is that so?" Isabella glanced to Captain MacGalloway and swallowed hard to keep her stomach from sloshing and her head from spinning. Perhaps sampling the wine had been a bad idea. "Did most of the men aboard follow you once you retired your commission—I assume you would have retired a commission, did you not?"

The question seemed to cause the captain some consternation. His eyebrows pinched together and a shadow crossed his face. He even shuddered, as if in a blink, his mind was cast back to the horrors of war. "Aye to both questions," he replied with unconvincing cheerfulness. "Most of the men aboard are Highlanders who fought beside me—survivors of the Battle of Lissa."

"The very sea battle that claimed me da," said Duncan, his expression troubled as he gave a sidelong glance toward the captain, who did not meet the boy's gaze.

"Come, lad." Cookie ushered Duncan toward the door. "There's work to be done below decks."

After they left, silence swelled through the air, as if the Battle of Lissa had taken place only days prior. Isabella wanted to know more, but by the somber aspects of everyone's faces, she thought better of it.

Without uttering a word, Captain MacGalloway picked up the carving knife and fork and set to slicing the roast leg of lamb, his strokes short and hard—almost violent. Perhaps he was back on the decks of the naval ship, fighting for his life?

But by the roiling of Isabella's stomach, she was unable to contemplate the sudden somber mood that had settled in the cabin along with the incessant swaying of the ship. She shifted her gaze to the bowl of boiled potatoes, though doing so only made her discomfort worse.

"Lamb, miss?" asked the captain, putting a slice on her plate.

As the scent of roasted meat wafted to her nose, Isabella closed her eyes and clapped a hand over her mouth.

"Ye'd best eat your fill," said Mr. MacLean. "The fare willna be anywhere near this good by the time we reach America."

Mr. Erskine passed her a plate of biscuits, so flat that they couldn't have an ounce of leavening. "If yer feeling a wee bit queasy, Cookie's ship's biscuits always help."

She took one and gave the young man a grateful

smile, the fingers of one hand still firmly pressed against her lips. "Thank you," she managed to squeak.

Everyone at the table stopped and watched as she clipped a bite with her teeth. "My, 'tis hard."

Mr. MacLean popped an entire piece of potato into his mouth. "Cookie makes them that way to keep the weevils and maggots at bay."

At the mention of maggots, Isabella's stomach could take no more. Suffering an involuntary heave, she covered her mouth. "Pardon me," she said, pushing her chair away from the table.

Bile burned her throat as she made a frantic and mortifyingly ungraceful dash toward the door, the ship pitching and rolling beneath her feet. Halfway across the floor, Isabella lost her balance, stumbling and flinging out her arms, reaching for anything to stop her fall. As she was certain she was about to topple backward, a strong arm slipped across her waist while another swept her legs upward.

"Och, lassie. Sometimes it takes a day or three for a sailor to develop his sea legs," purred the captain in his deep burr. "Ye'd best have a wee lie-down until the sickness passes."

# 5

Secure in Gibb's arms, Miss Harcourt curled toward him, her color quite a bit more ashen since the ship sailed into the North Sea. "You mustn't fuss over me. All I need is a moment and I'll be set to rights."

He ignored the woman's feeble attempt to downplay her seasickness. She was in the wars and most likely would be for a time yet. "Duncan!" he bellowed while he kicked open her cabin door. In two strides, he rested her atop the bed. "I'll fetch the chamber pot."

"I do not neeeeeee..." Miss Harcourt's words transformed into a cry of agony and gurgled choking in her throat. Lunging across the floor with the handle of the pot in his hand, Gibb managed to reach her just as the poor woman lost the contents of her stomach.

"Argh!" Miss Harcourt cried, heaving in a breath and clutching the pot with both hands. "Is acquiring one's sea legs always this awful?"

He handed her his handkerchief. "For some."

She had barely slipped the cloth from his fingers when her heaves resumed again.

"Ye wanted me, Cap'n?" asked Duncan, arriving at

the door, his gaze immediately falling to the chamber pot, the sight making the lad scrunch his nose. "Gadzooks!"

Still gripping the pot by the handle, Gibb nodded toward the bow. "Inform Miss Hume that her lady is ill."

"Straight away, sir."

"Argh!" Miss Harcourt again cried, doubling over.

"There, there—we shall have you serenading the sailors with arias soon," Gibb said, bending forward and rubbing her back. She had quite a lovely back—slender, with square shoulders and a long neck made all the more feminine with wisps of fine black hair that had sprung loose from her chignon. Gibb might have admired the image were the woman not doubled over, losing her nooning and most likely every other meal she'd eaten in the past week.

"Beg your pardon, Cap'n," said Duncan, popping his head in. "I'm afeard Miss Hume isna able to come—she's hangin' over her chamber pot as well."

"God save us, we'll have to nurse them both." Gibb dug in his sporran and motioned for the lad to enter with an incline of his head. He pulled out a key ring and selected the smallest. "Fetch the black bottle from my medicine chest, then ask Cookie for two cups of peppermint water."

Miss Harcourt rubbed her forehead. "Is the entire boat spinning?"

"Nay, but the North Sea has begun to give us a good show. Not to worry. Soon waves like these will be lulling you to sleep." Gibb resumed rubbing, up and down, back and forth, ever so slowly, ever so gently. "Tell me about the contents of the trunk at the end of your bed—it must contain something of import if you dinna want it stowed in the hull."

"Tablets," she said, the word seeming to be too much to utter, because the poor woman launched into a succession of dry heaves.

"Where did the tablets come from?" he asked after she'd managed to take a stuttering breath.

"The villa."

"Ah, yes." Gibb grinned, recalling their conversation in Newhailes' private park. "The Roman ruins you and your father unearthed in West Sussex."

"Mm-hmm." Miss Harcourt rocked back and forth, pressing the heels of her hands against her temples. "I'm...t-translating them."

"Interesting indeed."

Duncan reappeared, this time with the black bottle and two of the ship's mugs with flared bottoms to keep them from tottering. "Peppermint water and the tincture you requested."

"Thank you, lad. Set them on the table, then clean the chamber pot, if you will." Gibb made quick work of mixing two helpings of what he called his sleeping potion, used only for the sickest of men, and not often, because the black bottle contained laudanum—a fact that he revealed to no one. But if Miss Harcourt's maid was anywhere near as sick as her lady, they both would fare better with a night of uninterrupted rest rather than a night with their heads hanging over their chamber pots.

When the lad returned, Gibb handed him one of the mugs. "Take this to Miss Hume and tend to the maid's needs."

That freckled nose wrinkled again. "Ye mean for me to hold the chamber pot for her like ye've been doing with Miss Harcourt?"

"Aye. Empty it as well. Sit with her until she grows drowsy and then help her into bed."

"Och, I have to do all that? Sh-she's a lass."

"Mayhap, but she's ill and needs our help. As I recall, I tended you for an entire week the first time you set foot aboard the *Prosperity*. Go on, off with you."

As the door to the cabin closed, Gibb returned to his charge and offered her the mug. "Drink."

"I cannot." Shaking her head, Miss Harcourt pushed the cup away with her palm. "If I drink anything, it will only come right back up."

"It may, but if you manage to keep a wee bit of my tincture down for even a quarter of an hour, you'll sleep, and by the time you wake, the worst of the sickness ought to be behind you."

Miss Harcourt eyed the cup and shuddered.

Not about to be dissuaded by a wee wisp of a lass, Gibb shifted the mug toward her. "Just one sip and we'll see how it settles. That's all I ask."

"Gah," she managed, taking it in both hands, the cup trembling while she drew it to her lips. She took a sip, then sputtered with a cough and pushed it toward him. "No more."

"For now," he said, taking the mug and carefully placing between the arches of his feet to keep it secure. Still, if the ship encountered a big wave, the tincture might be lost, even though the mugs were hewn of wheel-thrown pottery with heavy, flared bottoms.

Gibb considered urging her to ease back on the bed, but not only was it highly improper, it was too soon—proven by the fact that the poor woman convulsed with a series of dry heaves.

She wrapped her arms across her midriff and fought to catch her breath. "Dear God, this is miserable."

It was. Over his career at sea, Gibb had seen the hardiest, most rugged men come aboard ship and be reduced to crying milksops, lying on their sides with their knees tucked up, barely able to lift their heads while they spewed their guts.

And the only thing that cured the bastards was time.

He ought to make Miss Harcourt drink the tincture and leave her alone to her misery. Except Gibb had promised to take care of her. During this voyage, the woman was in his charge. Sailing across the Atlantic wasn't for the feeble. Healthy men oft succumbed to sicknesses like scurvy and the ague. Though the *Prosperity* didn't sail with a surgeon, like most ships in the Royal British Navy, Cookie oft posed as their healer. Gibb also had spent a great deal of time reading articles and texts about how to keep his men healthy. That was why he made them drink from a barrel of lemon juice every morn, and Cookie served each sailor a dollop of pickled cabbage at the evening meals. Since they'd started the practice, there hadn't been a case of scurvy aboard ship.

*Unfortunate I canna find a cure for seasickness.*

Gibb watched Miss Harcourt out of the corner of his eye. When her posture relaxed ever so slightly, he said, "Shall I tell you the story of how I came to be in command of the *Prosperity*?"

She dabbed her mouth with the handkerchief. "I think you ought to leave me to my misery and go on about your captaining duties."

"Och, I'd like nothing more, but I gave my brother and your father my word that I'd see you safely across the ocean, and that is what I aim to do."

She shook her head, her complexion still far too pale. "Heaven forbid I die on this voyage and pose an inconvenience for my father."

"Oh? Is your da profiting from your marriage to

Mr. Schuyler? He mentioned the man keeps accommodations in Savannah, which indicated his domicile must be elsewhere."

She gave a nod, gulping as if she'd just controlled another surge of sickness. "Papa is profiting. Though who am I to question a man's desire to live out his remaining years in comfort?"

Gibb was such a hardened sailor that nothing could make him seasick, but his gut roiled at her overwhelmingly altruistic reply. "I beg your pardon? What of *your* comfort?"

"I believe my father *was* thinking of my comfort. In some way, at least. After all, once Papa passes away, my cousin will inherit. Not I."

Gibb grumbled under his breath. He had never imagined he'd inherit a thing, but thanks to Martin, he had landed on his feet quite handsomely. "And your cousin isna generous enough to see to your care?"

"No." She pressed the heels of her hands against her temples. "Forgive me, but I'm not feeling well enough to converse at the moment."

"Forgive me. I ken ye must be miserable." Gibb offered her the cup yet again. "You'd best take another sip, lass."

She grasped the handle and met his gaze, her eyes filled with pain and indecision. "Must I?"

He nodded, using his fingertips to urge the mug toward her mouth. She slightly parted her lips while he sat taller and watched as, with the sway of the ship, the liquid sloshed over them, sending a good-sized gulp over her tongue.

Gasping and coughing, she pushed the cup into his stomach. "No more. Please."

"I was about to tell you about the *Prosperity*," he

said, knowing full well that convincing a passenger with seasickness to drink down a tincture always took time and patience. Gibb wasn't patient by nature, but the sea had matured him, helped him to realize that a man must know when to bide his time and when to act decisively with haste.

Miss Harcourt sighed. "If you intend to remain here, then by all means, tell me about your ship." She clapped a hand over her mouth with a heave—just one this time. "I shall do my best to pay attention, though forgive me if I should soil the buckles on your shoes in the interim."

Gibb kicked up his leg, showing off his shoe and making his kilt flick up a bit. "You've been kind enough to miss them thus far."

"I make no promises."

He chuckled. It seemed the lass had a sense of humor even in sickness. He didn't know many women who could jest in the face of misery, but he liked that this one did. "It wasna long after me da died that Martin met me on the wharf at the Pool of London. At the time I thought he'd come to gawk at his brother aboard the *HMS Cerberus*, but he took me to the tavern across the street and told me our mother had said that she couldna bear to lose me in a sea battle so soon after losing her husband."

"Your mother seems like a very sensible woman."

"Aye, she is. Bless her, she birthed eight children. And I'll say every last one of us has given her cause to call for smelling salts at one time or another."

"Especially you?"

Gibb ran his finger around the clan brooch at his shoulder, as he often did. "As it turns out."

Closing her eyes, Miss Harcourt rubbed her temples while the ship continued to pitch and roll. "What happened in the tavern?"

"Martin and his steward told me that they were forming a new venture and the missing piece of their scheme was a ship's captain."

"Which they offered to you?"

"Aye. If I resigned my commission, the duke intended to buy me a ship—said it was my birthright."

"Yours? But are you not doing His Grace's bidding?" she asked, doubling over and grimacing.

"Because I choose to. The duke also established a cotton mill on the River Tay for my twin brothers Andrew and Philip."

"Cotton?" she asked, sounding suspicious, and it wasn't difficult to guess why.

Gibb picked up the chamber pot and held it at the ready. "Aye. Mind you, the MacGalloways have an exclusive agreement with a coalition of Irish sharecroppers—free men."

Bending over the pot, Miss Harcourt heaved, producing nothing but spittle. "Truly?" she asked, doing her best to converse regardless of her discomfort.

Gibb gave a nod, amazed at how this woman fought through her misery. "They were the only suppliers Martin would consider—though I must say that those poor blighters have their share of trials from the big plantation owners in America. It isna an easy life. I fear I'll reach her shores one day and there will be no one left."

"What does Martin think of this?" She sat up and grimaced. "Is there nothing the MacGalloways can do to protect them?"

"From Scotland?" Gibb shrugged, setting the chamber pot aside. "Martin has talked about sending

Frederick to help, but only after the lad graduates from St. Andrews University, and that willna be for a couple of years yet. Not to worry, the Irish are a hardy lot. I reckon they can look after themselves for a time longer."

Miss Harcourt yawned behind her hand, her eyes drooping a tad.

"Are ye feeling as if you could have a wee sleep?"

"I'm too queasy to lie down."

"Then let's have another wee sip of my tincture."

Through a fan of black eyelashes, she regarded him. "You're a fiend."

"Aye." He gave her the cup. "Though I reckon I've been called worse. Why not drink it down this time?"

"Must I?"

"Mm-hmm."

She glanced at the tincture. "Just remember that I'll be aiming at those buckles."

"Then I suggest ye keep in mind 'tis Duncan who'll be shining them."

"Fiend," she growled, then tipped the cup up and took a good swallow. "Gah! I'll never be able to withstand the taste of peppermint again."

"All in time, lass, all in time."

The poor woman yielded to the constant pitching of the ship and swayed in place. By the half-cast of her eyelids, she was well on her way to succumbing to the mind-numbing effects of the opium. Gibb rubbed her back for a time until she collapsed against him, dropping her head on his shoulder.

He shifted his nose toward her hair and inhaled—so sweet, so entirely feminine. His heart squeezed as he reached up and pulled a pin from her hair, hesitating for a moment to see if she might object. But she did not. With a gentle sigh, the woman nuzzled into him as if his shoulder provided the comfort she needed.

"I'll just remove these pins," he whispered.

Within a few heartbeats, he had every one of them removed, marveling as her black hair fell everywhere in waves. He ran his fingers through it—softer than ermine and so very thick, not to mention extraordinarily long. If she were standing, her locks most likely would fall past her waist, perhaps even past her buttocks.

He twirled a lock around his finger. If only he could have this woman in his bed with this feral mane draped across his chest. With a guttural moan, he let the hair fall away, doing his best to ignore his imaginings.

Miss Harcourt sighed—not a sigh of bliss, but a semblance of a groan filled with discomfort.

"You're still quite ill, are you not?" he asked, berating himself for his wayward thoughts. The only reason he had entered her cabin was to care for her, not to ogle her.

She nodded against his shoulder.

Blast it all, Gibb couldn't leave her to sleep alone. Considering the dose of laudanum he'd given her, she mightn't wake if she had another wave of sickness. The odds that she might choke were high enough for concern. Nay, he had best remain at the lady's sickbed, regardless of if she wanted him to do so or not.

He moved his hand up her spine. "I reckon you'll feel better if you loosen your stays."

She shook her head against his shoulder, mumbling something imperceptible.

Ignoring her protest, he slowly pulled open the bow at the back of her dress. "That's right. Just rest against me," he whispered, expertly working the laces open until he was able to slip the gown from her shoulders. "How's that? Better?"

Again, she shook her head, the corners of her eyes crinkling. "Don't feel well."

He pushed his finger inside the edge of her corset and wondered how the woman was able to breathe. "Your stays must be removed."

"No!" she argued, pushing him away and then crumpling forward, with her head in her hands, her breathing labored.

Giving her a moment, Gibb busied himself by collecting the pins and sliding them into the drawer of her table. When he again sat beside her, Miss Harcourt had not moved, but her breathing had grown deeper and slower.

"Are you asleep, miss?" he softly asked.

When she didn't answer, he made quick work of unlacing her stays—something he'd done hundreds of times, most often with women of easy virtue in rooms above taverns, but never aboard his ship and never with a gently bred lass.

"I'll pull this contraption away now," he said while she flopped to her side, her lips parted, those dark lashes fanning her ivory cheeks. "Och, 'tis for the best that you're nay fighting me, lass. It is miserable enough to be ill, let alone suffering seasickness whilst wearing one of these torture devices."

He cast the set of stays onto the trunk at the foot of the bed before returning his attention to his patient. She wore a fine shift of Holland cloth, but he would not have been a man if he didn't notice the lovely form beneath—sculpted breasts, a slender waist, a womanly flare of hip, all framed by a tangle of wild black hair.

"Good God," he growled beneath his breath, trying

to think of anything to distract his attention. Nay, Miss Harcourt wasn't his to ogle, and he'd not allow himself to gawk. Instead, he busied himself by removing her dress and draping it over the back of the chair. Then he levered her legs onto the bed, his throat growing dry when the lady's shift hiked up over her knee, revealing two lovely calves, and ankles so slender that he wondered if he'd be able to close his finger and thumb around each one.

Such a question was not to be answered—*never to be answered*. It took a will of iron, but Gibb forced himself not to admire the way her hair sprawled across the pillow, or the way the slight parting of her lips seemed to beg for a kiss. Instead, he covered her with a blanket and stood back. Aye, she looked like an angel. Unable to help himself, he kissed her forehead. "Sleep well, my raven-haired lass."

Gibb had no right to be so familiar with a woman who was all but a stranger, but it felt right in this hour when she was helpless and unwell. He would look after her this night, and come the morn, they would resume their roles—he of captain and she of a betrothed fiancée sailing across the sea and into her lover's arms.

# 6

Isabella rolled to her side, her head feeling as if it had been stuffed with wool. Worse, the change of position only served to increase her agony. A wave of nausea roiled in her stomach as she restlessly moved again, scratching her arms. Everything itched, and the dratted bed refused to stop its loathsome rocking.

Someone dabbed a cool cloth cross her forehead.

Feeling as if she were about to retch, she batted the hand away.

"Miss Harcourt?" asked a deep voice.

A decidedly masculine voice.

Every muscle in her body clenched taut.

Why was a *man* swathing her head with a cool cloth?

Isabella didn't dare breathe.

For a moment she couldn't think. But as she inhaled deeply, everything came flooding back. She remembered the kiss in the park and the devilish smiles and the cool captain who had greeted her aboard the *Prosperity*. She recalled the dinner in his cabin, followed by the horrible sickness overcoming her when the ship sailed into the North Sea.

He'd carried her into her chamber while she was

unable to control the convulsions of her wretched stomach.

He'd held the chamber pot for her.

Isabella groaned, mortified with herself. If only she could melt into the mattress.

*Please be a dream. Please at least be an apparition.*

"Miss Harcourt?" he asked again.

*I am most definitely not dreaming.*

Isabella's eyes flashed open. With a jolt, she sat up, making the blanket slip down to her waist while her head spun like a top.

The captain loomed beside her bed, his gaze first meeting her eyes and then drifting downward.

"Why are you still here?" she demanded, pulling the blanket up to her chin as she caught sight of her dress draped over the back of the chair. Good Lord, her stays were atop the table in plain sight for all to see. At least, if there was anyone else in the cabin, they'd be able to see her undergarment on display as if it were suspended from the main mast.

She glanced beneath the blanket and cringed. "And how did I end up in this *scandalous* state of dress?"

Captain MacGalloway turned his back, doused the cloth in the bowl, and wrung it out. "Miss Hume was also afflicted by seasickness and was unable to attend you."

"Oh? And thus you felt my illness gave you the right to remove my gown and stays?"

He draped the cloth over the rack at the side of the washstand. "In my opinion, you needed to breathe."

"Your opinion? Are you a physician as well as a sea captain?"

"I am not, but I have studied a great deal in the interest of keeping my men free of illness and out of their hammocks. Your breathing grew labored and your stays needed to go—especially after the tincture."

She clutched the blanket tighter beneath her chin while a wave of nausea crashed over her. Thankfully, the sickness left nearly as fast as it came.

*What did he say?*

Isabella scraped her teeth over her bottom lip. *Ah, yes. The tincture.*

The captain had been rather insistent that she drink it down, and she eventually did. And now, she couldn't remember a thing after finishing the contents of the cup. "How long have you been in my cabin?"

He checked his pocket watch. "Near enough to twelve hours."

"I've been unconscious for twelve hours?"

"Aye, and as small as you are, I'm surprised you are awake so soon. Laudanum can have some latent after-effects."

"You gave me laudanum?" she shrieked.

"Mixed with peppermint water."

"You, you...unmitigated swine!" No wonder her head felt as if it were packed with wool. Laudanum was nearly pure opium. "You could have poisoned me."

"Not likely, but I'll admit that someone needed to sit up with you to ensure I got the dosage right. I dinna want to take a chance on creating a scandal, thus decided it was best if *I* remained at your side until you woke."

Good glory, things were only growing worse. Isabella was about to be married, albeit to a man she didn't know or love, yet a man who had already proven himself to be a salacious rake had just spent an entire night in her cabin. "I am ruined."

Captain MacGalloway tucked his thumbs in his belt and rocked back on his heels. "Och, lassie, you were far too ill to worry about such drivel."

"Oh, that makes me feel so much more assured. The renegade who tricked me into kissing him behind a tree only paces away from his ancestral home sits in my cabin all night and insists I have not been ruined. You know as well as I that your presence here is *scandalous.*"

"I've already apologized for the wee kiss behind the tree, and I'm not about to do so again." He brushed out the sleeves of his leather doublet, seeming to grow taller. "I am the captain of this ship and live by a code of honor. I also made a promise to your father that I'd look after you throughout this voyage, and that's exactly what I am doing."

"A code of honor, did you say?" she asked with an edge to her voice. "But not when approaching unsuspecting ladies in parks."

Those blue eyes grew intense and stormy, his expression hard. "As I recall, the lass I met in the park was far more adventuresome than the *frosty* woman before me now." He took a step toward the door. "It was my decision to personally see to your care rather than appoint a sailor to the task. Had I known how affronted you would be by my presence, I might have opted differently."

"Wait." Isabella cast a longing glance at her gown and decided it was best to stay put with the blanket securely gripped beneath her chin. What would she have done if she'd awakened to some crusty old sailor staring down at her? "I may have overreacted a tad."

"*May* have?"

"Yes. I-ah...am...*thankful* that you did not assign someone else to watch over me. But..."

"Hmm?" he asked.

"Did you assign a sailor to tend Maribel?"

"Aye—Duncan."

"The cabin boy?"

"I thought the lad would cause the least stir below decks—given the whole idea of ruination and so forth. Forgive me, madam, if you did not approve of my decision."

Isabella gulped against another wave of nausea. Perhaps she wasn't yet thinking clearly. "You haven't slept, have you?"

"I often dunna sleep when asea." Captain MacGalloway folded his arms and eyed her. "And how are you feeling? Still a wee bit off, I'd imagine?"

"A little queasy—antsy as well."

"Aye, that would be from the tincture." He pointed to the bowl and ewer on the washstand. "Perhaps after you freshen up, we might take a turn around the upper deck. A bit of fresh air ought to help set you to rights."

"We?" she whispered, glancing at the washstand. "What will the sailors think?"

"About?"

"The fact that you have spent the entire night in my cabin?"

"First of all, no one aside from Duncan has seen me inside this cabin. Secondly, every member of this crew is well aware if they spout off about their captain sitting by the sickbed of a guest aboard this ship, they will be assigned to the bilges for the duration of the voyage." He gave her a gallant bow. "Good day, miss."

SHORTLY AFTER ISABELLA had washed her face and cleaned her teeth, Maribel came in with a change of clothes. "I'm so sorry I was unable to attend you last eve."

"It seems we both were afflicted by the seasickness." Isabella pulled her rather pale lady's maid inside, made note of the empty corridor, and closed the door. "I understand Duncan took care of you."

"Aye, the boy gave me a tincture. He was awfully sweet."

"Did he sleep in your cabin?"

A deep blush spread up Maribel's face. "He's only a lad."

"So, he stayed?"

"He slept in the corner." Maribel opened a small satchel that contained Isabella's toilette items and pulled out the hairbrush. "I understand the captain himself tended your bedside."

The statement made the air whoosh from Isabella's lungs. "He did—but only because he felt I was too sick to leave alone and you were unable to sit up with me."

"Yes, that is what Duncan said." Maribel worked the brush through Isabella's long hair, miraculously releasing the snarls at the ends, as she always did. "Were you..."

"Hmm?"

"Was he...?"

"Hmm?"

"You know what I'm trying to say. Was the captain respectful?"

"Indeed he was." Isabella had not and would never tell Maribel about the kiss in the park. "I might even venture to use the term heroic...or perhaps valorous."

"Valorous?"

"Yes." She nodded emphatically. "He is the captain of this enormous sailing ship, yet he held the chamber pot while I regurgitated everything I think I may have eaten for the past fortnight." Isabella ran her hands along her aching ribs. "At least, it felt that way. I do not recall ever being so sick I prayed for death, as I did last eve."

"It was awful, was it not?"

"Definitely not my finest hour."

"Then I suppose it is a good thing you are marrying Mr. Schuyler and not Captain MacGalloway."

A stone thudded in the pit of Isabella's stomach. The captain had behaved rather gallantly, and she'd not been very appreciative in return. But now that he'd seen her doubled over and sicker than she'd been in all her days, he most decidedly would never want to kiss her again.

"Yes," she agreed, though the word came out rather flat and unconvincing. To allay any further questioning, she grabbed her set of stays and held them against her chest. "Come, I want to dress quickly so that *you and I* might take a turn around the upper decks. The captain said a bit of fresh air will do us both a wealth of good."

"Very well." Maribel twisted Isabella's hair into a chignon before attacking the laces of her stays. "Are you hungry?"

A bit of queasiness snaked through Isabella. "Not yet. You?"

"Not at all." The laces tightened. "But I daresay stepping outside sounds quite refreshing."

It took only a few minutes more, and together they stepped through the outer door to the upper deck.

"Good morning, Miss Harcourt, Miss Hume," said Mr. MacLean from his place at the ship's wheel.

They both replied with a good morning, which seemed to prompt everyone on deck to stop what they were doing and greet them.

Captain MacGalloway pattered down the steps, his kilt slapping the backs of his legs. "Ladies, would you like to try your hand at steering the ship?"

"Truly?" asked Maribel.

"It is nay as easy as it looks."

"No?" Isabella gestured to the three masts full of sails above. "Even when you have a strong wind like today?"

"The stronger the wind, the more difficult it is to change course." He took her hand. "Come, I'll show you."

Duncan slid in beside Maribel and took her hand as well. "The cap'n allows me to steer in finer weather as well."

The quartermaster grinned. "Only when I need to take a—"

"I beg your pardon, Mr. MacLean. There's no need to go into such explicit detail when there are ladies present."

"Forgive my impertinence," said the quartermaster, stepping back and allowing Captain MacGalloway to take the wheel.

He looked Isabella in the eye. "If you'll move in front of me, I'll let you have a go."

"Oh, no. I would look rather silly, would I not?"

"No, miss," said Maribel. "When will you ever have a chance to see what it feels like to place your hands on a ship's wheel and gaze out over the sea? And the day is fine."

"Och aye," agreed Mr. MacLean. "The weather is ideal."

Isabella glanced at the captain. "Must you stand so close?"

He cut her a look full of arrogance and daring, but his feet remained planted solidly on the deck, both hands gripping the handles.

Mr. MacLean sniggered.

"Come now, lass," the captain urged.

"Oh, very well." She looked to Maribel and huffed. "How difficult can it be?"

Isabella stepped in and grasped the handles, the brush of the captain's sleeves hardly noticeable through the fabric of her pelisse, yet it made her quite self-aware. "There, I have it."

"Do you feel secure?"

Squaring her shoulders, Isabella tightened her hold. "Of course I do."

But when the captain released his grip, the wheel jolted and torqued right out of Isabella's grasp. She skittered aside while Mr. MacLean lunged up to the helm and stopped it from spinning out of control.

Clutching her hands over her heart, she drew in a few deep breaths to calm herself. "My heavens, this is nowhere as easy as it looks. Do you mean to say you *fight* the sea all day long?"

"It's no' so bad once ye grow accustomed to her," said the quartermaster.

Maribel chuckled and pointed to the sails. "I do believe you have quite an audience, miss."

Sitting atop one of the mainsail's booms, three sailors had become idle, doing nothing but gawking. The mops on the deck had stilled, each one of them with a sailor leaning on its handle, eyes wide and watching their every move.

"Enough entertainment, men," shouted Mr. Erskine as the boatswain marched aft. "Back to work!"

The captain offered his hand. "Will you ladies do me the honor of a turn about the decks?"

Isabella hesitated for a moment, but after receiving a nudge in the back from her lady's maid, she placed her fingers in his palm. As he closed his fist around them, a warmth spread through her. She didn't want to succumb to his charm, but everything about him was so incredibly tempting and ever so attractive to her soul. And as he led her along the ship's rail, her spirits soared as if she were floating across the timbers.

# 7

Though Gibb was seated with his back to his cabin's door, he knew Miss Harcourt had entered by the way the fine hairs tickled the back of his neck. Perhaps the admiring expressions suddenly on the faces of the other men at the table gave her presence away as well, a fact that made him want to assign each one of them to pumping the bilges or rearranging the cargo in the hold.

The men all pushed back their chairs and stood in unison. If they had rehearsed the action fifty times, Gibb doubted they would have been able to all rise together so precisely. Perhaps each man had strings connected to the same marionette handle?

Having risen as well, he turned and bowed. "Miss Harcourt, forgive us for not waiting. I had wrongly assumed that you were still restricted to a diet of broth and ship's biscuits."

She graced them with a lovely smile, the lanterns overhead catching a glimmer in her dark eyes. "Believe it or not, I am feeling rather peckish."

"That is a good sign," said Mac Lyall, pulling out a chair for the lady.

Gibb scowled at the hulking young officer. The

largest man aboard, Mac had barely turned nineteen, and this was his maiden cruise as first mate. He'd earned the post, for certain, but had no business flirting with a guest who was engaged to be married.

Once everyone had resumed their seats, Miss Harcourt rubbed her hands together. "I do believe the fare smells rather good."

"Chicken pottage this evening," said Archie. "The only livestock we sail with is chickens."

"Oh? Isn't that unusual?" she asked.

"Not on a ship this size," Gibb explained. "A larger brig has the capacity, but we are rarely ever asea more than two months, and livestock in the hold means there's less room for whisky and cotton."

"We always have plenty of salted pork and the like," said Gowan Erskine, offering the chicken pottage to the lady. "The fare aboard the *Prosperity* is better than any I had in the navy, for certain."

She spooned a dollop onto her plate. "I take it you treat your men rather well, Captain MacGalloway?"

Not one to boast, he shrugged, reached for the bottle of wine, and filled her glass. "Every man deserves to be well fed. Moreover, a sailor who eats his fill is more likely to put forth a good day's work."

"And if ye keep them busy, they're more likely to stay out of mischief," Archie added.

Miss Harcourt took a sip of wine, the liquid making her lips glisten with the light from the lamps lazily swinging overhead. "Are there many discipline problems aboard?"

"Not many," Gibb said, pouring for himself.

"But we must always pay attention, aye, Cap'n?" asked Mac. "That's what ye told me."

"Indeed it is, Mr. Lyall." Gibb set the bottle down in the center of the table.

"And then we act swiftly," Mac said as if he were an expert on disciplining the crew, which he most definitely was not.

Miss Harcourt helped herself to a biscuit and broke it. "How so?"

"The punishment must fit the crime," said Gowan, who was only two years Mac's senior and nearly as wet behind the ears.

"Well, I hope there's no need for anyone to be punished during this voyage."

Archie smirked—if there was anyone aboard who knew as much as Gibb about running a ship, it was Archie MacLean. "I've heard that miracles happen, but I've yet to witness one."

The door to the cabin swung open and Duncan popped his head in. "Beg your pardon, but the wind's shifted and Danny reckons we're drifting off course."

Archie shoveled a spoon of pottage in his mouth and stood. "I'll take care of this."

"Excuse me," came a sailor's voice from the corridor. "The rigging on the fort topmast staysail is busted."

Gowan pushed his chair away from the table. "I suppose I have my marching orders as well, then."

Cookie appeared next. "I hate to spoil your fun, lads, but there's a wee leak in the hull—right below the food stores. If it isna fixed by morn, we'll be starvin' by the time we reach America."

Mac stood and bowed over Miss Harcourt's hand, planting a sloppy kiss on the back of it. "There's no rest at sea, miss—not for any of us."

Gibb sat back and listened to the footsteps fade away while the lady sitting at his right looked from her plate to the door and back. "Are you not going with them?"

"They are all capable officers. If I followed and looked over their shoulders, I wouldna be much of a captain, would I?"

"So, if there's a problem they cannot tackle, then you step in?"

"Aye, and believe me, there are plenty." Gibb took another drink. "Tell me about those tablets of yours. What do they say?"

She smiled, her eyes flickering with interest. "Mind you, I've only managed to fully translate four, but I believe they comprise some sort of journal."

"Only four? It must be slow going."

"Yes." She scooped a bite of pottage with her spoon. "Most of them are in pieces, and it takes painstaking hour after painstaking hour to figure out how they all fit together."

"Fascinating. Have you received assistance from the Society of Antiquaries?"

A lovely blush flooded the lady's cheeks while she shook her head. "After they took all the credit for finding the villa and sent in their own team of men, pushing me aside, I decided to keep the discovery of the tablets to myself—at least until I've pieced them together."

Gibb liked that—liked that she had the backbone to thwart the "establishment," which so often made a right muddle of everything. He grinned over his glass. "Have you any idea who wrote them?"

"I'm not certain. They're only small, but the person —a man, I'm guessing—has mentioned in each one how much he misses the person to whom he addresses each entry."

"*Te desidero*," Gibb mused, using the Latin words for "I miss you."

"That's right. You speak Latin?"

"Aye, 'tis a prerequisite for the son of a duke, even the son of a *Scottish* duke."

"You say that as if a Scottish dukedom were less important than an English one."

Gibb held up his glass and watched the liquid slosh with the sway of the ship. "That is because the English mistakenly believe it to be true."

Miss Harcourt took a bite of pottage. "I don't know about that."

"Oh? Scottish peers are rarely as sought after as those born south of the border. You must have had a Season, did you not?"

The lass raised one shoulder, nearly touching her ear. "I suppose I attended a few balls and the like, though I'm not a good dancer, and even worse at flirting."

"Hmm, I'd rather disagree with the latter. In my opinion, you are naturally gifted at flirting."

"Sir, I assure you, I do not flirt."

"I'll have to disagree with you on that point. After all, in the park you managed to flirt with me most convincingly." He set his glass down and offered his hand. "As to your first self-deprecating statement, however, the jury is still undecided."

"Jury?"

"At sea, my rule is absolute. I am the captain—judge and jury of dancing maidens who are promised to...an American from Georgia?"

She placed her fingers into his palm, making frissons of energy crackle up his arm. With her nod, she stood. "Mr. Schuyler."

He tugged her away from the table and toward the open space in front of the row of windows. "I trust you have met the man. Did he come to West Sussex and sweep you off your feet?" Gibb asked, placing his hand on her waist, preparing for a waltz.

"No," she whispered, following his lead. "I have never met him."

He wanted to ask for clarification, but he'd heard her plainly enough. How did a lovely, enterprising daughter of a knight end up wrangled into a marriage of convenience? Had Gibb known this when he met with her father at Newhailes, he would have demanded an explanation. Had Martin been aware?

*Surely not.*

Gibb led her into a series of slow, waltzing turns while his heart burned. Good God, how could she pick up and blindly shift to a country that was rugged, wild, and uncultured without so much as an introduction? Moreover, how could her father have allowed her to do so? "Do you feel it is your duty to marry a complete stranger?"

Miss Harcourt did not meet his gaze, her dark lashes lowered, making two distinct crescents against ivory cheeks. "Mm-hmm."

*Pity*. Rather than utter the word aloud, he hummed the *Sussex Waltz* and watched as the raven-haired lass effortlessly moved with his every cue. She was lovely and graceful and...

*Sad.*

*Lonely.*

*Afraid.*

Suddenly, Gibb couldn't recall the rest of the tune.

When he stopped, she drew away and clapped her fingers over her mouth. "I warned you that I am not a good dancer."

"You must excuse me, but I am convinced that you are wrong. In my opinion, you are gifted at both flirting and dancing."

She curtsied. "Then I'm afraid we shall have to disagree, my lord."

As she started toward the door, Gibb caught Miss Harcourt's arm. She turned her face up to his, those black eyes alive and full of want, her pink lips parted. A wisp of straight black hair had come loose and slashed across her throat. By God, she was lovely—a lonely, vulnerable damsel who made his blood thrum with yearning. With his next breath he might be struck dead by the Almighty, but he could not deny that he'd never wanted to kiss a woman as much as he wanted to kiss Isabella Harcourt in this moment.

But she was not his to woo. Not even her feet were his to kiss. Bowing, he settled for a whisper of a peck on the lady's hand and escorted her to the door. "Sleep well."

~

As THEY SAILED SOUTHWARD, the days grew warmer. Isabella had not only opened her portal window, she had propped the door open to allow a gentle breeze to provide some relief while she worked. Thumbing through her Latin dictionary, she found the word she'd been looking for: "*succid* – to cut down." She recorded the English translation in her journal, but once she read the sentence, something didn't seem right.

"Hard at work, are you?" a man asked from behind —the same deep voice that had come to make gooseflesh skitter across her skin.

She turned to find Captain MacGalloway leaning against the doorjamb. Holy help, the man looked as cocksure as a pirate, one ankle crossed over the other. As usual, he wore a worn-in leather doublet, his kilt belted low across his hips with a sporran covering his loins, a dirk and *sgian dubh* sheathed on either side. How he managed to stir her blood every time he was in her presence, she could not understand. Lord knew she had oft chastised herself for such unbidden adoration.

She affected a smile—one somewhat aloof, concealing the pure pleasure thrumming through her blood merely from the sight of the blue-eyed devil. "I've been searching for the fragments to complete this tablet for days, but it just doesn't seem to make sense."

He sauntered inside. "Mind if I have a look?"

She sat back and pointed with her tweezers, careful not to touch the bit she had just pieced together. Then she referred to her journal. "I've translated this passage as: *Before the battle, the lieutenant pledged his head to the gods of the dead in return for victory. But after the last sword stilled, it seems I was to be a cut down.*" Isabella pointed to the tablet. "He has used the word *succid* here, but the translation doesn't seem to flow. Perhaps it is '*I was to be cut down.*"

The captain leaned in, the scent of spice and the sea wafting over her just as it had done when he placed his hand upon her waist last eve and began to waltz.

Being near him was dangerous and hypnotic, yet something deep inside her craved closeness, challenging all sensibility.

"Look here," he said, slipping the tweezers from her grip, his light touch causing her to gasp. Thank heavens it was a quiet gasp. At least the captain pretended not to notice. He pointed to the *d* at the end of *succid*. "There's a bit of ink trailing. I think the word is not complete."

Isabella referred back to her dictionary. "Might it be *succidaneus*?"

"I think you may be right. It wasn't unusual for a solider to pledge his life to the gods of the dead in return for victory. Perhaps your man was saying that he was used as a substitute sacrificial victim." Captain MacGalloway leaned over her crate of fragments. "What else do you have in here that might prove us right?"

"Well, I'm not sure if it will fit, but there's a passage that mentions that the *legatus* and a band of *legionnaires* all swore an oath to the *generalis*..." She nudged him aside a fraction, found the section to which she was referring, and pointed. "There."

Biting down on the corner of his mouth, the captain carefully tried to lever the piece out with the tweezers, but he stopped as soon as a sliver flaked away. "These are only good for tiny bits," he said, tossing the tool onto her table.

He unsheathed the razor-sharp *sgian dubh* from the scabbard on his belt. Before he could do any damage, Isabella grasped his wrist and stayed his hand. "I've never used a knife on the tablets."

Completely motionless, they regarded each other, his pulse thrumming beneath her fingers, her mouth dry. Their gazes held as if linked by a charged current until one corner of his lips turned up.

"Not to worry, lass," he said in his deep brogue as if confident those four lilted words would render her unable to argue. "I'll only use it to slide under the piece. It ought to remain intact that way."

She gave a nod but bit her bottom lip while he carefully moved the piece and placed it into the hole. Isabella nudged it a tad with the tweezers. "This is it. See, the edges on the right fit perfectly."

Though there was a craggy void where the *aneus* was missing from *succidaneus*, it was clear that the Roman who'd written the texts had suffered a grave misdeed.

"Now we absolutely must find out what oaths the men swore to the general."

The captain fetched a second chair from his cabin, and together they worked, their shoulders touching, their knees brushing, their breath often catching, and their gazes meeting and holding for a time before shifting back to the work at hand. Tirelessly, they sat beside each other for hours until the tablet was nearly complete.

Isabella recorded the entire translation in her journal and read it aloud while the captain leaned in, his breath skimming the back of her hand. They exchanged an expectant grin before she read aloud:

"*Before the battle, the lieutenant pledged his head to the gods of the dead in return for victory. But after the last sword stilled, it seems I was to be his victim. The lieutenant and a band of legionnaires swore an oath of blood to the general that I had betrayed the cohort's location and had informed the Aquitanians of our weakness. And now all I love is stolen from me. In chains they brought me to this frigid land, fighting for the air I breathe. The only thing keeping me alive is your memory, Flavia. Kiss our son for me.*"

"Astounding." The captain tapped his finger beneath the newly pieced-together tablet. "From this we can deduce quite a bit. Our man was married and had a son. He was betrayed by a lieutenant, and he is not in Britain of his own free will."

"Agreed." Isabella nodded. "I fear this Roman is a slave."

"Aye." Perusing the notations she'd just made in

her journal, the captain leaned nearer. "You said you had translated four more—what did they say?"

Isabella glanced toward her trunk. One was rather salacious in nature and not something she could possibly read aloud—especially not to this man. "He speaks a great deal about how much he misses his wife."

"Flavia."

"Yes."

"Cap'n," said Duncan from the door. "Cookie has dinner ready, and Mr. MacLean is asking if you'd like to inspect the helm afore you sit down to eat."

The captain checked his pocket watch. "It is after seven already? How the devil did that happen?"

# 8

After two days of rain and rough seas, the weather turned balmy, as it oft did in the heat of summer. Gibb and his officers had enjoyed a dinner of roast chicken and a bottle of particularly delicious wine. Of course, Miss Harcourt had joined them, expertly flirting with every man at the table. It was odd that the woman saw herself as not good at flirting. In Gibb's opinion, she didn't need to try. A woman equipped with such wit and in possession of such mysterious black eyes fanned by inordinately long lashes could make a man's heart stutter with a mere blink. Every evening she dined while entertaining them with diverting conversation before slipping behind the door of her cabin.

As usual, Gibb took a turn about the decks long after the crew had headed for their hammocks, leaving only the night watch up top—a few able seamen who had spent their lives at sea, most of whom were restless souls like Gibb.

After he'd made his way to the bow of the ship, he climbed onto the rigging that supported the jib sails out over the prow. The hemp ropes were just wide enough for his wingspan, and he balanced there, daring the gods of the sea to thwart him. An indescribable sense of excitement touched his soul when he balanced out over the water in the dead of night, a wind tousling his hair, the ropes digging into the flesh on his palms. Wings spread like a seabird, he sang a Highland ditty to the rhythm of the sails flapping overhead and the whisper of the ship's wake.

"Far have I travelled and much have I seen,

"But there's nay so bonny as the blue waters of Scotland,

"Be it the beaches of Orkney or the brooding waters of the firth,

"I sail the seas of Scotland in me dreams—"

A soft footstep cut him short. A footstep that shouldn't be on deck this hour of night.

"Please do not stop on account of me," said Miss Harcourt. "I had no idea you possessed such a riveting bass voice."

Now Gibb truly was flying. At least his heart had grown a pair of wings. He glanced over his shoulder and hopped down, landing beside her. "You oughtn't be out here this late at night."

"Oh?" she asked, tilting up that delicate chin. "But those rules do not apply to you?"

"I dunna oft sleep but a few hours. Besides, I like the quiet of the night sea."

"It is different out here at night," she said, toying with a button at the top of her pelisse. Her hair had been tied back with a ribbon, but a lock had escaped its bounds and was plastered across her damp forehead.

"How so?" he asked, sweeping the hair away and tucking it behind her ear.

"There's nothing restricting us like there is on land—no fences, no trees to circumvent. Having never crossed an ocean, I'm surprised not to see any seabirds." She raised her arms, stretching her fingers upward. "Above us, the night sky is filled with innumerable stars. It seems to go on infinitely. It is almost as if..."

"As if?" he asked.

"...we are the only two people in the world."

"It does seem that way. Aside from Danny at the helm and Rupert in the crow's nest, we are very much alone, miss." He took her hand. "Are you a stargazer, perchance?"

"I cannot say I am."

Gibb led her to the starboard rail and pointed. "We all are familiar with the moon."

"Mm-hmm. That's a waxing crescent, is it not?"

"Aye." He shifted his finger downward. "That bright spot below and to the right just a tad is Mars."

"Oh my goodness. It seems so vivid. I had no idea one could see Mars without a telescope."

"Only at certain times, but the planets and the constellations are far more vivid when at sea than anywhere else."

"Fascinating."

Gibb placed his hand in the small of her back and moved his finger. "Do you see the bright dot to the left, almost touching the horizon?"

She leaned toward him ever so slightly, but enough to cause his heart to skip a beat. "The fuzzy one?"

"That's it," he whispered into her ear. "'Tis Saturn."

"Truly? But there are so many bright dots everywhere, I cannot believe that you can pick out two planets so easily."

"It might be easy now, but only after years of training, and learning to navigate in the navy." He shifted his hand, realizing it was still pressing against Miss Harcourt's back, which had grown a tad moist with perspiration. Gibb fingered her sleeve. "What are you wearing?"

"With the heat I was rather restless and wasn't ready for sleep. Rather than wake Maribel, I donned a pelisse."

"But this is wool."

"Yes."

"You must be sweltering."

"A little, though the breeze out here feels heavenly on my face."

He tugged her into the bow, not up onto the ropes where he'd been, but right into the point of the prow. "If it is wind you're seeking, gaze out over the sea and let her speak to your soul," he whispered, urging her to stand in front of him, and quite subtly slipping the ribbon from her tresses. "Let the wildness of the breeze whisk through your hair and breathe its life into your verra being."

"I feel..."

"Hmm?" he asked, closing his eyes as her hair swept around him.

"So free."

But she wasn't free enough, not with her hands gripping the rail and her feet flat on the deck. Gibb closed his hands around her waist. "Spread your arms wide, lass," he said, lifting her above his head. "Now fly!"

Her skirts batted around his face, but the thrill of

her gasp made the effort worthwhile. "I feel entirely weightless!"

"Are your eyes open?" he asked, weaving his face out from the shroud of her gown.

She arched toward his palms as if she expected him to set her down. "I'm afraid I might fall."

"I have you—now open those bonny black eyes and ride the waves!"

"Oh, oh my!" Miss Harcourt called out. "No wonder you like it up here. The view is astonishing."

Chuckling, he set her down. "I do believe you have the spirit of an adventurer."

"I'm afraid you may be right, though aside from my recent trip to Scotland to meet your ship, I have never left the South of England."

"And now you are making a potentially perilous crossing to join in holy matrimony with a stranger."

By the swell of heavy silence on the air, his words had changed the tenor of their chance meeting. He also knew it was necessary to do so before he did something stupid, like pulling her into his arms and kissing her until she promised to stay aboard the *Prosperity* for the rest of her days...which would be a grave mistake.

Gibb loved women as much as the next man, but he had pledged his life to the sea. He was not meant to be married or attached to any female. He'd known other sailors who'd taken wives, and it never turned out well. Someone usually ended up being unfaithful or gravely unhappy. Children were raised without their fathers, a fact that bothered Gibb to his bones. If he were to impregnate a wife, he couldn't imagine not being a part of his child's life. To see a son's first smile or to experience a daughter's first steps were wonders not to be missed.

But Gibb would have none of it. His dreams were of voyages, of battling the briny deep, and of seeing new shores in faraway places. He was a second son, and now that Martin's wife had birthed James, Gibb was no longer next in line for the dukedom. He was free to make his mark upon this world, and he'd chosen the sea.

Miss Harcourt looked to her toes—which happened to be bare. "Yes, I suppose I am on an adventure of sorts. I only hope the destination comes with a happy ending."

"Do you have any reason to believe it will not?" he asked, his gut clenching.

"Papa gave me Mr. Schuyler's letters. From them I thought my intended seemed nice enough."

Nice enough was not half good enough for this woman. In the short time he'd come to know her, Gibb had been fascinated by her intellect, by the excitement she imparted when talking about her tablets. Like him, she had strived to educate herself on matters she deemed important. And regardless if she thought so or not, she was a graceful dancer. What other hidden talents lay beneath Isabella Harcourt's cool exterior? If only he had more time to come to know her.

"But not incredibly nice?" he asked. "Or incredibly romantic?"

"Oh, no. His letters were all quite formal and earnest—mostly about the transaction at hand, as well as a bit about his work and his house."

"Odd you should refer to your pending nuptials as a transaction."

"But is that not what an arranged marriage is? Is that not what happens to most young ladies on the marriage mart?"

"Perhaps, but they dunna usually marry a complete stranger on the other side of the world."

Her face fell with a wee groan. "No."

"You mentioned his work. What is his trade?"

"He owns a silver mine."

"I see." Gibb had spent enough time in America to know there were a great many mines. Whether they were profitable was yet to be seen. "Your father mentioned Mr. Schuyler maintains rooms in Savannah. I'm guessing his house is not in the city?"

Miss Harcourt shook her head. "His house is near the mine. One of his letters mentioned that it's near a township called Lockhart."

Gibb also knew a bit about Southern townships. Most of them consisted of a shack they called a general store, and the townsfolk were fortunate if there as a church within twenty miles. "Will you marry right away?"

"Papa said Mr. Schuyler is an older gentleman and is rather anxious to..."

"Hmm?"

The lass hid her face in her hands. "He is anxious to start a family."

Dear God, that was the last thing Gibb wanted to hear standing on the deck in the dead of night with a woman with raven's hair billowing about her hips as if she were the last woman on earth. He cleared his throat and swiped a hand across his eyes. He'd been gazing at far too many stars this night. It was best if he turned the topic toward something more terrestrial. "I'd like to see the tablets you've already translated."

Her face brightened with her smile. "Would you truly?"

"From what I've seen so far, I believe they are extraordinary examples of an ancient Roman's existence and must be preserved for future generations to see."

"I agree, and that is why I am following the Society of Antiquaries' recommendations for preservation of texts and tablets of this nature. Once I have the pieces put together for a tablet, I build a frame around the work and secure it under glass."

"Aha, which is why your trunk is so incredibly heavy, is it?"

"Yes," she said while the wind picked up her mane of tresses and blew them out over the bow. "The glass and the stone box in which I found the tablets is quite heavy as well."

Gibb captured a lock of silken hair and drew it to his nose. The woman's scent nearly brought him to his knees—so sweet, so feminine, so alluring. "May I see them?"

"Perhaps tomorrow, when—"

"Not tomorrow." He kissed the lock of hair and let the strands slowly cascade from his fingertips. "Now."

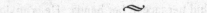

~

THE CAPTAIN HAD STOPPED to speak to the helmsman while Isabella slipped into her cabin. Overhead, the oil lamp squeaked in harmony with the rocking of the ship. She glanced upward as she opened her trunk. "I am well aware," she said to the noise as if it were her conscience. "I should have said no."

But she had not. His words had not been a request. No, no, Captain MacGalloway had issued a command—one given by a man who was accustomed to ordering people about and having them bend to his every whim.

*Including me, dash it all.*

And now Isabella was heaving ho like one of Lord Gibb's sailors. Of course she wanted to show him the tablets, especially after he'd shown so much interest when he helped her identify the word *succidaneus.* Isabella's father was a learned man and had initially been interested in the ruins when they first unearthed them. But Papa hadn't given much consideration to the tablets. Perhaps he cared more about the money he'd earn when the antiquarians began charging visitors to view the site.

*How odd that before he sold my hand in marriage, I had never thought of him as a fortune seeker.*

She opened the trunk and pulled off the quilt she had packed atop two of the framed translated tablets that were safely stowed in the topmost wooden tray. Carefully, she lifted it out and placed it on the bed. Two frames rested atop another quilt and were packed securely with wool padding on all four sides.

She stared down at the first tablet she'd translated —the one that was rather salacious in its content. In truth, Isabella had never felt it was terribly off-color, even though she ought to have been mortified by the translation. Nonetheless, it was a piece of antiquity, an item that reflected the history of its time. After all, the Romans lusted for gladiatorial sport, and were renowned lovers. Why would this slave not be akin to his contemporaries?

Glancing downward, Isabella considered hiding the piece beath the quilt.

"Do you require assistance, miss?" asked the captain, appearing in the doorway.

*Too late.*

She straightened and forced a smile. In no way would Isabella show him the page in her journal with her translation of that particular piece. He'd have to figure out the content for himself—and she doubted he was fantastically skilled at translating Latin without referring to a dictionary, son of a duke or not.

"The first one I found is rather brief," she said, her voice far too high-pitched. She cleared her throat and continued, "But the second one tells of our man's sailing across the sea."

The captain's gaze slid to the first tablet—of course. The man was a natural-born rake, after all.

He reached for it, but Isabella stopped him by holding up her palm. "Please, I'd prefer to leave them in the tray."

"Verra well," he said, leaning over with his hands clasped behind his back.

Isabella bit her lip as she watched him read, the back of his neck growing uncharacteristically red.

"You said you translated this one?" he asked, straightening and looking her directly in the eyes.

Unable to hold his stare for all the butterflies flitting about her stomach, she cast her gaze to the floor, her face warming considerably. "Yes."

"And the translation is in your journal?" he asked, moving to her writing table and placing his hand atop the worn-in leather volume embossed with the pet name her father had given her, Issy. "May I?"

She heaved a sigh. "Must you?"

He handed her the journal. "If you do not wish it, then I will honor your desire. Obviously, you are aware that he has written about—"

She stamped her foot. "Yes, I am well aware of what he has written about, and notwithstanding its salacious nature, I strongly believe this chap's writings give us an important window into the life of a man during Roman times."

"That is verra...avant-garde of you."

Isabella wasn't about to go that far. Yes, she might be a bit forward-thinking and a bit daring, but not radically daring. "It is very *practical* of me, mind you."

"Aye, it might be practical, but it also proves you're no supercilious lass. No wonder you were averse to the *ton*. Your aversion surely wasna caused by your dancing—or your flirting expertise."

"Oh, pshaw!" She batted a hand through the air. "Perhaps my dancing with you was passable because we were alone and there weren't dozens of bystanders watching and judging my every step."

A crooked smile stretched his sensual mouth, making smiling back utterly irresistible. "A bit bashful, are you? Ye ken there's no need to be. I reckon young ladies would become green with envy while watching your *every* step." He handed her the journal. "Will you do me the honor of reading your translation of the second tablet? My quick perusal suggests it contains nothing untoward."

Isabella opened to the page she'd transcribed and ran her pointer finger down to the first translated word.

"*My dearest Flavia, I traveled to Britannia by boat, my leg shackled to a bench, one arm shackled to an oar. The drum beat continuously, the drummers working in shifts. But there were no shifts given to the miserable souls below the deck, sitting in their own urine while a tyrant with a whip ripped our flesh raw. More than once I thought I would meet my end and present my miserable soul to the gods of the dead. But my rage fueled me. I fixated on plotting my vengeance. Nonetheless, when the ship arrived in Britannia and I stood on the slaver's podium where they sold me for a mere ten denarii, it wasn't revenge that kept me alive. It was love. Love for you, Flavia, and the promise*

*I made to one day return to your arms. No, I have not forgotten, nor will I.*"

Captain MacGalloway stood without uttering a word for a moment before he swiped a hand across his mouth. "He wrote to Flavia again."

"Yes, his wife. If you recall in the tablet you helped me translate, he asks her to kiss their son on his behalf."

The captain rubbed the back of his neck. "Poor bastard."

Isabella closed her journal and set it on the writing table. "I can think of nothing worse than being condemned for a crime I did not commit."

"Condemned and sold into slavery. I'd rather be hung and have my misery over with."

"Perhaps our Roman proves his innocence in time."

"Now I ken you believe in fairy stories. He's more than likely to die of the ague than find his wife and son—and who kens what has happened to *them*. Life wasna easy for the families of soldiers who were convicted traitors."

Isabella replaced the tray with the tablets in her trunk. "No, but perhaps someone has given Flavia safe harbor."

"Let us hope so," the captain said, stepping beside her.

As she straightened, the hair at the nape of her neck tingled with the brush of his fingertips. Out of the corner of her eye, Isabella watched as he lazily let her tresses slip across his palms, falling in a cascade of black. Before she ventured outside, she had tied it back with a ribbon, but her hair was so fine it was terribly difficult to keep tied in place, especially when there was a wind.

"You hair is like silk," he whispered, his breath skimming her ear.

Isabella's palms grew moist, her skin hot. Would he kiss her? Heaven knew she desperately wanted him to kiss her again. She closed her eyes and touched her fingers to her lips, remembering their single fleeting kiss behind the wood. And now they must never kiss again. She was promised to another. Even thinking about kissing the captain was sinful.

"May I ask you a question?" she said while her hair whooshed against her back.

"Aye."

She faced him. He knew the contents of the first tablet yet hadn't judged her. Perhaps there were many facets of Captain MacGalloway she was yet to understand. "Why did you kiss me in the park?"

In tandem with the darkening of his blue eyes, a grin slowly stretched across his lips. "I thought I apologized for that misstep."

That was not the answer she sought. Was it entirely difficult to explain his reasoning? "So, you believe it was a mistake to kiss me?"

He cringed, looking toward the door. "Weeeeeeell..."

She huffed, shifting her hands to her hips. Perhaps he was a fiend—at least deep down a little elfin fiend existed in his character. "Did you believe me to be a woman of easy virtue?"

"Och, nay, not at all. I thought you were—" He raked his fingers through his sun-kissed hair, making him look all the more fiendish, as well as captivating, possibly charming and enchanting, and most definitely difficult to ignore.

But Isabella desperately wanted him to an answer the question that had been keeping her awake at night. "Hmm? Please continue. I truly want to know what drove you to make, in your words, such a *misstep.*"

He held up his palms. "Truth be told, I assumed you were attending my mother's luncheon and had stolen away for some time alone."

Ah, yes. She'd always been a consummate wallflower. This time she might have appeared to be a garden flower—or garden nymph, as it were. But Isabella was not satisfied with his reply. "Aside from being mistaken about my being one of the dowager's guests, I must admit I had very much desired to enjoy a bit of time alone. But that does not explain *why* you kissed me. Please. What compelled you to do it?"

Again those fingers raked his hair, but this time they continued backward until he gripped his nape. "As I recall, the wee kiss was in payment for our wager."

"Perhaps, but you didn't offer an alternative. You were quite emphatic about receiving a kiss. Tell me, captain, do you have a soft spot in your heart for bluestockings? For rather plain, bookish wallflowers?"

Groaning, he dropped his hands to his sides. "First of all, there is nothing plain about you. Though I will admit it did cross my mind that I might have a wee bit of fun with a shy young lady."

"Young? Hardly." At five and twenty, she had already crossed into spinsterhood and would have been quite content to remain unmarried, had her father not intervened. "I shall ask once more, did you think me a woman of easy virtue?"

"Och, nay. Quite the opposite. Truth be told, I thought you'd tell me to go take a chilly dip in the Firth of Forth."

She snorted. "I probably should have done so."

"Then why did you not?"

*Why?* Isabella bit the inside of her cheek. At the time she'd hardly been able to think, let alone verbally spar with a man as skilled at flirting as Lord Gibb MacGalloway. "Tell me, captain, what would you have done if you'd been me—a woman who had never been courted, who had never been kissed, a woman whose father had sold her hand in matrimony to a stranger twice her age in a faraway land? What would you have done when a handsome, blue-eyed Scottish man wearing a kilt challenged you to an archery contest with the wager being a kiss?"

One corner of his mouth turned up as he hooked his thumb into his belt. "Handsome, did ye say?"

Isabella crossed her arms and began examining the buckles on his shoes—anything not to have to look into those piercing eyes, eyes that so obviously could see into her soul. "Devilishly so." Dear Lord, had she actually spoken those two words aloud?

He fingered the collar of her pelisse. "Did you shoot poorly on purpose?"

Arms dropping, she coughed out a guffaw. "Never. I am a very good shot, mind you. It just seems you are an *astonishing* shot."

"I suppose I wasna quite forthright on that count. Growing up in Martin's shadow, I did everything possible to best my elder brother, be it archery or muskets. Even as a lad I spent years perfecting the art of the slingshot."

"Now that I can believe." Isabella thwacked his elbow. "You knew your wager was won before I fired the first arrow."

"Let us just say I was confident as to the outcome." The captain cupped her cheek, the pads of his fingers rough against her skin. "Ye ken if you werena promised in marriage, about now I reckon I'd be begging for another one of your kisses."

Isabella leaned into him, her lips pursing, her heart racing.

He dipped his chin, but rather than give her the type of bone-melting kiss she wanted, the fiend pressed his warm lips to her forehead, then dropped the ribbon from her hair into her palm. "Goodnight, Miss Harcourt. Sleep well."

# 9

During the sweltering days, Isabella settled into a routine of dressing in the morning and breaking her fast with a cup of tea and a bowl of porridge with Maribel and Duncan on the deck. The lad had mustered up a couple of half-barrels for them to sit upon while they enjoyed looking out at sea. With a bit of a breeze, it surely was far more comfortable to be on deck, but it was no place for working on the tablets.

After breakfast, she usually headed back to her cabin and tolerated the heat while Maribel tended to her duties. Today, however, Maribel stayed while Duncan paid a visit.

"The cap'n taught me a shanty and a hornpipe."

"Is that so?" Isabella asked. "Do you sing and dance at the same time?"

The lad thumped his chest. "Aye, 'tis no' so difficult."

"Forgive me, I should have known." Isabella gestured to the floor. "Well then, I think we need a demonstration. What say you, Maribel?"

The lady's maid clasped her hands together. "Oh, yes, I'd love to see your performance."

Isabella patted the bed, indicating for Maribel to join her while Duncan removed his cap and bowed deeply. "For your particular enjoyment, 'Whisky-O.'"

The two ladies clapped while the boy crossed his arms and kicked up his heels. "*Whisky-O, Johnny-O, rise her up from down below.*"

Isabella tapped the rhythm on the bed while Duncan made quite a show of fancy footwork.

"*Now whisky gave me a broken nose, and whisky made me pawn me clothes!*"

Patting her chest, she nudged Maribel. "Such a topic for a child."

"Mind you, he's exposed to a wealth of adult conversation below decks," Maribel whispered behind her hand.

Isabella gaped. How did the lady's maid know what the boy overheard when below decks?

Duncan kicked his feet high while hopping from one to the other. "*Now whisky is the life of man, whisky from that old tin can.*"

The lad stamped his feet and tapped his heels, and by the uproar coming from beyond the main door, the entire crew was doing the same. Isabella sprang to her feet. "What is happening out there?"

The lad stopped and thrust his fists into his hips. "I reckon they all heard me and are dancing a hornpipe."

Outside, angry voices rose with a great deal of shouting. "No, something has gone awry," Isabella said, taking a step toward the door.

"Nay, Cap'n MacGalloway sent me in here to entertain you two ladies." Duncan tugged her arm, urging her to resume her seat. "I reckon it is best to ignore whatever—"

Refusing to listen to another word, Isabella twisted her arm from the lad's grip and hastened outside.

The deck was alive with sailors shouting and thrusting their fists into the air.

Duncan tugged Isabella's hand. "You'd best go back inside, miss."

She rose onto her toes, shifting her head from side to side. "What is happening?"

A sudden hush swelled across the deck, followed by the sound of a whip hissing through the air. A bellowing yelp of pain startled her as if she'd been struck.

The men roared like a mob of crazed patrons at a Roman coliseum.

Isabella pushed through the crowd, finding a man tied to the mast with stripes of blood across his back and the captain wielding a vile cat-o'-nine-tails. Captain MacGalloway's arm swung back to deliver another strike.

She marched forward. "Stop this insanity at once!"

Mr. MacLean moved into her path, his arms crossed over his chest, his expression deadly serious. "Ye'd best go back to your cabin, miss."

"Go back to my cabin and allow this barbarism to continue? I cannot believe what my eyes have beheld, and you"—she thrust her finger at the captain—"you sent a boy to keep the sensible ladies from venturing out here to witness this atrocity!"

Captain MacGalloway's icy stare shifted her way as he ran the knotted tails of the whip through his fist. "Woman, you may be a guest aboard my ship, but you are not the lord high magistrate, and you have absolutely no business poking your nose where it does not belong."

"Keel-haul the bastard!" shouted a sailor from the ranks.

"Who kens what else he's filched! Mind your sporrans, laddies!"

"Mine's guarding me loins for a reason!"

The captain again ran the cat-o'-nine-tails through his hand. "I advise you not to further question my absolute authority aboard this ship and suggest that you and your lady's maid retire to your cabins." He nodded to Mr. Erskine. "Take the ladies aft and see to it that they remain in their berths."

Isabella clutched her fists to her midriff while the men parted, making a pathway for her departure. When the whip struck behind her, she jolted even before the pitiful soul tied to the mast shrieked.

"You should not have gone out there, miss," whispered Mr. Erskine. "You as well, Maribel."

The lady's maid stopped inside the corridor and grasped the boatswain's hands. "I thought there might be a reason for Duncan to try so desperately to distract us."

Isabella could have blown steam out her nose. "How dare Captain MacGalloway speak to me as if I were a complete idiot?"

"Dunna mind the cap'n, miss. He barks at everyone, especially when someone has been stealin'."

Isabella wrung her hands. What could she do to help him? "That poor man. What did he steal? A ship's biscuit?"

"He was caught with his fingers in Cookie's effects—took two gold sovereigns, he did."

"Who would steal from Cookie?" she asked, still trying to come to grips with what she had just witnessed.

"Clyde Briggs, that's who. This is his first voyage with us."

"And his last, I would presume," said Maribel.

Isabella paced the corridor. "But whipping a man

seems so barbaric. Why not throw him in the brig, for heaven's sake?"

"Och, he'll spend the rest of the voyage in the brig for certain." Mr. Erskine gave Maribel a wink before he turned to Isabella. "I'll tell ye true, if the cap'n dinna issue a few lashes, the men would have been hankering for vengeance. 'Tis always best to discipline thieves and the like quickly, lest the fellas take it upon themselves to do it."

Stopping, Isabella shuddered as another round of shouting came from the deck. "I take it the punishment would be worse if left to the men?"

"Ye're no' wrong there. Clyde most likely wouldna have survived if the men had their way." The boatswain bowed to Isabella, then took Maribel's hand and kissed it. "If ye ladies dunna mind, I'll return to my post."

Maribel clasped her fingers over her heart and smiled with an enormous sigh. "Thank you for explaining, Gowan. We're so very grateful."

After the boatswain took his leave, Isabella pulled her lady's maid into her cabin. "You have a fondness for Mr. Erskine."

Maribel blushed scarlet. "Oh heavens, does it show?"

"Show?" Isabella flipped open her fan and cooled her face. "You practically swooned into his arms."

"I say I wouldn't mind too terribly if I did swoon into his arms."

"Goodness." Isabella turned the fan toward her lady's maid. Obviously, Maribel was far more in need of fresh air. "I also noticed that you are referring to him in the familiar. How often have you crossed paths with the boatswain?"

"Dunno." Maribel tittered with a giggle. "A few

times. Often enough to give him leave to call me Maribel."

"You aren't going below decks, are you?"

"Oh, no. Only..."

Isabella pulled the maid into her cabin and shut the door. "Tell me."

"'Tis nothing, really. When you go inside to work on your tablets, he sometimes accompanies me on a stroll about the upper deck. It is so awfully stuffy being cooped up inside all the time."

Well, a stroll on the deck wasn't anything to balk about. Isabella had done enough strolling on the deck with the captain, and no one seemed to find it out of the ordinary. "As long as Mr. Erskine is acting as a gentleman, I see absolutely nothing wrong with befriending him."

"Oh, thank you, thank you!" Maribel drew Isabella's fingers to her lips and kissed them. "He's ever so kind, and I do adore listening to his Scottish accent."

As her heart fluttered, Isabella reflected back to the tall captain who had also lulled her with his charming brogue. "The Scots do have a delightful way with words, do they not?"

GIBB PUSHED through the outer door and headed for his cabin. Three strides in, he stopped outside Miss Harcourt's door and clenched his fist around the cat-o'-nine-tails' handle. The bloody bleeding heart had come close to inciting a mutiny. Either that or she'd come close to having her arse thrown overboard—possibly by Cookie, who rarely ever lifted a finger to harm anyone.

The woman was too soft—definitely not made for

a life at sea. If he had let Clyde Briggs go without a good lashing, the men would have rioted for certain. There was nary a soul aboard the *Prosperity* who would tolerate a light-fingered mate, and if Gibb hadn't locked the thief in the brig, Briggs would have been dirked in the back before morn.

He stood for a moment, too angry to confront Miss Harcourt. Growling under his breath, he proceeded into his cabin, stowed his whip, and poured himself a dram of whisky. After a reviving drink, Gibb moved to the windows and stared out at the ship's wake, the gentle rolling of the sea foam cooling the fire in his chest.

Of all the duties a captain must face, he detested issuing punishment the most. He didn't ever take on a sailor without a recommendation. Most of the men aboard had served with him in the navy. Mr. Briggs had come aboard with a letter of recommendation from a captain Gibb once met in Edinburgh.

Gibb didn't expect another captain to be deceitful, especially a Scot. But then again, Gibb was unfamiliar with the man's signature. Perhaps the letter had been forged.

He threw back his drink and poured himself another. He might have been raised in the fantasy world known only by the aristocracy, but he was no dupe. Aye, his nursery had been in an enormous castle on the northern tip of Scotland. Every spring of his youth he'd hunted with his brothers at the Dunscaby lodge in the mountains—a castle with its own loch fed by mountain snows. He'd spent countless hours at Newhailes, dubbed the "wee cottage" by his da, where he'd learned to be a gentleman. He'd even spent a few years at St. Andrews University before acquiring his naval commission. But that was where his fantastical life of a nobleman had ended.

War had a way of making men hard—depriving them of sleep for the rest of their days as well. Gibb had fought his share of sea battles, and it turned out to be a damn good thing he was an ace with a bow and a musket, as well as bloody accurate with a pistol. Give him a sword and he'd fight like a man possessed. Though he hadn't been able to save Duncan's da.

That mistake was one that would plague him with night terrors for the rest of his days. As Gibb closed his eyes, he saw the cutlass make its deadly blow as if it had happened yesterday. At least he'd made certain the French bastard who took Farley Lamont's life never drew another breath.

But that didn't make up for the loss of a good man. A better man than Gibb himself—a father who, only one month prior, had lost his wife to consumption, leaving wee Duncan an orphan.

A rap came at the door.

"Enter," he barked, not bothering to turn around. Most likely, Archie had come to report that Clyde had been securely locked in the brig.

The door creaked open rather slowly for Archie. "I've come to apologize."

Gibb gulped. He had not expected Miss Harcourt to pay a visit. He'd been harsh with the lass and didn't want to face her now, not when his gut was twisted in knots. Without turning, he remained where he stood, watching the wake. No footsteps approached. The latch did not engage.

"You should not have intervened," he said, then took a sip, the liquid burning a pathway through his gullet and warming him all the way down to the soles of his feet.

"Mr. Erskine was kind enough to explain what happened and why."

"But you disagree?" Gibb asked, his tone as fiery as his tot of whisky.

"I believe that any sort of corporal punishment is a form of barbarism."

Gibb tightened his grasp on his glass. If she thought him a rogue, then so be it. "Perhaps it is, but when we weigh anchor and sail away from civil society, the brutality of a life at sea turns some into thieves, as the case happened to be this day. There is much to endure for a sailor, cut off from all the comforts of home for months. They live in cramped conditions and daily face the dangers of the sea—not only the weather, but it is perilous simply to walk the decks when the sails are shifting. I've seen a rope snap and kill a man. I've seen men fall from the rigging to their deaths."

Gibb turned and faced the woman standing in the doorway like a queen, listening to his explanation, though he did not need to give her one. "Tars are hard-drinking brigands. But I'll back my men any day, at any time. The sailors aboard this ship work tirelessly through sickness, through the cold and the wet. They fight the weather just to stay alive, only to fall into their hammocks exhausted. Most of them have come from the gutters of our cities, knowing nothing of our polite society—of our comfortable coaches, rococo fainting couches, and proper manners."

Miss Harcourt raised her chin. "But they appreciate justice."

"In their own way. They understand that I will tolerate no subversion and will treat every man fairly as long as he gives me a day's honest labor and does everything in his power to prove his loyalty."

"And for that, you are their master and commander."

Gibb tipped up his chin. Was she judging him? He cared not, for her opinion held no water in this matter. "I am," he said without an iota of remorse, for if he ever questioned himself, his crew would do the same.

The lady stood motionless for a moment, her lips quivering as if she had a great deal to say but was at a loss to put it into words. After a sharp inhalation, she said, "Since you surrendered your naval commission, have you engaged in battle?"

"Against pirates, aye. That is why I sail with twelve guns. Believe me, I'd rather have barrels of MacGalloway whisky in place of them—there is no finer currency in all of Christendom."

She curtsied. "Forgive me for my intrusion. I will leave you to your duties."

He stood like a dolt while she took her leave, quietly closing the door. Dammit, Gibb hadn't even accepted her apology. He'd just held forth, giving her a litany of all the reasons it was necessary to maintain order aboard *his* bloody ship.

Blast the woman, anyway. She wasn't his to care for, aside from his promise to safely ferry her across the Atlantic. Once he delivered Miss Harcourt into the arms of her betrothed, Gibb planned to forget she'd ever set foot on the *Prosperity*. For the love of God, Gibb had sworn an oath to himself never to lose his heart, and he stood by his word, especially when it came to women who were promised in marriage.

# 10

Several days had passed following the incident with the sailor who had been caught stealing, and since, Captain MacGalloway had scarcely looked Isabella's way. Of course, he had been cordial enough. After all, she dined in the man's cabin every evening, but gone was the cocksure Scot who had captured her hair and drawn it to his lips. Neither had she seen the man who had kissed her forehead when she secretly desired more. And nowhere aboard this ship was the swaggering lord who had tricked her into wagering a kiss.

And she desperately wanted to see that chap again.

Except she should not.

She ought to be happy with the fact that he had grown aloof and seemed to never be on deck when she took a stroll out of doors. Isabella had done her best to pay attention during the evening meals when the men discussed the repairs that would be needed the next time they were in port, or the carpenters needed aboard, or the fact that Duncan had tied a thumb knot rather than a double Carrick bend when he secured the spritsail, which had come loose and caused a significant stir among the crew, not to mention a delay.

Yes, she had paid attention, but that was about all she could do, given Duncan obviously knew far more about tying knots than she ever would. Isabella had followed every conversation while stealing glimpses of the dashing captain out of the corner of her eye. To her chagrin, never once did he look her way. Well, he greeted her when she entered and said goodnight when she left, just as he did to every other person who came and went from his cabin.

*But that is how it should be, is it not?*

She groaned as Maribel tugged the laces on the gown Isabella would be wearing to dinner.

"I'm sorry, miss. The pitching of the ship made me jolt."

It had rained quite a bit today, and the seas were white-capped and angry. "Not to worry," Isabella replied, quite glad that Maribel had no clue as to what had caused her to groan in the first place. "Have you been spending time with Mr. Erskine?"

The laces cinched tighter, this time causing a well-deserved *oomph*. "We usually meet for the noon meal."

"How lovely." Isabella stretched her shoulders to enable herself to take in a deep breath. "Are you growing fond of him?"

"I daresay I am," the lass replied, a touch of sorrow in her tone.

"You're not thinking of leaving me alone with Mr. Schuyler, are you?"

On a sigh, Maribel tucked in the laces. "Oh heavens, of course not. I couldn't ever do such a thing."

Turning, Isabella grasped her maid by the shoulders and looked her in the eyes. "Well, if you decide to follow your heart, please know that I would never stand in your way."

"Truly?" The maid took a step away and shook her head. "I am in service. My mother and her mother before me were in service, and you have always been so kind to me. I could not turn my back, especially at a time when—"

The cannonball churned—the same one that had been lodged in Isabella's stomach since her father's announcement. "Hmm?"

"You'll be alone in a strange land. I reckon you will need me more than ever."

"Perhaps you're right." Isabella pressed her fingers against the ache. "But I do believe Mr. Erskine will be back in America at some point. The *Prosperity* sails to and fro, bringing MacGalloway whisky from Scotland and returning home with American cotton. Your paths may cross again."

"True. It would be nice to see the crew as well as Mr. Erskine. Mayhap they will not forget us."

"Let us hope Mr. Erskine doesn't forget *you*. One day he might make his fortune and kiss the sea goodbye."

"And you were born with stars in your eyes. He's as likely to make a fortune as I am."

"I'm not so certain. Captain MacGalloway could find treasure and share it with his men."

"Very well, I shall add the discovery of treasure for the crew of the *Prosperity* to my nightly prayers."

Making her way to the captain's cabin, Isabella chuckled. As always, she gave a little knock, though His Lordship never actually answered the door.

Except for tonight.

As soon as those fathomless blue eyes met hers, she couldn't hold in her gasp. Captain MacGalloway stood motionless for a moment, staring with a most discombobulating intensity. "Good evening, Miss Harcourt." As if he hadn't been staring, he bowed like a man who had been trained to exhibit impeccable manners—which, of course, as the son of a duke, he had been. "Have the rough seas made you queasy?"

She patted her stomach. "Actually, I've been so absorbed in my translations today, I've hardly noticed, aside from the inconvenience of having to keep everything in a box to ensure it didn't fall off the writing table."

He stepped away and gestured inside. "Duncan will be bringing the meal up shortly. I'm afraid we'll be having cold fare tonight—ship's biscuits, as always, but served with butter and plum jam. There ought to be some cold chicken as well. 'Tis too dangerous to light the hob when the seas are this rough."

She weaved her way to her place at the table, noting that she was the first to arrive. "Where are the other officers?"

"Tending to their duties, as I should be doing as well."

"You should?"

"As soon as we've eaten, I'll go out to inspect the deck. They'll send someone to fetch me if I'm needed beforehand." He held her chair—something Mr. Lyall usually did. "Please, have a seat. Can I pour you a mug of wine?"

"Mug?" she asked.

"I dunna allow glasses in rough seas, lass."

"Then yes. Wine would be lovely, thank you." She glanced over her shoulder, realizing she'd never been alone with the captain in his cabin before—at least not with the door closed. "You said Duncan would be bringing the food soon?"

He pulled the stopper out of the bottle and filled her mug. "Aye." Then he poured for himself, giving her a glance, a bit of a spark returning to his eyes—or had the light from the lamp swinging above caught the glint just right? "Would you prefer to take your meal elsewhere?"

She sipped the wine while the patter of rain pelted the windows. "Not particularly." After all, they had been *in her* cabin alone with the door closed and it hadn't caused a scandal. Surely her husband-to-be would understand that guests aboard this ship took their meals with the captain, and his officers mightn't always be present—not that she'd ever willfully declare such a thing to Mr. Schuyler.

The ship listed so far starboard that she was forced to clamp both hands on her mug while the liquid sloshed and the chair beside her toppled backward. "Oh my," she said, starting to rise, but the captain placed his large hand on her shoulder.

"I'll fetch it. Drink your wine before it spills."

Isabella took a healthy sip. "Do you think we've come through the worst of the storm?"

He replaced Mr. Lyall's chair where it belonged, then slid back into his seat. "I hope so, but the skies are awfully dark. At least I reckon it shouldn't get much worse...unless we're unfortunate enough to be sailing into the eye of a hurricane."

"Hurricane?" she asked, clapping a hand to her chest. Everyone knew a hurricane was absolutely one of the worst calamities that could befall a ship.

The captain shuddered. "That word is worse than a curse. And this is just a fierce summer storm. Mark me."

"I truly hope you are right."

The door swung open, and Duncan tottered in,

carrying a tray. "Here we are—jam, biscuits, and a bit of cold chicken, compliments of Cookie."

His Lordship tapped the center of the table. "Put it here, son."

As Duncan did as he was told, Captain MacGalloway patted the lad's shoulder—not a thwack like you'd normally see a man give to a lowly cabin boy, but his touch imparted a deep sense of caring. "Are your chores done, laddie?"

"Aye, all except the washing up."

"Well, do what you must, then head for your hammock. I dunna want you on deck when the wind's blowing a gale and the rain's coming down in sheets."

"But I'm needed to man the yardarm of the foresail."

"You're needed for far more than tending sails, lad. Now go on and do as I say."

Duncan cast a flabbergasted look to Isabella and rolled his eyes. "Aye-aye, Cap'n."

The man picked up his mug and grinned behind it as the little chap took his leave.

"I believe you have developed quite a fondness for that boy," Isabella said.

"Duncan?"

"Yes. You are aware that he looks up to you?"

A deep crease formed between the captain's eyebrows. "I suppose it is natural for him to do so. After all, he is an orphan."

"Poor lad—growing up on a ship is no kind of childhood."

Captain MacGalloway glanced her way while a dark shadow crossed his face. Something she'd said bothered him deeply, yet judging by the white lines forming around his lips, Isabella didn't feel comfortable pursuing the conversation further.

They ate in silence for a time, the captain's visage gradually becoming less brooding.

With the ease of tension in the air, he sat back and rubbed his belly. "You mentioned that you've been spending a great deal of time working on your tablets. Tell me, what have you found?"

She smiled, always at ease when talking about her tablets. "Well, I believe I've pieced together part of another—our man and Flavia's son's name is Titus."

"How fabulous. Is that as much as you've restored, or is there more?"

"A little more—our man wishes he were home so that he can teach his son how to ride a pony and wield a sword." Isabella dabbed the corner of her mouth with her serviette and neatly folded it. "Oh, and he tells Flavia not to let Titus become a soldier. The Roman wants his son to become a learned man of books and scrolls."

"I think if I were to have a son, I'd tell him the same. War is brutal, and it leaves men with scars no one can see." Gibb waggled his flaxen eyebrows. "I wonder what *your* Roman's name is."

Ah, he'd caught her reference to "her Roman," as she'd come to think of the man who appeared to have been wrongly enslaved. "As do I." Isabella popped the last bit of biscuit into her mouth. "Oh, and this tablet mentions that he has been away for five years."

"Dear God, that is a long time to suffer."

"And he could have done so for far longer, the poor ma—" As she spoke, the ship listed so far to port that the back legs of her chair came off the ground. Screaming, she planted her hands on the table, trying to hold steady while the dishes were hurled to the floorboards and shattered.

The ship violently rocked toward the starboard

side, making Isabella lose control. Flinging her hands over her head to protect herself from a fall, she screamed again as her chair toppled backward. Her backside lost purchase with the chair. She squeezed her eyes shut, preparing for impact.

But miraculously, the captain's powerful arms encircled her, pulling her close. He held her securely against his chest for a moment, standing firm as if the ship weren't rocking from port to starboard. Those fathomless blue eyes stared into hers, harboring a thousand secrets and unspoken desires.

"In rough seas, always remember to bend your knees and ride the waves," he softly growled beside her ear.

If her chair hadn't almost toppled and cracked her head on the floorboards, Isabella was certain she would have swooned. Instead, she struggled to catch her breath, curling into his warmth, jolting at the bangs and booms sounding around them. She glanced to the floor. If only Captain MacGalloway would hold her forever. "Once you set me down, I shall give it a try."

He obliged, leaving her feeling cold, but he didn't step away. Instead, he kept hold of her elbow with a firm hand. "Easy, lass—ye must move with the tempest, lest it get the better of you," he said as if the entire case of books hadn't just crashed to the floor.

Trembling, she closed her eyes and tried to make her knees unlock. "L-like this?"

"Aye. Now breathe in."

She tried to draw a deep breath but only managed a sharp inhalation. Blast it all if Maribel hadn't tied her stays too tightly.

"And out," he said. "Focusing on your breathing will calm your nerves."

But by the groaning of the planks below their feet, Isabella was anything but calm, regardless of how many breaths she took. "Are we going to die?"

"Not on my watch."

"Shipwrecked, then?" she asked, her voice incredibly shaky.

"Nay. The *Prosperity* has met with worse than this."

She whimpered as he bent down and gathered her into his arms once again. "I must head for the helm at once," he said, carrying her to her cabin. "I strongly advise you to pull the bedclothes over your head and stay put until the storm has passed."

"Mayhap I should fetch Maribel."

"That would be a verra good idea." He pressed his lips to her forehead. "What must you remember?"

"To fetch Maribel?"

"Bend your lovely knees—and your lady's maid must do the same."

"Yes, I'll bend my knees." In truth, she'd figured out that rule of sailing on the first day, but it was rather difficult to do when one was being thrown about the cabin like a doll.

"Grasp the latch."

"What?"

"Before I put you down, you must first grasp the latch of your door. Doing so will help you balance."

She reached for it, and her feet slowly descended.

"You will be safe here, ye ken, do you not?"

As she touched the floor with her back to him, she gave a nod, wishing he would stay, but knowing she had no right to ask.

He pressed his lips to her neck and lingered for a moment. Sighing, Isabella leaned her head back against his mighty chest, drawing from his strength, his warmth.

"Do not leave the safety of your cabins. If the storm should grow worse, I'll come for you. Agreed?"

"Yes," she whispered, forcing herself not to turn around and wrap her arms around him.

And then he was gone—that heavenly, warm body was no longer pressed against her back. Cold and trembling, Isabella clung to the latch and looked toward Maribel's door.

*Just a few paces.*

The ship wildly listed from port to starboard as she hastened there, balancing by placing her hands against the walls. "Maribel!" she shouted over the roar of the tempest, pounding on the door. "Are you in there?"

When there was no answer, Isabella feared the worst and flung it open. "Maribel! Where are you?"

She lost her hold on the latch, and the thrust of the ship sent her careening into the wall. Isabella barely had time to gather her wits before she heard a thunderous boom and the shattering of glass coming from her own cabin.

"Dear God, no!"

# 11

After battling the storm for hours, exhausted with every muscle in his body aching, Gibb finally saw a break in the clouds to the south. "Prepare to shift all booms fine on the starboard bow!" he bellowed, confident the *Prosperity* would withstand anything else the tempest might throw at them.

"Aye, Cap'n!" Gowan shouted before spreading the word through the ranks.

"The undertow is already easing," said Archie, only able to stand on his feet because he had a hold of the wheel, but the man was spent, as was the entire crew. During the grueling night, Gibb had spelled the quartermaster several times—in the worst of it, he had no option but to hold her steady alongside the man for a good three hours, mayhap more.

"You're not wrong." Gibb pointed to the clearer skies just over the bow. "The worst is past us."

Archie cast his gaze to the heavens. "God willing."

"Aye, and you'd best pray the good Lord is willing, else there willna be anyone left with the strength to fight."

Down below, Miss Harcourt stumbled out of the

cabin hold and steadied herself by grasping a belaying pin.

"What the devil is she doing?" asked the quartermaster.

"I aim to find out." Gibb marched down the steps, grinding his molars. Even if there were blue skies ahead, the storm was still too savage for her to be on deck. What was it about women and their inability to follow orders? "Miss Harcourt, did I not instruct you to stay in your cabin?"

She had moved to a water barrel, levered off the lid, and dunked a cloth. "Forgive me, but I—"

Holy hellfire, the woman had tracked a swath of blood across the deck. "Good God, what happened?" Rivulets of blood streamed from her hands, and her dress was slick and wet. It took but two strides before he pulled her into his arms. "What did you do?"

"My trunk toppled." She curled into him while a sob racked her body. "Th-there was glass everywhere."

He didn't wait for her to say more. "Mr. MacLean, you have the helm. Sail us to clear skies!"

"Aye-aye, Cap'n."

A hundred questions rifled through Gibb's mind as he glanced through the open door of her cabin. God on the cross, it looked like a battlefield. "Where is Miss Hatch?"

Miss Harcourt shook her head. "I've no idea. She wasn't in her cabin all night."

"Dammit all, the lady's maid is paid to see to your care. It isna as if she was required to be *anywhere* else."

Still curled over with her fists pressed against her forehead, Isabella whimpered. "She must have gone below."

A tic twitched above Gibb's eye. He'd told both women not to go below. He'd have words with the lady's maid, but not before he saw to Miss Harcourt's wounds. He kicked the door to his cabin open, marched across the littered floor, and rested her atop his bed. Hell, his chamber was nearly as destroyed as the lady's, riddled with broken plates and books scattered everywhere.

"No," she said, trying to stand. "I'll bleed all over your bedclothes."

"To hell with my linens," he growled. "What did you do in there? Surely you dinna try to light your lantern."

"No, it was dark—almost completely so. I tried to pick up the glass and put everything back in its place, but I'm afraid I made a frightful mess of myself."

He levered open the half-barrel of water he kept for his own use and dunked a cloth, then returned and kneeled beside her. "What hurts the most? Do you ken if there are any shards of glass still lodged in your skin?"

"I don't know. Everything hurts. My slippers fell off whilst I was trying to bend my knees with the waves, and I cut my feet." She held up her palms. "My hands are a mess. Especially my fingers."

"How about your head? Did you have a fall?"

"No."

*Thank God.*

Allowing himself to breathe, Gibb grasped her right hand and began cleaning away the blood from her fingers, carefully searching for glass fragments. "By the blood smeared across your face, I was afraid you'd suffered a head injury."

"No, my head is perfectly fine, though it should be examined by a physician for allowing me to bend to my father's whims and set out on this godforsaken voyage." She kicked up a leg. "I'm afraid it will be a few days before my feet are healed enough for a stroll about the deck."

He pulled a sliver of glass from her thumb and pressed the cloth firmly over it. "If you canna walk, then I shall carry you."

"Pshaw!" She kicked the other foot. "You are far too busy to worry about the likes of me."

"I can make time." Finishing with the right, he picked up her left hand. "I reckon you'll have quite a task putting your tablets back together."

"Ugh," she groaned. "Do not remind me. I am sick —*physically* sick to see all my work tossed about by that horrible storm."

"Then I shall help you repair them."

Miss Harcourt emitted a wee gasp, and for a moment, Gibb thought he might have hurt her. "You would do that for me?" she asked, her voice soft and utterly vulnerable.

If only she knew how much he wanted to do for her. If she weren't betrothed and he weren't a ship's captain, he'd be happy to spend his days by her side translating her tablets, helping her discover more about the man who wrote them.

But rather than acknowledge how those black eyes brightened, Gibb moved to her feet and cleansed them. "A few of your cuts are deep. They'll need to be bandaged, else you'll bleed all over my ship," he said, giving her a wink.

She graced him with a lovely smile, wild black hair shading one eye, her face still smeared with blood. But it didn't matter. She was the bonniest woman he'd ever seen in all his days, and though her feet and hands were cut, she had just made his heart soar with her wee grin. "Heaven forbid I spill a drop of blood on your pristine timbers, my lord."

His hand stilled for a moment. It didn't bother him that she'd referred to him as lord, not really. He'd been "my lord" most of his life. However, aboard the *Prosperity* he did not want to be seen as a lordling—not by anyone. "Captain, never *my lord* when we're asea."

"Forgive me. I misspoke."

"I'll not hang you from the gibbet today. Tomorrow, mayhap, but not today."

"You're awful."

"And you're tenacious."

"I am, rather, am I not?" She flexed her toes. "'Tis my curse."

"I wouldna venture that far. Your persistence is an admirable quality. If I had a dozen men as dogged as you, my timbers would be even more pristine."

She threw her head back and laughed. "Be still, my thundering heart."

Gibb laughed with her, admiring those eyes. God save him, the woman who had haunted his mind for the past weeks was lying prostrate atop his bed, and there was absolutely nothing he could do about it.

"Beg your pardon, Cap'n?" Archie said from where he stood in the doorway, his shoulders bent, his face drawn. "The storm is behind us. We've a damaged yardarm. We also have damned uncountable yards of tangled rigging. Besides that, nearly every sail is in need of repair."

"And the cargo?" Gibb asked.

"Mac reported two barrels of whisky lost."

"Is that all?"

Archie scratched his head, making his hair stand on end. "Thus far."

"Verra well. Send Duncan to me, then find your rack. We'll make our repairs and pray we dunna drift too far off course."

"Aye, Cap'n." Archie turned his shoulder, stopped, and glanced backward. "Beg your pardon, Miss Harcourt. Are you well?"

"Just a few cuts and bruises, is all," she said. "Thank you, Mr. MacLean. Captain MacGalloway told me we wouldn't have come through the storm without you."

After the door closed, Gibb regarded Isabella—her namesake after all, even though he had purposefully made himself think of her as Miss Harcourt, engaged to an American miner. "I dinna tell you that."

She brushed her fingers over the stubble on his cheek, and no matter how hard he tried not to moan, a rumble of longing swelled from his throat. "You didn't need to. Over these past weeks, I've watched how you put your trust in Mr. MacLean. You listen to him far more than you do any of the others."

"Aye, he's a brilliant navigator—taught me most of what I know about the sea."

"You were in the navy together?"

"I entered with an officer's commission, but he was forced to fight his way through the ranks. And not a day passes when I dunna thank God the man took me under his wing."

Her fingers brushed his stubble along the other side of his jaw. "He was kind to you."

"Not at first, but after we fought together in a few battles, he decided I wasna one of those fops who idles away his days in London gentlemen's clubs smoking pipes and sipping brandy."

"Did you impress him with your skill at archery?"

"Hardly. The King's Navy issues muskets and cutlasses in this century—cannons as well."

Duncan arrived, his hair mussed, bags under his eyes. "You asked to see me, Cap'n?"

Gibb pushed to his feet. "Och, lad, you look as if ye've been in the wars. Did you not stay below decks as I ordered?"

"I tried, sir. But I fell out o' me hammock and thumped me head." The lad rubbed his temple. "Got a knot the size of a walnut to prove it."

"Well, you'd best not overtax yourself today. Stay here with Miss Harcourt and tidy up this mess whilst I inspect the ship's damages—and find out where the devil Miss Hatch is hiding."

Duncan threw a thumb over his shoulder. "She's back in her cabin now, but Gowan thought she'd be safer if she stayed in the wee storage room behind the galley."

Gibb blinked at the lad. Good God, had his boatswain fallen in love with the lady's maid?

"I'll speak to her," said Miss Harcourt. "You have far too much with which to concern yourself. Moreover, Maribel is my responsibility."

~

After the captain wrapped Isabella's feet in bandages and told her to stay put, she watched Duncan methodically pick up the books that had scattered across the floor during the tempest. Interestingly, the lad put them all back where they belonged, first by topic and secondly in alphabetical order.

"You can read," she said.

The boy glanced her way, running his hand over the cover of a book. "Aye, miss."

"How did you learn?"

One of Duncan's bony shoulders twitched up while he slid a volume into place. "The cap'n makes me take two hours of lessons after the morning chores are done every day except Sundays. He reckons I only have to do my chores on the Lord's day."

Isabella found it touching that the swaggering captain would ensure the boy was educated. "My, you ought to be obliged to him for giving you an education. Men who know their letters as well as mathematics and languages can always find a position in Britain."

"Aye, that's what Cap'n says, though my da dinna ken much about reading and writing. He was in the navy—an enlisted man, ye ken."

"Was he?" Isabella sat up and swung her feet to the floor. "Pray tell, what happened to your parents?"

"Both dead."

Though she knew Duncan was an orphan, she thought he might have answered with a bit more information. "Oh my, you poor boy, how awful for you." When Duncan did not respond, she opted to pursue a different tack. "Goodness, your story must be astonishing. Tell me, how did you end up on the *Prosperity?*"

The lad opened a cupboard and pulled out a broom and dustpan. "Once Cap'n MacGalloway resigned his navy commission, he came to fetch me at the boarding school."

Isabella shook her head. It appeared there were several missing facts. How did an orphaned boy end up being "fetched" by His Lordship? "Wait a moment, I don't quite understand. How, exactly, did you come to know the captain?"

"Och, he kent me da. My father was a petty officer aboard the *HMS Cerberus*, and the cap'n was a commander. They fought side by side fending off the French bastards in the Battle of Lissa. The cap'n said me da fought like a Spartan right up until the verra end."

As she drew in a deep breath, she blinked away her tears. "Though I'm sure losing your father must have been dreadful, it is good to know he died valiantly."

Duncan swept the shards of pottery into a pile. "The cap'n said he'd never met a man braver than Farley Lamont."

"Then your father must have been a hero indeed. Was he away at sea when you lost your mother?"

"Aye, she died of consumption a month afore me da. That was awful, it was." The lad pushed the pile into the dustpan. "I dinna ken what to do, and then the magistrate took me to the orphanage. I reckoned I was done for, until Cap'n MacGalloway had words with the orphanage's mistress."

"He did?" Isabella put a bit of weight on her feet, testing the cuts.

"Ye sound surprised," said Duncan, dumping the dustpan into the rubbish bin.

"I am a bit. After all, it is not common for an officer to visit the orphanage of the son of a fallen man, is it?"

"I dunna think it is all that odd. Me da asked Cap'n MacGalloway to look after me—those were his last words."

Isabella stood without much pain, though donning a pair of shoes might be another matter. "Then after he visited you in the orphanage, did he bring you aboard the *Prosperity*?"

"Och, nay. At first he took me to a boarding school that wasna a great deal better than the orphanage—aside from all the books and the learning of me letters."

She chuckled. "I was schooled by tutors, but from what I understand, boarding schools can be a tad severe—however, a good education tends to work out for the best in the long run. I say, you are still of schoolboy age. Did you complain to the captain about being mistreated? Why are you aboard ship and not there?"

Duncan returned the broom to the cupboard. "When the cap'n came to visit, he asked me if I wanted to be a cabin boy aboard his new ship. And I couldna say yes fast enough. Then he told me I could join the crew as long as I kept up with my studies—two hours per day, mind ye."

Reaching for the back of a chair, Isabella took a couple of steps while she reflected back on several times when she'd been on deck midmorning. At that time of day, the captain was usually near the helm. And never once had she noticed the lad taking lessons in his cabin. "*He* teaches you?"

"Nay. He has me read to him and whatnot. But Thane—the oldest sailor aboard—sees to my lessons on account of he used to be a schoolteacher in the Highlands. After the clearances, all the children were gone, and the only way Thane could make a living was to join the navy."

"Let me guess, he was aboard the *HMS Cerberus* with His Lordship as well?"

"Cap'n, mind you."

"I know, but he wasn't a captain then, was he?"

Duncan opened the door and held it for her as she gingerly tiptoed through. "I reckon he wasna."

It shouldn't have surprised Isabella to find Mr. Erskine in the corridor speaking to Maribel, but, nonetheless, it did. She waited until Duncan took his leave before addressing the pair. Then she squared her shoulders, doing her very best to appear commanding as she strode toward them. "I am glad you are both here, because I believe each of you needs to hear what I have to say."

Hat in hand, Gowan bowed. "Beg your pardon, miss, but the cap'n already had words with me—stern words, mind you, words not meant for a lady's ears."

"Did he now?" Isabella wasn't about to allow the boatswain to take the wind out of her sails. "Well, I might add that I was quite—"

"I'm ever so sorry, miss," Maribel said. "I didn't intend to remain below, but when the storm started—"

"It was my fault," Gowan cut in. "For a moment it looked like the tempest was easing a wee bit, so I asked Maribel to go below with me for a bite to eat."

The maid nodded emphatically. "But then the storm grew far worse and—"

"I told Maribel she'd be far safer if she remained there rather than try to make her way back to her cabin."

Isabella sighed, the wind in her sails waning. "Which is Mr. Lyle's cabin, and I am occupying your cabin, am I not, Mr. Erskine?"

The boatswain took Maribel's hands. "Och, nay. The cabins are yours whilst ye're aboard the *Prosperity*."

The lady's maid blushed a lovely shade of rose. "Thank you, sir."

Though the display of affection was endearing, Isabella needed to take charge of things before the lad bent his knee and proposed marriage. Not that Isabella minded, but the corridor of the ship was not the place for such an overture. She cleared her throat. "Let us agree that it was best for Mirabel to stay below decks last night. However, there are two things that I want to point out. First of all, given the storm, it would have been proper for you to inform me that you were going to dine with Mr. Erskine before you followed him below. Secondly, when we came aboard this ship, we were told most emphatically that we were not at any time to venture below decks. Maribel, you broke the only rule Captain MacGalloway gave us, and that is unacceptable."

Growing even redder, Maribel gripped her hands over her midriff and cast her gaze downward. "I am so very sorry."

"But that was my fault as well," Mr. Erskine explained. "I told her it was all right to go below decks as long as she stayed near the galley and away from the sleeping quarters."

Isabella looked the man in the eye. "That may very well be, but as an officer aboard this ship, I would think you would give more consideration to your captain's orders. After all, the men look to you for guidance. If you willfully disregard Captain MacGalloway's orders, what are the crewmen to think?"

Now both of their faces had turned scarlet. Mr. Erskine offered a bow. "Forgive me, miss. You have me word it willna happen again."

"Thank you." Isabella gave him a quick curtsey before turning to Maribel. "We have a great deal of cleaning up to do."

# 12

Fortunately, the weather cooperated over the ensuing days, which gave the crew time to make repairs. They had already passed the two-week mark, and it was likely they'd not quite make the Atlantic crossing within a month, but Gibb was no longer in a hurry. He was keen for the opportunity to help Miss Harcourt repair her damaged tablets.

Also fortunate, though the glass had shattered on three of the tablets she had already translated, the pieces remained reasonably intact. Cookie had given Isabella a flat baking sheet from the galley, which she used to slide under the fragments before flipping them over.

Nonetheless, every evening after dinner, Gibb had visited her chamber, leaving the door ajar, of course. Most of the time Miss Hatch remained as chaperone, sitting on the bed and tending to the crew's mending (punishment that Gibb assigned after the storm, while Gowan had spent the better part of a week pumping the bilges).

But this evening was unusually warm, and Miss Hatch had asked if she might take a stroll around the upper deck for a time. Gibb allowed it, knowing full well his boatswain would find the lass within the blink of an eye.

They sat side by side at Isabella's small writing table, each holding a pair of tweezers with their heads bent over the box of fragments. A box of larger pieces was behind it, pushed up against the wall where there was barely enough room for it to fit.

With his tweezers, Gibb joined two fragments that nestled together perfectly. "Look at this—here is the name *Hadrain.*"

She leaned forward, her soft curls brushing his cheek. "Oh my! That very name ought to enable us to date the tablets. At least now we know this could not have been written *before* Hadrian's rule. We absolutely must find the remainder of the text."

Gibb stretched his neck and scanned the larger pieces. About halfway through, he spotted three words. "I think this is it: *in nomine Imperatoris.*" Very carefully, he picked up the name *Hadrian* and placed it beside the second piece and released a whooshing breath. "Have a look at this. Translated, it reads, 'in the name of Emperor Hadrian.'"

Isabella examined his work, her knee lightly touching his as she leaned inward. "Have a look at that!" Her leg didn't shift as she reached for her notebook. "I simply must record this at once."

Did she actually realize that their legs were touching? And if she did, why had she not shifted away? Very careful not to shift his knee by a hair, Gibb watched her work as she made the notation. By the saints, this woman had the longest neck he'd ever seen. Her skin was incredibly pale, made more so in contrast with her black hair. Without forethought, he traced his finger along the arc.

Miss Harcourt's quill stilled. In fact, she seemed to

freeze in place. "Why did you do that?" she whispered as a splotch of ink dripped onto the paper.

Gibb snapped his hand away. "Forgive me. I shouldna have touched you."

The quill resumed, and she finished her notation. When she sat back slowly, Isabella's smoldering gaze met his. The lady's delicate tongue moistened her lips, making them shimmer in the amber lamplight.

Dear God, she was as tempting as a hot scone slathered with whipped cream and plum conserve.

"You're not going to tell me, are you?" she asked.

"What?" he asked, trying to sound as if he had no idea to what she was referring.

"It seems you are avoiding my question and are not inclined to tell me why you touched my neck."

He shifted in his seat and rubbed his chin. Though he'd shaved this morning, he could do with another. "It...ah...happened to be there." One corner of his mouth turned up. "Your neck, was...there."

She smoothed her lithe fingers around to her nape as if she needed to verify his featherbrained explanation. "Yes, it has been for quite some time. 'Tis attached to my head."

"Aye. But since you described the attachment in such unadorned and ordinary words, allow me to elaborate." Damnation, he ought to be struck by the hand of God for saying more, but the woman had absolutely no idea how alluring she was. And it was nigh time someone told her. "Your neck is not only long, it has an alluring arc that reminds me of a woman's waistline. At the back, your hair frames such loveliness with feminine curls, bringing out the creamy alabaster of your skin, and silken smoothness that could only be possessed by a woman."

Gibb leaned near enough to blow on the object of

his desire, and was rewarded with a pebbling of gooseflesh.

Miss Harcourt drew in a gasp. "I...ah...thought you were here to assist with the translations."

"You would be correct, madam. I am enjoying solving these puzzles of yours." He blew on her neck once more. "But I would be lying if I said the tablets were the only things from which I am deriving pleasure."

She crossed her arms and leaned away from him a tad, given there wasn't much room to move one way or another. "Oh, please, Captain. I am well aware I am not the type of woman born to adorn ballrooms."

Unable to help himself, Gibb brushed the pad of his pointer finger over the velvety soft skin on the lobe of her ear. "Are you referring to the empty-headed darlings of the *ton*?"

"Mm-hmm," she whimpered.

Och aye, if Gibb were wagering, he would bet a treasure chest full of guineas that she wanted to kiss him every bit as much as he wanted to devour her. "I must admit, I'm not one to loiter about in ballrooms, or in London, for that matter. But I believe if I were attending a grand ball, the only woman in the entire hall who might—and I stress *might*—draw my attention is seated beside me now."

The corners of Miss Harcourt's lips turned up as she reverted her attention to the tablet they were so painstakingly trying to piece together. "I gather from your inability to admit to having anyone command your attention, you are altogether averse to dancing."

"Inability to admit?" he asked, coughing out a guffaw. "Me?"

"Yes, it appears so." Using her tweezers, Isabella lined up a couple of pieces. "Why?"

Gibb gripped the sides of his chair to prevent himself from touching her again. She wasn't wrong. Even if he found a woman at a ball who made his cock stand at full attention, he wasn't likely to request an introduction. Gentlewomen of her ilk were off-limits and had been since he came of age.

Miss Harcourt regarded him over her shoulder. "Hmm?"

"I'm a sailor—always at sea. You ken as well as I that fancy balls serve only one purpose."

"I'm guessing the correct answer to the supposed purpose is not to dance and make merry."

"Absolutely not—I enjoying dancing as much as the next man. But I firmly believe the only reason women invented balls was to trap men into marriage."

She tapped the piece she was working with, then gripped the tweezers in her fist, brandishing them under his nose. "Right, so men had nothing to do with this *untoward* matchmaking ritual?"

"Aye, because if a woman doesna marry, she usually becomes a burden on her family for the rest of her days. Furthermore, if my mother were on the committee that got together and decided balls were a good idea, I would definitely say the women had the upper hand."

Miss Harcourt laughed—an unfettered laugh, the sound skimming across Gibb's skin like warm water, or even better, warm cream. "I had the pleasure of spending a little time with your mother before the *Prosperity* came to ferry me to my doom. She truly is a spitfire."

"She was a fabulous duchess."

"Still is."

"Dowager."

"Perhaps, but she is still Her Grace, and a spitfire, as I said. I wouldn't want to cross her, not ever."

Gibb released his grip on his chair and drummed his fingers. At least the conversation had reverted to something that definitely had a deflating effect on his cock. He loved his mother dearly but had never and would never allow her to poke her nose into his pursuit of women. However, as he watched Miss Harcourt return to her work, something she had said needled at the back of his mind. "Am I indeed ferrying you to your doom?"

Color flooded her cheeks as she placed two more pieces in her string of words. "How can I know? My father has made a transaction for my hand as a man might conduct when selling a piece of furniture. I have no idea what I will face when I step off this ship. 'Doom' seems as good a word as any other."

Gibb moved to smooth his hand over her shoulder, but Miss Harcourt's back shot straight. "I cannot believe this." She tapped the writing table. "Never have I been able to piece a string of words together so quickly."

After shoving his errant hand into his doublet and reading the Latin, Gibb translated:

"*At one time I was a proud centurion under General Quintus Pompieus Lusius. But when I led my legion into Aquitania in the name of Emperor Hadrian, I was betrayed...*"

"OCH, this is far too great a find to ignore," said the captain as he studied the fragments. "Now we absolutely must find the rest of the entry afore we turn in for the night."

Isabella's heart soared. She adored having Gibb MacGalloway work beside her. He was quick-witted and brilliant. Of course, he was incredibly beautiful, masculine, alluring, and too dangerous for her own good. And now that Maribel had stepped out for a walk, he had become nearly impossible to resist.

Before this night, they had both behaved with remarkable propriety. In all honesty, proper conduct wasn't unusual where Isabella was concerned, but she continuously had to remind herself that before they were introduced, he'd proven himself to be a womanizer. And though she had been isolated in West Sussex throughout most of her lifetime, she did read the news reports about the mischief in which unwed lords embroiled themselves. It was awfully common for young men to be rakehells before they married. In truth, many chaps continued such behavior after they had taken their vows.

But there was far more to this man than she'd ever dreamed, exemplified by his care for the cabin boy. "Duncan told me about his father."

"Oh?" A deep crease formed between the captain's sun-kissed eyebrows. "He was a good man."

"It seems his son is following in his footsteps."

He took a fragment and placed it beside another in front of him. "Aye, the lad shows a great deal of promise. If only I could interest him in reading more."

"He seems to know his letters. At least, he did a fine job of alphabetizing your books."

"He kens them, he just doesna want to read." The captain again studied the crate of fragments. "He'd rather be up top scrubbing the decks. It makes no sense at all."

Isabella set her tweezers aside, parallel to the crate

as she always did. "Have you given the lad story books?"

"Not certain. I've left that bit up to Thane. After all, he was a schoolteacher."

"Hmm. I'm wondering if Duncan might be enthralled by an adventure book. Perhaps something like *Robinson Crusoe.*"

"That might be an idea."

She sat a little taller. Perhaps he would act on her suggestion. "I wager he'll like it."

The captain glanced up from his work, his hawkish eyes homing in on her. "Would you care to place a wager, miss?"

Ignoring the fluttering of her heart, Isabella met his stare. "As I recall, the last time I made a wager with you, it nearly led to my ruination."

His gaze meandered to her lips. "Then never ye mind. I agree with you anyway. Duncan ought to enjoy *Crusoe*. Mayhap I'll be able to find a copy the next time we step ashore."

Before she did something entirely daft, like lean in and steal a kiss, she picked up her tweezers and reverted her attention to the partially translated tablet. "You are aware that the boy looks up to you, are you not?"

"I dunna ken about that. Aboard ship he has no choice but to look up to me."

"I disagree. His affection for you goes much deeper. And you are quite fond of Duncan as well."

"Wheesht. Ye dunna ken what ye are on about."

Isabella shook her tweezers beneath his nose. "I have two eyes."

"Enough." Gibb regarded her, white lines forming around his lips. "His da died on account of me."

Her bravado deflated. "Duncan said his father lost his life in the midst of battle. Is that not correct?"

The captain hesitated for a moment, his fists clenching. "Aye, but I couldna save him. I turned my back for a mere second, stopped one of Napoleon's louts from running the captain through, and when I turned back, Farley Lamont was down, his life's blood spreading a sea of red across the deck."

"But it wasn't—"

"Dunna say it. Dunna even think for one minute that I wasna at fault. The man not only had a son to care for, the poor bastard had just lost his wife. Damnation, I swore an oath to protect him." The captain pushed to his feet and tossed the tweezers on the table. "I think we've done enough for the night."

Isabella jolted as he marched away and slammed the door. Blinking back tears, she wiped her eyes. No wonder Captain MacGalloway had trouble sleeping. He carried the guilt of Duncan's father's death around his neck as if it were an anvil.

From her own father's experience, she was well aware that war had a hellacious effect on men. In their dreams they relived the horrors they'd faced--yet without resolve.

She sat for a while, staring at the wall. The fact that Gibb had walked out was for the best. If he'd stayed, she might have done something completely ridiculous, like ask him to kiss her again. Heaven knew, the thought had crossed her mind dozens of times. How did a woman who was en route to meet her future husband ask the ship's captain to kiss her?

Such a thing simply was not done. No matter how many different scenarios she played out in her mind, Isabella hadn't come up with anything suitable. No request for a kiss would sound innocent or unintentional or even spontaneous. She would know it wasn't spontaneous, and that would make her look like a harlot.

*And I am no harlot.*

Perhaps his exhibition of anger was a warning to keep her distance. But the man was so confounding. Every time she hit a nerve with Gibb, he groused at her. She shouldn't stand for it. He needed to know that he might be captain of this ship, but he was not lord and master over her.

She glanced over to the fragments that Captain MacGalloway had assembled and translated them:

"Good Lord," she mused, her heartbeat thudding in her chest. "His name is Marcus Antonius."

She arranged the lines in front of the sentence, putting the few that she'd found at the end. Until dawn, Isabella worked tirelessly on the tablet until the entire piece was complete and she translated the text in her journal:

*This is the journal of Marcus Antonius, husband to Flavia, father to Titus. At one time I was a proud centurion under General Quintus Pompieus Lusius. But when I led my legion into Aquitania in the name of Emperor Hadrian, I was betrayed by a younger officer intent upon ruining me and taking my place. Everything I fought for has been stripped from me, and I am wallowing in the filth of this ludus.*

Isabella reflected back to the excavation of the villa. At least the antiquarian had said it was a villa, but if it was a *ludus*, it was far more. And though Marcus Antonius might be a slave, he had been put into service as a gladiator, which most likely meant there was an arena nearby.

# 13

Gibb spent the next two days on deck, barking orders like an obnoxious troll. Duncan even tucked tail and sought refuge in the crow's nest. Though Gibb had sent the lad up there, he must have filled his pockets with ship's biscuits, because he hadn't come down for hours.

He wasn't angry with Duncan, nor had he been angry with Miss Harcourt, but the fact that she hadn't joined him for the past two dinners set him even further on edge. Yes, he had snarled at her, but she spoke of things beyond her understanding. Nonetheless, whether he was in the right or she was in the wrong didn't make him feel any better. He'd never admit it to a soul, but whenever he barked at anyone he felt like a damned heel—doubly so when it came to revealing his testy side to a woman.

And now regret had a hold of his gut with the gripping force of an iron vise.

No matter how anyone tried to rationalize it, Gibb would never forgive himself for Farley Lamont's death, full stop. Before the battle began, he'd found the petty officer holding his head in his hands. When Gibb pressed him for an explanation,

Farley bared his soul and admitted to the recent loss of his wife and his concern for the son left behind in Edinburgh. That was when Gibb swore an oath to himself to keep Farley out of danger—he'd even gone so far as to lock him in his cabin. At least, Gibb thought he'd done so, but the blasted sailor found the spare key in Gibb's writing desk and let himself out.

*I should have taken both keys.*

But Farley was gone, and the only thing Gibb could do about it was to ensure Duncan received an education and landed on his feet. If the lad wanted to attend university, Gibb would see to it he succeeded. Once Duncan was of age, no matter what he decided he wanted to do with his life, Gibb would help him. But for the time being, he was raising the boy for a life at sea—except not a life in the navy. Duncan might decide to be a seaman, but he'd fare better if he remained on a merchant ship—mayhap one day he'd captain a ship in the MacGalloway fleet. He deserved as much.

Archie nudged Gibb away from the helm and took over. "Och, ye've been skulking about the deck for long enough. I reckon it is high time ye go on and apologize."

After hours of gripping the wheel, Gibb rubbed the stiffness out of his hands while he leered at the quartermaster's craggy face. "I beg your pardon? What the devil are you on about?"

"I ken you were helping Miss Harcourt with her Roman tablets. Miss Hume told Gowan the pair of you worked together like a couple of honeybees, and then it stopped a few nights back...about the same time you turned into an ogre." Archie set his gaze on the horizon. "And now Miss Harcourt has all but made herself invisible. She hasna even come to dinner, and all the while ye've been bellyachin' like a sore-headed bull."

Gibb scowled. "Watch your bloody tongue."

"Aye? Someone has to give ye a kick in the arse, and the only person aboard who you'll listen to is me, though I wonder about that at times."

"What do you ken of the details from our wee rift? I'll wager you reckon it's all my fault, do ye not?"

"Aye. Isna it always? Just like when you saved the captain and turned around to find Farley smote by one of Napoleon's bastards. You blame your beefy-arsed self."

Gibb clenched his fists. "Farley's death *is* my damned fault."

Archie's nostrils flared. "Of course it is, on account of ye bein' the Almighty."

With a growl, Gibb removed his bicorn hat and raked his fingers through his hair. If he didn't take charge of the conversation now, he'd likely come to blows with the miserable cur. "We're nearly to Virginia. We'll be saying goodbye to the lassies soon."

Archie grinned, his teeth crooked and yellow. "All the more reason to make amends."

"Why would you care?"

"Because she's a nice lady and deserves to remember us fondly."

"Aye, whilst she rides off into the sunset with her groom," Gibb grumbled, shoving his hat atop his head.

"With her *old* groom. Ye ken he's over twice her age?"

Gibb nodded. Sometime during their work on the tablets, Miss Harcourt had mentioned something about Mr. Schuyler being older, but never said how old. "Tell you, did she?"

"Heard it from Gowan."

It was no secret that the lady's maid had been keeping company with the first mate, and Maribel knew everything of import about Miss Harcourt. "That lad is going to pine for Miss Hume something awful."

"He'll get over it. He always does."

Gibb smirked. Gowan, like most young sailors, fell in love as often as possible, then made himself miserable with yearning until he found a new wench in the next port. "Well, since you're tending the helm, I might have a word with Cookie—make certain he serves us something palatable this eve."

Archie nodded. "Then will you also ask Miss Harcourt to join us?"

"I might." Gibb gave the wheel a rap. "Och, you have a soft spot for the lass, do you?"

"Aye, as does every other man aboard this ship, especially you."

Gibb had heard enough. As he walked toward the bow, over his shoulder he signaled the quartermaster with an indecent finger, the one described by the Romans as *digitus impudicus*. Though Archie was the only man aboard the *Prosperity* who could pester him without fear of retribution, the bastard was close to crossing the line.

As Gibb traversed the deck, the wind seemed to catch his foul mood and blow it out to sea. Perhaps the change in his disposition was because it wasn't as hot today. Perhaps something else had released a valve within his chest.

Gibb didn't care. He was just glad that the anger and melancholy had taken a rest for the time being. "Cookie!" he bellowed, climbing down the steep steps.

The big fellow popped his head out the galley,

wiping his two-fingered hand on his apron. "Aye, Cap'n?"

"Have you a couple of nice roasted chickens for tonight's dinner?"

The cook glanced to the pot of stew boiling on the hob. "I reckon there's enough time to prepare a pair if that'll meet with your fancy. Ye could be dining a wee bit late, though."

"Fair enough. What about dessert? Do you have something unique stowed away in the larder?"

"Ye mean something to appease an unhappy lassie?"

"Good God, does everyone aboard this ship ken I had a wee quarrel with Miss Harcourt?"

"Aye." Cookie pulled the string of the larder key from beneath his shirt. "Except the tale is it wasna so much of a quarrel as a scolding."

"Wheest your gob." Gibb thrust his upturned palm toward the storeroom door. "Do you have a treat or nay?"

"I've a tin of Christmas pudding I've been saving—swimming in rum. Added currants, dates, and nuts as well."

"Plenty of sugar?"

"Aye, plenty—just the thing for an apology."

Gibb snorted. He could wager not one of the men on board kent what he and Miss Harcourt had disagreed about, yet it seemed they all believed him to be the guilty party. Regardless, he had asked for the damned dessert, and it was, indeed, intended to make amends. Since his mood was decidedly improving, he let Cookie's remark go. "If it is verra sweet, then I reckon your Christmas pudding will do nicely—but we'll call it holiday pudding, since it is August."

"Are ye certain ye dunna want to save it for the lassie's last night?"

"Nay. Ye ken we'll be dropping anchor in Norfolk afore we reach Savannah. Replenish your supplies and make something tasty sweet for the entire crew to enjoy."

With that tidbit of business accomplished, Gibb took a route where Archie wouldn't gloat, and made his way across the mizzen deck and up to the cabins. Miss Harcourt's door was slightly ajar, though not propped wide open as she usually set it before their spat.

He stood unmoving for a moment, watching her work. The woman was so incredibly feminine, her every move graceful. How he had possibly thought her plain when he first came across her in the park, he had no idea. From the soft curls pinned on her head, to her slender shoulders, tapering to an exquisite waist, everything about her was womanly and alluring.

She held her tweezers aloft, looking from one box of fragments to the next, pulling out a bit, shaking her head, and putting it back.

"How go the translations?" he asked, crossing his ankles and leaning against the doorjamb.

The tweezers fell from Isabella's fingers and clattered to the floor. "Captain?" She turned in her seat.

Before the lady could bend forward, Gibb hastened inside and picked up the tweezers. He bowed and presented them to her. "I believe you dropped these, madam."

She slid the tool from his grasp, soft fingers brushing his ever so lightly, but the touch was enough to make his knees grow wobbly. "Thank you," she said rather curtly, and definitely without a smile.

Remembering his manners, Gibb removed his hat and tucked it under his arm, resisting the urge to comb his fingers through his hair as he usually did. "How are the translations coming?" he asked again.

Miss Harcourt returned her attention to the tablets. "Fine."

At her single-word answer, he looked to the cross-beams in the ceiling above. She wasn't going to make this easy. Bless it, he might have been short with her, but he also felt strongly about everything he'd said. Gibb did blame himself for Farley's death, and no matter who tried to tell him he was wrong, it didn't make a lick of difference to his bedamned heart. "I... ah...came to say...ah...something."

"Is that so?" she replied, her tone quite sardonic.

He huffed a sigh. He most likely deserved her ire. "The other night, I dinna mean to hurt you. As you might realize, the Battle of Lissa is a verra tender subject with me—one I dunna care to discuss overmuch."

Miss Harcourt picked up a fragment and moved it to the tablet she was reconstructing. "My father fought in the wars, and he, too, is unable to talk about it. Though I do not believe..."

Gibb didn't ask her to finish her sentence. He knew what she was going to say, or near enough, and hearing it might turn his mood sour again, which he definitely could do without. "Och, I'm making a muddle of this." He took her hand between his palms. "I am sorry for being an overbearing brute. It was unforgivable of me to bark at a woman who is a guest upon my ship, and I am truly embarrassed by my outburst. I hope that you will find it in your heart to forgive me."

For the first time since he entered the lady's cabin, those black eyes shifted upward and met his gaze.

Within a heartbeat, a thrill of yearning pulsed through his blood. Isabella eased her hand out from between his palms while the corners of her lips turned up slightly. “Thank you. I’ll wager that wasn’t an easy apology to make.”

“No, but it was necessary.” He rolled his shoulders with a deep inhalation to cool his unbidden lust, then gestured to the empty chair. “Do you mind if I join you?”

“Be my guest.” She pointed to a framed tablet that hadn’t been there before. “Were you aware that *you* had found our author’s name before you left?”

Gibb took note of the name, shook his head, and blinked. “I did?” he asked. While they were discussing Duncan and the battle, he had found a string of fragments that fit perfectly but hadn’t bothered to stop debating and take the time to translate.

She nudged his arm, making him gasp while tingles spread across his body. “After you left, everything came together as if by magic. Read the whole passage.”

The room grew quiet while Gibb leaned over the tablet. “My word, Marcus was a centurion.”

“Mm-hmm, then he was betrayed and sent to Britannia, where he was sold into slavery.”

“And he ended up in a *ludus*. Is he a gladiator?”

“Yes, I do believe so.” She took a fragment and aligned it with her current work. “I say, it is getting easier to find pieces that fit. I’m nearly finished with this one as well. The last bit is from a couple of the larger pieces—though I’m afraid the ink is quite faded.”

Gibb leaned toward her, inhaling the scent of lavender and something sweet he couldn’t put his finger on. Perhaps honey? “What does it say?”

"Like many, it begins with a salutation to his dear Flavia." Isabella referred to her journal. "*There is but day upon day of misery in this ludus. During the reenactment of the battle of Silva Arsia, the only two men I trusted in this vile place were sent to the underworld. I fear my time is coming near, for my sword is heavy and my armor worn. How I long to hold you in my arms once again before I...*"

Miss Harcourt stopped and pointed. "This is where I cannot make out the writing. I'm sure I have the pieces in place, but the ink is too faint. The remainder of it reads as follows: *I long to wait for you beside the statue of Mars. I long to see your smile as I wrap you in my embrace.*"

Gibb leaned in and squinted at the faint passage. "I canna make it out either, but given the fact that Marcus has said he believes his time is short, I think we can assume he's saying that he wants to hold her in his arms again before he dies."

"I assumed the same as well, though there is too much space in the passage for a single word like *moritur.*"

"Aye, though it could say, *occurrit mihi finis.* 'Meet my end' would fit, I'd reckon."

Nodding, she bit down on her lip. "Perhaps you are right."

"Well, why not assume so, at least until you have an opportunity to consult with an antiquarian who specializes in Roman texts?"

"After the unpleasant exchanges I had with the chap in West Sussex, I think I'd rather find a linguist who can verify my translations."

"Smart of you." Gibb picked up his tweezers, realizing she hadn't moved them. Neither had she moved the chair he'd been using. "I wonder where Marcus was raised. He must have come from a high-ranking family if he was a centurion."

"I'm glad you asked." She gave him a grin that made his heart sing. "I believe I have pieced together the beginning of another tablet where he says he longs to see the shores of *Valentia* again. I think that is a very telling clue that his home must be coastal. In addition, I also found the words *Platja de la Garrofera*."

"*Platja* means beach—'tis Catalan," he said.

"Yes, I am well aware."

Gibb grasped Miss Harcourt by the hand. "We have two very strong clues, and I have rolls of world maps in my cabin. I reckon we ought to be able to pinpoint Marcus' origins."

~

IN AN EFFORT TO tamp down her excitement, Isabella clasped her hands and watched while Captain MacGalloway sifted through his maps like a lad on Christmas morn. His exuberance made her want to dance a jig, but she squeezed her fingers and did her best not to appear too happy. After all, she mustn't forget that he'd shown his temper when she questioned him about Duncan's father.

Thank heavens he had apologized. For the past few days, she'd been racking her brain trying to figure out how to approach him without appearing to yield. She had stood her ground because she didn't care to be shouted at when she was only trying to be cordial. Hopefully he'd understand that she wouldn't tolerate such boorishness in the future.

Except they had no future. She pressed her hands against the sudden sinking in the pit of her stomach.

"Here we are," he said, unrolling a map atop his writing table. "This is of southwestern Europe."

Together they bent over and studied the map. "Have you heard of a town named *Valentia*?" she asked, her mind boggling at the sheer number of seaside villages and cities that were part of the empire during Hadrian's reign.

"No, but we're talking about ancient Rome. The name could very well be something different now."

"Oh, that makes this task easier," she said sardonically while reading the names of the Italian coastal cities.

"Think about the tablets you have already translated. What do you ken thus far?"

"Well..." She drummed her fingers atop the map. "We do know he mentioned *Platja de la Garrofera*. He also fought the *Aquitanians*—which I believe would be part of France now, so it is highly unlikely that he was from the northern Roman territories, especially given the seaside element."

"Wait a moment." The captain moved to his bookcase and ran his finger along the spines. "Here it is. I'd almost forgotten about this old text."

He pulled an enormous leather-bound volume from the shelf and opened it atop the map. "My father employed a Mr. Ramsey as my tutor of languages. When I showed an aptitude for Latin, he gave this to me. 'Tis a history of the Roman Empire." He thumbed through the pages. "If my memory serves, there are a few maps showing the empire's borders through the ages."

He stopped at the first one, giving her a chance to lean in and take note of the date. "No, this one's from 555 BC, far too early."

"I reckon we'll find a map from *Anno Domini* near

the back. After all, the Roman Empire fell two or three centuries after Hadrian."

Isabella anxiously watched him thumb through the pages. "I believe by the time Hadrian was emperor, the Romans weren't as bent on conquering as they were on preserving what they had. After all, Hadrian built a wall to keep out the barbarians, not to allow more in."

"Och, those barbarians to whom you are referring would be my ancestors, mind ye."

"Yes, and they were known to be the fiercest fighters in all the lands—unconquerable. You ought to be proud."

"I am, and that is why I employ fine Scotsmen to man my ship." He turned the last page and jammed his finger atop the book. "This map is more like it. 'Tis of 117 AD."

"That's the year Trajan died."

"Is it?" he asked.

The first thing Isabella saw was the Atlantic. "Heavens, I never noticed it before, but the Romans called this very ocean *Oceanus Atlanticus*."

"Some things never change." The captain leaned over the map. "Look here—*Valentia* is on the eastern shore of *Hispania* between *Saguntum* and *Dianium Ebusus*."

"I guarantee you we will not find *Dianium Ebusus* on a nineteenth-century map."

"I wager you are right. But now we ken where *Valentia* is." He moved the book aside, giving them a clear view of eastern Spain.

The captain placed his finger on the unmistakable promontory of land that was named *Dianium Ebusus* on the ancient map. "Aha. It is now Xàbia."

"Yes, but look up there." Isabella used the feather

end of his quill to point. "That's the city Marcus referred to—Valencia—only a slight difference in spelling! And Platja de la Garrofera is just south."

"At least the beach's name is unchanged. And look there—to the north is Port de Sagunt. It is too similar not to be adapted from the Roman town of *Saguntum*."

Isabella clapped her hands over her mouth and moved to the windows. "Oh, if only we were sailing through the Mediterranean Sea and not across the Atlantic. Do you have any idea how many times I've dreamed about Marcus and Flavia? If only I could go to Platja de la Garrofera and see if any ruins remain of their farm—of their villa—of the statue of Mars."

The captain moved in behind her. "It would be an adventure of a lifetime for certain," he said, his breath skimming the back of her neck.

Closing her eyes, Isabella reveled in his nearness, wanting him to touch her. "But I don't even know if I'll ever see West Sussex or Britain again, let alone take a voyage to Spain."

A sigh escaped her lips as he slipped his hands on her waist, his fingers sliding into place as if they belonged there. "None of us ken where we'll be tomorrow or a year hence, or ten years from now. But that doesna mean we canna dream. If you truly desire to go to find Marcus' *Valentia*, then wish it, *mo leannan*."

As Isabella opened her eyes, she watched the wake foam behind the *Prosperity* and made her wish just when Gibb pressed his lips into the arc of her neck. She nearly swooned as the intimate caress imparted so much more than a kiss. How in all of creation could a man convey so much emotion by kissing a woman's neck? Unable to help herself, she dropped her head against his chest while he trailed those kisses along her shoulder.

"*Mo leannan*—it is Gaelic, is it not?" she whispered.

"Aye," he said, his lips returning to her nape and rendering her helpless to flee.

"What does it mean?" she asked, breathless.

Behind her, Isabella sensed the captain stiffen. "I should not have uttered it."

"The words sounded beautiful."

"My thanks." He placed his hands on her shoulders and urged her to turn and face him. "Will you please join us for dinner this eve? Cookie has a surprise dessert for you."

"*Cookie* does?" she asked, a tad disappointed.

"Well, if you must know, I asked him if he had something that might help raise your spirits, and he had just the thing tucked away in the larder."

Somehow knowing that the captain had inquired on her behalf made her feel as if she were floating inside a bubble. "Then I shall be delighted to join you."

"Excellent." Together they walked toward the door. "We ought to be arriving in Virginia on the morrow."

He could have said anything else without destroying the moment, but reminding Isabella that their voyage was about to come to an end took her bubble and violently popped it. "Oh dear."

"Are you nervous about reaching America?"

Cringing, her gaze meandered upward until she met his beautiful blue eyes. "Terrified."

# 14

Captain MacGalloway had not been wrong when he said that Cookie was to prepare a surprise. It wasn't simply the dessert that was delicious, the whole meal was spectacular, with three courses—a flavorful consommé, perfectly roasted chicken served with cabbage and a loaf of real bread rather than biscuits, and a holiday pudding so sweet it made Isabella's mouth water.

The captain reached for the wine bottle and topped up her glass. "I wish we had a wine cellar on board. I do believe a wee dram of port would complement the pudding perfectly."

"This vintage is nice, though I've most likely had a tad too much wine for one sitting," Isabella said, nonetheless reaching for the glass.

"I'm right fond of Islay whisky." Mr. MacLean pushed his chair away from the table and looked to the other officers. "The meal was delicious, but it is time to make our rounds, men."

Mr. Lyall stood and bowed. "As always, it was a pleasure dining with you, Miss Harcourt."

"Och aye," Mr. Erskine agreed. "You have been missed."

She raised her glass and bowed her head. "Thank you, gentlemen. I have greatly enjoyed our meals throughout this voyage."

"There are a few dinners yet to be served before we reach Savannah." The captain pushed to his feet as well and offered his hand. "Would ye care to accompany me on a stroll across the deck?"

She placed her fingers in his sturdy palm. "I'd like that very much."

Once they were outside, a gentle breeze greeted them, taking away the swelter from earlier in the day. Isabella turned her face to the wind, ever so glad she hadn't bothered to don a bonnet. "I daresay the temperature is absolutely perfect at the moment."

The captain brushed away a rogue lock of hair from his face, but it slid right back into place, nearly covering one eye. "I reckon nights like these are what keep men sailing."

"Is that so?" she asked as they strolled to the ship's rail. "I thought sailors took to the seas because of the promise of wages and the temptation of treasure."

"Some do."

She resisted the urge to twirl that roguish lock of hair around her finger, rather busying herself by running her hand along the hickory balustrade instead. "But not you?"

He followed her lead, walking beside her while the sails flapped overhead. "The sea is in my blood."

"And so is the nobility—dukes, duchesses, and all that goes with the aristocracy and polite society."

He flashed a discordant glance. "I left that world behind when I accepted my commission to the navy—havena looked back since, especially since my brother's heir was born."

"Hmm," she mused. "No longer next in line?"

He picked up a cork bung that must have dropped onto the deck from a water cask and slid it into his sporran. "Thank the saints."

"Why do you abhor the idea of inheriting a title? Your family seems to care for you very much."

"My family is the best thing about the nobility."

Isabella watched him as he strode forward, his tall frame solid, like that of a man capable of heavy labor. His kilt, always worn low on his hips, accented a pair of powerful calves. He turned toward the sea, shifting his fists to his hips, the stance making him seem as if he were in command of the world.

"Simply put, I might have been born into a dukedom, but being a lord with a courtesy title never suited me. I have too much of an adventurous spirit thrumming through my blood."

Isabella patted her hand over her heart, trying to convince herself that she merely admired the captain's physique—trying to convince herself that she had developed a fondness for him merely because she was in a tenuous state of uncertainty. Furthermore, insisting to herself that once she arrived in Georgia his memory would fade, replaced by a dashing image of Mr. Schuyler with splashes of grey hair at his temples. "Hence joining the navy and risking your life for king and country."

Captain MacGalloway faced her, those eyes ablaze as if she'd struck a nerve. "Aye, and I'd do it again a hundred times over. The navy turned me into a man—showed me a life far more rugged than anything I ever could have imagined growing up in a nursery and the drawing rooms of the various homes and castles owned by the duchy."

Clearly, whatever had contributed to compose the sum of this man's character, it had truly turned him into a force to be reckoned with, regardless of if he was on the deck of a ship or carousing among London's *ton*. "Yet you were—still are—a man who can command any ballroom, handsome and lofty enough to marry anyone he may choose."

He smirked. "I shall never marry."

"No?" *Such a pity*. "Whyever not?" she asked, her eyes meandering down to his chest.

Offering his elbow, the captain started off again. "I've known many married seamen, and not a one was happy. And I'm not about to become a blackguard who woos his wife and leaves her alone to bear the children whilst I'm off hauling whisky to the Americas and ferrying cotton to my brothers' mill on the River Tay."

"But surely if you fell in love with the right woman, you might decide to kiss the sea goodbye."

"Not me. I'm married to my ship. I canna imagine saying goodbye to her. No more adventures, no more tempests to fight, no watching the sunrise alone on calm seas with nothing but water stretching to the ends of the horizon. I reckon I'd go mad."

As they approached midship, music started by a group of sailors drew Isabella's attention. They had made themselves comfortable, sitting amidst coils of rope and water barrels. "Good evening, gentlemen," she said.

"Good eve, Miss Harcourt. Ye are just the person I wanted to see!" Duncan hopped up, grabbed her hands, and pulled her into the center of the circle. "Play us a hornpipe, Thane!"

"You'd best make it a reel," warned the captain as the men made room for him to join them. Goodness, he stood a head taller than most of them.

Thane, the former schoolteacher, must be a man

of many talents, because he raised a fiddle to his chin and started to play a reel while another sailor rapped the hilt of his dirk on a quarter barrel to keep time, and another expertly played the spoons.

Isabella did her best to follow along while Duncan kicked up his heels like an overzealous sailor, his reel looked almost identical to the hornpipe he'd demonstrated for her during the Mr. Bogg's incident. But the boy's enthusiasm was infectious.

Laughing aloud, she let Duncan twirl her into circle after circle, until her head swam. "Stop!" she cried, only to have him release her hands and send her staggering and toppling straight into the captain's chest.

Those strong arms wrapped around her and held her steady. "Easy there, lass," he whispered against her ear.

She nearly swooned. "Perhaps I did imbibe in a little too much wine."

The captain didn't release her, his chuckle rumbling through Isabella's body, making everything tingle. "I dunna think it is the wine so much as it is the experience of your dancing partner."

"Och aye?" Duncan folded his arms over his boyish chest. "I can kick my legs higher than anyone on this ship!"

"That may be, lad, but ladies prefer a waltz to a hornpipe, or a reel, for that matter." Captain MacGalloway gave Thane a nod. "Allow me to demonstrate."

Isabella's mouth grew dry as the big Scot placed his hand on her waist and took hold of her right hand in preparation for a slow French waltz. Boldly, she shifted her gaze upward until she stared into those deep blue eyes. Beneath the night sky they seemed dark with want, staring at her with such intensity he made her feel as if he were able to see into her soul.

"But I'm a rather poor dancer," she muttered feebly.

"Wheesht. Have you forgotten that we've shared a waltz?" He winked, a sly smile spreading on his lips. "I ken ye to be quite accomplished, lass."

Thane began to play his fiddle, the tune sounding nothing like the raucous reel he'd played for Duncan. The instrument suddenly became an airy violin expertly singing a Mozart waltz fit for any ballroom in London. The ethereal notes swirled around them, as if attempting to merge their souls. Captain MacGalloway proved that expert marksmanship was not his only virtue. Yes, she'd danced with him before and noted his skill, but at the time she'd thought him an unscrupulous rake. Tonight the man demonstrated indisputable grace while maintaining unquestioned command, and Isabella had no difficulty following his lead. She also had no difficulty losing herself in the deep pools of blue presently captivating her attention.

She ought to be worrying about how closely he held her—only inches from his body—or whether she appeared to be smitten, or if she ought to put an end to the dance, because at least a dozen sailors were staring. But she would be unable to back away even if someone offered a chest full of Spanish silver. Isabella's feet moved without effort as her heart soared, her attention utterly captivated by the Scot.

If only she could take this moment and freeze it—capture it in a bottle where she'd be able to revisit it time and time again. Even if she were able to seize this moment, how could she ever be able to replicate the feelings thrumming through her blood?

Captain MacGalloway led her through a series of

turns, the last in concert with the end of the piece. He bowed while she curtsied, the breeze carrying the last vestiges of the final note out to sea—out to the place where history was kept.

"Cor," croaked Duncan, his eyes wide, his mouth agape.

The others also appeared a tad stunned as they applauded. Isabella's face warmed and she bit down on her bottom lip, praying no one else on the upper deck realized how much she had been captivated by the leader of their ship.

"I dinna ken ye could dance like that," said the cabin boy.

The captain mussed Duncan's hair, then looked to Thane. "Perhaps the lad's ready to move on from hornpipes and reels. After all, he'll most likely find himself in a ballroom one day."

"Aye-aye, sir."

Isabella took Captain MacGalloway's elbow and, as he led her past Thane, she tapped the old teacher on the shoulder. "Thank you for the Mozart. Your mastery is truly inspiring."

The voices of the men also faded with the breeze while Gibb led her to up the steps and to the bow of the ship. Isabella reflected back to when they began the journey—after she recovered from seasickness, she'd taken a stroll about the deck and found him there. "It wasn't all that long ago we stood in this very spot and you showed me how incredibly liberating it is to look out over the abyss of the sea with the wind in my face, my arms opened wide. It was as if I were standing on the top of the world."

"This has always been my favorite place of solace —to come here at night and listen to the sound of the sea and clear my head."

Isabella glanced over her shoulder. She thought they couldn't be seen by the men below, but she checked just to make sure. And once she had confirmed it, she gripped her hands tightly together over her midriff to calm her nerves and raised her chin until she again met his gaze. What she wanted was terribly taboo. What she wanted was unspeakable. Yet she knew that, deep down, she had the wherewithal to ask.

*There are no bottles in which to trap memories.*

She licked her lips.

He brushed an errant lock of hair away from her face and tucked it behind her ear. "You look as if you have something to say, lass."

A shiver of nervousness coursed through her. "I do."

"Would you like to fly again?"

"No... I mean, I would like to, but there is something else I've wanted to ask, and since we are here... alone...I was wondering if..."

He leaned in, those eyes searching hers. "Hm?"

"I was wondering if you wouldn't mind too terribly if you were to kiss me again," she said as if making a business transaction. "After all, the last time you took me by surprise, and I wasn't at all prepare—"

Placing his hands on her cheeks, Lord Gibb MacGalloway smothered her final word with his lips. For the briefest of moments she stiffened, shocked by his sudden agreement. But as she sighed, her body relaxed and her fingers grew minds of their own and moved forward, sliding onto the captain's waist. And with her sigh, a deep moan rumbled from the depths of his throat, sending frissons of energy crackling across her skin.

His full lips molding to hers, Isabella opened her

mouth for him. His tongue swept inside and took up where their waltz had left off in a swirling mayhem of emotion. The big Scot proved magical, stroking deep, allowing her to savor his taste, the remnants of sweetmeats and the overtones of rum together with spices of cinnamon and clove.

When she sighed again, he shifted his hand around her, pulling her close. He deepened the kiss while trailing his fingers upward and threading them through her hair gently, expertly, delightfully. God save her, she never wanted this kiss to end. It felt too good and too right to be wicked.

She whimpered when he eased his lips away, not ready to stop. But then he trailed his lips to her neck, teasing the skin with soothing nibbles, tracing kisses along the sensitive flesh beneath her jaw. Again, he ran his tongue down the length of her neck, lingering as he found a new spot of utter sensitivity in the curve transitioning to her shoulder.

Arching her back, Isabella pressed her body along the length of him, bringing yet another surge of intense desire. "Gibb!" she cried out, clinging to him for dear life.

He chuckled—not a laugh, but a deep, rumbling murmur, expressing the same longing within her. "Did ye mean to call me by the familiar, Isabella?"

"Yes, Captain," she replied, utterly breathless.

He kissed her again. "Then let it be so when we are alone. I adore uttering your name—Isabella, Issy, Bella. It is so very womanly, so incredibly irresistible."

Unable to find the words for an adequate response, she cupped his cheek, rose onto her toes, and savored one more succulent kiss.

As their lips parted and he touched his forehead against hers, there was nothing more tempting than to remain in his arms for the remainder of the night, but she had already taken too much and was hanging on a dangerous precipice of no return. Drawing upon every bit of fortitude in her body, Isabella slid her palm to his chest and gently pushed away, putting a few inches between them.

"Thank you," she said, not meeting his gaze. "I will never forget you."

Before he could respond, she dashed to the stairs and headed for her cabin.

# 15

Isabella did not ask Gibb for another kiss. In fact, she did not indicate that she desired to kiss him again even though he had a strong suspicion that if he pulled the woman into his arms, she wouldn't reject his advances. No, Miss Harcourt would not have balked as her lips yielded to him.

And heaven knew he wanted to do so much more than kiss. Since that unforgettable joining of the lips nights ago, if he dared to again kiss her, he doubted he'd be able to stop. And he would never, ever ravish the woman. Isabella was pure and chaste, and merely kissing him was the most daring thing she'd ever done in her life.

After the incredibly romantic night when they'd waltzed and kissed, it was as if she had closed off the passion thrumming through her blood and resolved to face her destiny.

As planned, the ship moored in Norfolk, Virginia, where Gibb dispatched a letter to Mr. Schuyler to let the miner know they would arrive in Savannah in five days' time—two days for the men to offload the barrels of whisky, a day to load the sharecroppers' wool, and, since the wind was waning, another couple for sailing to Savannah. While they were in Norfolk, Cookie replenished supplies while Archie took the thieving Mr. Briggs ashore and handed him over to the port authorities.

But all too soon, they had weighed anchor and pointed the *Prosperity* southward.

Regardless of his feelings, Gibb continued to spend a great deal of time with Isabella, helping with her translation work. No, she did not ask for another kiss, but he craved one with his entire being. And it was with every ounce of strength he possessed that he fought his craving. He relied on his training and good sense to constantly remind himself that he had no place in his life for a wife, and this particular woman was promised to another. She would never be his, could never be his.

It was pure torture to sit beside her every evening —and to resist temptation. He sat so close that all he needed to do was capture her dainty chin with the crook of his finger and turn her face just enough to brush his lips over hers. It was pure agony to be so near and yet powerless to pull her into his arms and onto his lap. And the worst torture was to be sitting directly beside a bed and not be able to lay Isabella down, pull the pins from her hair, and watch as those black locks sprawled across the pillow. To never make love to her haunted his dreams. To never tell her exactly how much she had entwined herself into his heart haunted his every waking moment.

Tomorrow they would arrive in Savannah, but tonight Gibb sat watching Isabella as she tilted her journal toward the lantern.

"*...I won my fight in the arena yesterday, which is why I am alive and able to take up my quill once again. My opponent was fiercer than any I've faced before. His short* *sword sliced through my armor and cut my side. Though the wound is deep, I told Dominum that I will be well enough to fight three days hence. For if I do, at long last I will earn my freedom. I cannot believe that I will be sailing for home soon and will once again feel your arms surround me. No sword in all of Britannia will be able to prevent me from winning. Wait for me, my love. I am coming to you."*

Gibb loved listening to Isabella read from her journal, and tonight's entry brought on an unexpected turn of events. "One more fight and Marcus will be free," he mused. "It is astonishing that the man survived so long. How many years was he a gladiator in the *ludus*?"

She closed her journal and put it aside. "I'm not quite certain. There is the one tablet where he mentions it has been five years since he last saw his son, but heaven knows how long he lived in West Sussex."

"If he had to fight to earn his freedom, I'll wager it was years—mayhap ten or more," Gibb replied, his mind boggling at the number of fights the man must have faced. Even if it was one per month, the odds of Marcus surviving had to be miniscule.

"If we assume that's correct, Titus could very well have been a grown man by the time Marcus made it home."

"That is, *if* he ever arrived home—in this letter he says he has one more fight."

Isabella's spine straightened and her eyes grew wider. "But he was so close. He absolutely must have earned his freedom. He pined for Flavia for such an inordinately long time, they deserved to have their happy ending."

Gibb doubted they'd ever know. There was enough debris from the tablets remaining for several more letters, and Marcus never dated a one. Who knew how often he wrote, or from where he sourced his writing materials? "For your sake, lass, I truly hope they did. History is fraught with a great many unhappy endings, especially for people who are wrongly accused and sold into bondage."

"I would give anything to go to Valencia and Platja de la Garrofera and hunt around for clues—perhaps find the remains of their farm."

Gibb flicked the quill's feather, making it rattle in the holder. "After nearly eighteen hundred years, I reckon finding any trace of Marcus and Flavia would be a miracle."

"Finding the ruins in West Sussex as well as these tablets was a miracle in itself."

"True, but you could very likely travel to Valencia and unearth nothing."

Picking up her tweezers, Isabella tapped one of the fragments and sighed. "At least I can dream."

"Aye, and dreaming is a good thing. It is what keeps our hearts full of hope." Gibb stretched and glanced back toward the open door. "I dunna believe it makes sense to start piecing together another tablet tonight. Would you care to take a stroll about the deck?"

"I'd like that."

As they headed outside, a fierce wind made the door slam open against the inner wall.

"Goodness," said Isabella, clapping her hands to her hair. "I should have donned a bonnet."

Gibb firmly pulled the door shut, then tugged one of her hands away from her head and tucked it into the crook of his elbow. "I like it better with your head uncovered."

Together they waved to the night helmsman on the way to the forecastle deck, which Gibb oddly thought of as *their* place, even though it had always been *his* place of solace. "Are you afraid of what's to come?" he asked.

"Not really." The jib sails flapped loudly along the bowsprit mast, and as she watched them, she shook her head. "No, that isn't true. I am terrified."

Gibb's gut clenched. He could not imagine being in her position. It was almost as abhorrent as Marcus' situation—at least the part about being betrayed and shipped to a foreign land. "Would you like me to disembark with you?"

Isabella hesitated for a moment, grazing her teeth over her bottom lip. "Would you?"

"I think it is the least I can do. Though first impressions are not always precise, I can learn a fair bit about a man's character by looking him in the eye."

"And what will you do if you believe him to be a blackguard of the highest order?"

The first thing that popped into Gibb's mind nearly made him laugh. "I reckon I might challenge him to an archery contest."

With a burst of laughter, she thwacked his shoulder. "You are awful."

"Not awful, just careful with my wagers." Gibb reached into his sporran and pulled out a leather pouch. "I wanted you to have this."

"What is it?" she asked, sliding it from his grasp.

"Something to remind you of this journey as well as show you the way home—wherever your home may be."

She slid the compass out of the pouch and turned until it was pointing northeast—in the general direction of England. "Is this yours?"

"Aye, but I have another." Gibb tapped the glass.

"The gift of a compass symbolizes safety, protection, and God's speed for your journey."

Tracing her finger along the needle's direction, Isabella sighed. "It is perfect."

"I hope you realize that you will always have my protection should you ever have a need of it."

The moonlight shimmered with the wind and reflected in her eyes as she looked up and smiled. "If you ever should venture back to Savannah?"

"One letter from you and I'll come with my guns a-blazing, madam."

The bonny lass threw back her head and laughed, making a pin fall from her coiffeur. A lock escaped and whipped with a gust. "Oh dear, my hair!"

"Nay," he said, urging her to pull her hand away. "I want to see it down. May I?"

Her gaze darted astern. "What will the men think? They'll see me looking disheveled when I return to my cabin and think the worst."

He plucked another pin. "I'll put it back up again."

"You?"

He gave a shrug. "I reckon I can wield a few hairpins well enough. At least I can make it sufficiently presentable for you to walk back to your cabin without drawing undue speculation."

"Very well." On a sigh, Isabella turned and presented her chignon. "It's awfully thick and unruly."

He pulled out three pins, watching the cascade of black come alive with the wind. "'Tis magnificent." Gibb took out the remaining pins and threaded his fingers through the long mane of black silk. "Your hair is so bonny it is a shame you must wear it up."

She strode to the point of the prow and spread her arms wide. "With it down, I feel wild as the sea."

Isabella had no need to glance over her shoulder. By the warmth spreading across her back, she knew Gibb had moved behind her. When, to her thrill, he placed his hands on her waist, a shiver coursed through her body.

"Climb onto the ropes," he whispered.

Isabella looked to the rigging, dangerously suspended out over the water. "No, no, I cannot."

"We shall do it together."

"What if we fall?"

"I will never allow you to fall, lass." He reached around her and grasped one of the dozens of taut ropes. "Follow my lead."

She wiped the perspiration from her palm by rubbing it on her skirts before she gripped the rope, her fist just in front of his. Upward they went, holding on to the ropes with their hands and scaling them with their feet.

"Here," he said, stopping. "What do you see?"

Isabella had been so focused on watching Gibb's hands and feet that she hadn't looked anywhere except at the rigging. As her gaze shifted, a heavy stone instantly dropped to the pit of her stomach. "Ack!" she screeched as his arm slid around her waist.

"Dunna let go," he growled in her ear. "Breathe with me. In, two, three, and out, two, three. In, two, three, out, two, three."

As she heeded his whispered commands, her tension began to ease.

"What do you feel?" he asked.

She dared to again glance downward to the abyss of the black sea, the glow of white foam breaking on the ship's bow. If she were to fall now, she'd be dragged beneath the hull and undoubtedly meet her end. "I-I feel as if I am cheating death," she confessed, even though she knew Gibb's arm was securely around her waist.

"Aye, lass. Up here, you are at your own mercy. A sailor experiences this fear every time he climbs the rigging. When at sea, repairs must be made, and they're not for the weak-hearted. Up here you must rely on your own strength and the knowledge that you alone are in control of your destiny."

Isabella watched the water break against the bow and gulped. "I think I prefer it when my feet are on the deck."

"Do you?" he asked, not sounding convinced. "Remember when we were here not all that long ago and you felt as if you were flying?"

"Yes."

"Close your eyes just for a moment."

She wasn't certain she wanted to do anything but climb down as fast as possible.

"Are they closed?" he asked.

Bless it, if she didn't humor him now, she'd always wonder what he would have done. Nodding, she did as asked.

Gibb's lips nuzzled her ear. "Imagine yourself riding a horse. You ken how to ride a horse, do you not?"

"I do. Sidesaddle."

"You cue him for a trot." As she imagined it, Gibb gripped her waist tightly and posted with her. "That's it, we're on a country road and the wind is freely blowing through your hair, taking it aloft like the flag at the top of the main mast."

Isabella hadn't even thought about her hair, but it

was sailing, the wind whipping through it and strong against her face.

Gibb's motion changed. "And now we're picking up a canter, going faster and faster. Are you with me, lass?"

Isabella's heart thrummed. "Faster!"

He pressed his chest against her back, urging her to lean forward. "Our horse's nostrils are flaring and he's pulling on the bit. The stretch ahead is wide open and he wants his head. Are we going to give it to him?"

"Yes!" She leaned farther forward. "Let him gallop!"

"He's off and racing, so fast his hooves have left the ground, and now we are upon a cloud, sailing out to sea!"

"We are a shooting star!"

"You are!" he shouted, his arm slightly easing from her waist. "Now open your eyes and experience what it feels like to be Titan in command of the seas."

Isabella opened her eyes, and the sight of the black sea before her stopped her breath, making her fists clench around the ropes. "Don't let go!"

"I have you," he growled. "But more so, you have yourself. You are in control of *your* destiny. No matter where you are or what you do, you make your own decisions and you are capable of anything, even flying into an abyss suspended over the bow of a ship."

With his words, Isabella completely handed her trust over to him. With her feet balanced on the ropes, she leaned against Gibb's powerful chest and released her grip. Her heart nearly burst while tears streamed down her cheeks.

On the morrow she would walk away from this man —a man who made a wallflower feel beautiful and showed her how to command the waves as if she were the queen of the universe. Though this man held the esteemed position of captain, he'd spent hour upon hour at Isabella's side helping her to translate her priceless tablets. Yes, at first she had considered him a rake, but now she knew better. This Scot was passionate and giving and thoughtful. He cared about his crew, and a little boy who had been orphaned by the war.

"Where are you now?" Gibb whispered, his breath skimming her ear.

*Madly, deeply, and passionately in love with you.*

But Isabella couldn't utter the truth aloud. Gibb MacGalloway had told her he was a man of the sea and would never take a wife. Her father was depending on her to perform her duty, else his later years might be fraught with poverty. She had no place to go, and no one to turn to except Mr. Schuyler, who had paid dearly to have an English gentlewoman as his bride.

"I am off the coast of Georgia, not far from Savannah, and on the morrow I will begin a new chapter in my life," she replied, no longer terrified, but now ready to face her lot.

The man behind her stiffened. He said nothing for a time, though the air grew charged as if stretched as tightly as the *Prosperity's* rigging. "What if—"

"Shh!" She'd had a monumental revelation and would stand by it. "I have just experienced the most exhilarating moment of my life, and there can be no 'what ifs.'"

Isabella turned her head and looked into his eyes. "Thank you, but I am ready to climb down now."

Once their feet were securely on the timbers, Gibb gripped her hand and kissed it. "Ye ken you are promised to a stranger."

"Promised to the only man who has ever made a proposal of marriage to me." Though Gibb's mouth twisted, she silenced him by tapping her pointer finger to his lips. She didn't want to force him to make an offer of marriage, and neither did she want him to feel cornered into doing so. "Come the morrow, Mr. Schuyler will no longer be a stranger."

Isabella pulled her hair to the side and twisted it into a rope, then wound it around, making a bun. "May I have my pins, please?"

Gibb didn't try to take over, he simply held out the hairpins and let her do it. When she was finished, she stepped back and patted her coiffeur. "How do I look?"

"Ravishing."

He was exaggerating, of course. Isabella might have corrected him by saying "passable," except he'd argue. Instead, she stood straight and tall while their gazes locked in an unspoken moment of utter longing. Then she turned and swiftly strode back to her cabin.

Walking away from Captain Gibb MacGalloway was the hardest thing she'd ever done in her life.

# 16

Gibb kept his expression so hard and stony that his jaw ached from clenching his teeth. The *Prosperity* had arrived before dawn and been given a mooring at the wharf at the Port of Savannah, allowing his crew time to hoist Miss Harcourt's trunks from the hold and offload them onto the dock before Mr. Schuyler made an appearance.

He had dressed in his finest—a kilt in the MacGalloway tartan, his dirk, *sgian dubh*, and sporran as usual. He'd donned a linen shirt with pristine neckcloth tucked into a white silk waistcoat. Over it all he wore a navy-blue sea captain's coat, lined with gold cording, its brass buttons polished and looking as new as they were on the day it was delivered from his tailor. Though he always wore a naval bicorn hat when on deck, this morning he'd stood in front of his looking glass as he put on the hat he kept for ceremonial purposes.

After the sun rose, Gibb had Duncan take the ladies their breakfast, but he stayed away from the officers' cabins altogether. He left orders with Archie to find him when the silver miner arrived on the wharf, then proceeded to take Mac below for a surprise inspection of the crew's quarters as well as an inspection of the hold.

"This place isna fit for a wallowing swine," he said, looking at the clothing and rubbish strewn across the mizzen deck where the hammocks hung in neat rows, side by side. Damnation, he'd let things slide. "What the devil have you been doing during this cruise?"

The enormous first mate seemed to grow five inches shorter. "Sorry, sir. It wasna this bad when we arrived in Norfolk."

"Is that so?" Gibb asked, pursing his lips and tapping a discarded wooden bowl with his toe. "I gave you this position because I thought you had the grit to manage this crew, which means the mizzen is neat and tidy at all times, the one exception possibly being when we are in the midst of a hurricane."

Gibb picked up a discarded shirt, wadded it into a ball, and threw it at a hammock, the thing unfurling as it sailed through the air, landing on the edge of the damned bed and dangling. "I am extremely disappointed."

"Sorry, sir."

"Have the men tidy this mess forthwith. I want it spotless before we set sail from Savannah or I will have your head."

"Aye, sir. We'll have it in shipshape."

"Not a speck of dirt, mind you, not even on the floor." Gibb scowled. "The next time I come below, I'll be wearing a pair of white gloves."

Things were worse once they got to the hold—at least, Gibb felt they were. The barrels were all lined up and stowed as they ought to be, but the floor was covered with chicken droppings, and he found a ladder with a broken rung. Furthermore, there was a hole in the gate that kept the ship's flock of chickens from escaping and climbing over the damn barrels.

Gibb was about to launch into another tirade about his expectations for cleanliness when Archie popped his head through the hatch. "Beg your pardon, Cap'n, but a black carriage befitting a duke has arrived."

Gibb's throat closed, making him. "Have Duncan fetch Miss Harcourt and Miss Hume."

"Aye, Cap'n."

Gibb pointed to his first mate. "Fix the broken rung and the hole, clean up the chicken shite, and dunna allow the wee beasties out of their coop ever again."

Mac tossed the broken ladder over his shoulder as if it weighed no more than a feather. "Straight away, Cap'n. We'll have it tidied within the hour."

By the time Gibb climbed up to the main deck, Miss Harcourt and Miss Hume were emerging from the officers' quarters. Unblinking, he strode toward the ladies and bowed. "Good morn. I hope you were able to finish your breakfasts. We had a good wind and arrived a wee bit early."

"Yes, thank you. Duncan was kind enough to bring us bowls of porridge and a bit of honeyed lemon juice that Cookie brought aboard in Norfolk."

"Excellent. Did you ken Captain Cook gave his crew lemons to prevent scurvy?"

"I had no idea. Did it work?"

"From the notations in his journal, it appears so." Gibb offered his elbow as the crew finished lowering the gangway into place. "I believe Mr. Schuyler has arrived."

Isabella's face blanched. "Oh."

Gowan stepped near Miss Hume, took her hand, and kissed it. "Will you promise to write to me?"

"You know I cannot read, but I will if Miss Harcourt is willing to help."

Isabella paused for a moment. "All you need to do is ask."

Gibb scowled. "Come, ladies, this is no time to dally. There's a miner on the wharf who has waited months to meet his bride."

The lady tightened her grip around his arm while she chuckled nervously. "And thus comes the hour in which my destiny will be revealed."

Those words were like a knife thrust into Gibb's gut. Nonetheless, he forced a smile. "At least you willna have to suffer the indignity of being lowered to a skiff on a boatswain's chair."

Miss Hume offered a wee titter. "I do like your ability to put a positive spin on things, Captain."

Allowing him to lead her to the gangway, Isabella sighed. "I rather enjoyed the boatswain's chair when we boarded."

Gibb recalled the day. Though he'd been a tad embarrassed by his behavior in the park, the lady's smiling face as the men swung her onto the deck emphasized her astounding sense of adventure.

By the time they reached the wharf, a well-dressed man wearing a coat, top hat, and white gloves stepped from the carriage. He was nearly as tall as Gibb, though not as broad in the shoulders.

Gibb patted Isabella's fingers before he straightened his elbow and tugged down the cuffs of his coat. In two strides he faced the dandy and bowed. "Mr. Schuyler, I presume?"

The man's gaze first shifted to the women before he addressed Gibb with a curt bow. "Yes, sir."

Gibb made the introductions while he watched the miner, careful to avoid looking into Isabella's eyes. With an enormous smile, Mr. Schuyler immediately grasped Isabella's hands. "Welcome to America, my dear. I cannot tell you how happy I am that you have arrived at long last."

The man gallantly removed his hat and applied an appropriate kiss to the back of her hand.

Gibb nodded to the sailors who had come ashore to load Isabella's trunks and then gestured to the wagon behind the carriage. "Please exercise particular care with the black trunk, lads." Then he turned to Mr. Schuyler. "Will you be traveling far this day?"

"My packet boat is supplied for the run up the Savannah River. It takes a bit over two days to reach my estate in Lockhart." The man motioned for the footman to open the carriage door. "My dear, I'll tell you now, the house is aflutter in anticipation of your arrival."

Isabella caught Gibb's eye, her expression wary. "Is it a large house?"

"Oh my, is it large!" Mr. Schuyler's eyes shone with pride. "I brought in an architect who replicated the Governor's Palace in Williamsburg."

"Goodness, that sounds positively colossal," said Miss Hume.

"Only the best for my bride," said Mr. Schuyler, leading Isabella to the carriage.

Before her foot reached the first rung, Gibb hastened forward. "I would like to thank you and Miss Hume for joining us on this voyage and to wish you all the best with the translation of your tablets. I hope they lead to a wealth of discovery."

"Thank you, Captain, and safe travels to you and

your crew," she said as her future husband handed her inside.

Gibb took a step away, his fists clenched so tightly that the fingernails he'd trimmed only this morning bit into his flesh. He didn't want to like the miner, but the man seemed genuinely excited to meet Isabella at last.

After the two ladies had boarded the coach, Mr. Schuyler gave another bow, offered his thanks, and climbed inside.

His heart squeezing as tightly as his fists, Gibb turned on his heel and headed back up the gangway. He was met at the top by his quartermaster. "Well, that's that, I reckon."

"Aye." Gibb looked to the *Prosperity's* furled sails. "Why are we not preparing to weigh anchor?"

"Och, I figured you'd want to give the men a wee bit o' leave. Replenish supplies as well as allow Gowan's men to make some needed repairs to the sails."

"Cookie replenished in Norfolk." Gibb headed for his cabin. "Tell Gowan he has this day only for his repairs. We sail at dawn on the morrow—after I've inspected the mizzen deck."

~

WITH HER BACK ERECT and her eyes on the man who had made an offer of marriage without ever meeting her, Isabella sat beside Maribel in the coach. Beneath Mr. Schuyler's top hat, he had grey hair peppering his temples and brown eyes that were weathered with deep furrows etched at the corners.

"How was the voyage?" he asked before coughing

into a handkerchief with a pained grimace. "Did you incur much foul weather?"

"There was only one severe storm, but the crew navigated through it well," Isabella replied.

"Thank heavens," he said, thumping his chest, then removing a flask from the inside pocket of his coat and taking a sip.

"Are you unwell?" Isabella asked.

"I am perfectly fine." He made a sour face as he pushed the stopper back into the bottle. "I have a pain in the chest that comes and goes. The doc gave me this tonic, but it tastes vile."

Maribel glanced at Isabella. "My mother always said the worse it tastes, the more potent the cure."

Mr. Schuyler replaced the flask. "And that's exactly why I put up with this...unpleasant tasting concoction."

"I thought we might be staying in Savannah," Isabella said. "My father mentioned that you have rooms here."

"I do, a small town house I use for conducting business, but I felt you would be more at ease if you saw the house first." He smiled. "Besides, I've the vicar waiting—and remaining in Savannah will only draw things out all the more."

Isabella gulped. "The vicar is at your house?"

"Nearby. Reverend Marshall oversees the services at churches in three townships, but he agreed to remain in Lockhart until your arrival."

"How very kind of him." A bead of perspiration slipped from beneath Isabella's bonnet and trickled down her neck. For some reason, she thought she might be given time to settle in before the wedding—weeks, or a month...a year would have been ideal. "Are you anticipating a hasty wedding?"

"Considering that I have been waiting months for your arrival, I wouldn't call it hasty, madam. But yes. If it meets with your approval, I hope we'll be able to recite our vows as soon as we arrive home."

"Immediately?" asked Maribel, her voice shooting up while Isabella's head spun.

Mr. Schuyler cleared his throat and thumped his chest. "Perhaps you ought to have a day to settle in, of course."

All Isabella could manage was a purse-lipped nod. Her heart was in shreds. She'd just said farewell to a man who had opened a Pandora's box of emotion inside her very soul. With every turn of the carriage wheels, it was less and less likely that she'd ever see Gibb again. With every step made by the team of horses, she was falling into an abyss of the unknown. Yes, Mr. Schuyler appeared to be a gentleman. He was well dressed, well spoken, and he truly seemed to be happy with her arrival, but she didn't know this man. She hadn't spent a month sailing across the Atlantic with him.

"I am certain the arrangements you have made will be perfectly fine," she heard herself say, her body numb. If only she could scream. If only she could tell him she wanted race back to the *Prosperity* and into Captain MacGalloway's arms. But Gibb had been so expressionless this morn. Perhaps he was ready to move on. After all, he told her that he was married to the sea. He didn't want a wife. He didn't want someone like her ruining his life. Was he not the man who had insisted that every married seaman ended up miserable?

She glanced out the window, noting they were travelling along the river's edge. "You mentioned we'll be taking a river packet?"

"We will. My boat is waiting for us at the ferry pier upriver."

Isabella clasped her hands tightly. "Will there be enough room aboard for my trunks?"

"Indeed. You'll find we don't make many things small in Georgia, and my *Silver Star* is as large as a ferry. We'll be able to drive the wagon and the carriage straight on board from the dock. I hope you two ladies don't mind sharing a berth below decks."

With relief, Isabella nodded her approval. Though Mr. Schuyler might be a Southern gentleman, he was still a stranger, and sharing with her maid brought a modicum of comfort.

"Is the *Silver Star* a steamer packet?" asked Maribel.

Mr. Schuyler sat a bit straighter. "Interesting you should ask, miss. I've been working with a gentleman in Augusta to finance the first steamer on the Savannah. They have made impressive strides, but there have been a few explosions. Needless to say, until they can provide me with a boat that won't sink, or worse, cause mortal injury, I'm still using sail."

Isabella nudged her lady's maid. "We've had plenty of experience aboard sailing ships of late, have we not?"

"Indeed," Mirabel agreed.

Mr. Schuyler smiled while Isabella studied the man to whom she was about to promise to love, honor, and obey for the duration of her life—or his life, considering that he was so much older. Though his face was deeply etched by the years, he appeared to be fit. His visage was attractive, his fingernails immaculately clean.

But would be a good husband?

*Only time will tell.*

# 17

Arent Schuyler proved to be true to his word with everything he had told Isabella along the journey up the Savannah River. Nonetheless, her trepidation mounted as the boat made its way into the American wild. The farther they sailed from the town of Savannah, the wilder the scenery became, the forest thicker, the distance between farms and homesteads growing farther and farther apart. And it seemed every domicile they passed was cruder than the last, right up until she spotted a woman cooking over an open fire with three children huddled together beneath the ramshackle eaves of a lean-to, of all things.

She was quite relieved when they moored in Augusta and loaded the boat with supplies—evidently where her future husband got most of his supplies. Though they'd only stopped for a few hours, Mr. Schuyler had taken Isabella and Maribel on a brief walking tour of the city. Augusta was nearly as bustling as Savannah had been, with stately homes and a myriad of businesses. But they were quickly hastened back on board the *Silver Star* to resume their journey. Unfortunately, only about a mile outside of

Augusta, the wilderness grew even thicker than it had been before.

Just when Isabella was convinced her betrothed was taking her and Maribel to a shack with a dirt floor, the crewmen furled the sails and took up the oars, directing the boat to the bank, where it docked beside an enormous estate. Her mouth fell open with unabashed awe. The mansion before them looked nothing like the sod-roofed houses and shanties they had recently sailed past.

The enormous red-brick house was set atop a mound and was a good distance from the river to keep it safe from flooding, Mr. Schuyler had said. Manicured gardens with hedged pathways and splashes of colorful flowers led the way up to the stoop, making the home look a great deal like an English manor befitting a peer.

After the housekeeper took Maribel under her wing, Mr. Schuyler himself escorted Isabella on a tour through the house. The circular entry walls were adorned with weapons much like the great homes she had seen in England—though these weapons were from America's War of Independence, fought against her own countrymen.

From the parlor to the ballroom, there was no want for space. Even the kitchens were large, including a pantry with shelves all the way up to the ceiling, and a warming room. In truth, she had never even seen a warming room before. Of course, many English manors had cold rooms in which they stored their perishables, but the warming room was complete with a cast-iron furnace, which Mr. Schuyler explained was far more efficient at warming great rooms. And he referred to the rather expansive dining hall as the supper room.

*How very provincial, indeed.*

The bedchambers were all on the second floor, including a fully appointed, never-used nursery. For a moment Isabella stood in shock, staring at the cradle, her heart shrinking, her chest tight. In that moment, she was hit with the stark reality that Gibb MacGalloway was gone and she would never see him again. Tears burned at the back of her eyes, and she wiped her face to hide her desperation.

Thank heavens Mr. Schuyler appeared not to notice as he continued on, animatedly showing her room after room, explaining many of the details, from the types of wood used for doors and moldings, to colors, to curtains and why he chose each of them.

Isabella trudged heavily, following him throughout the rest of the tour, though it all passed by her in a blur. She vaguely remembered the servants' quarters or the stables filled with dozens of horses of various breeds and sizes, all brought to the estate by her betrothed to fulfil specific needs.

Along the way, Mr. Schuyler introduced her to countless servants. There were so many names that Isabella couldn't possibly remember any—except for one, Mr. Booker, who ran the mine, which she discovered was located on the property. Everything was on the property, it seemed—after all, her intended owned over sixty thousand acres, the expanse of which was unheard of in West Sussex.

Mr. Booker dressed in shirt sleeves and leather breeches, and wore spectacles. Mr. Schuyler spoke to the chap with a great deal of respect, and later confided that the man had studied law at the University of Georgia.

Most of the laborers lived either in the bunkhouse provided by Mr. Schuyler or in the town of Lockhart, which had a measly population of seven hundred and thirty-one.

It was all overwhelming, far nicer than she had envisioned, and the man who had paid her father for her hand in marriage seemed affable and somewhat fetching, given his advanced years.

But he wasn't Captain Gibb MacGalloway.

He wasn't the man who had kissed Isabella behind a tree in a park without even knowing her name. He wasn't the mariner who had insisted he would never marry.

Isabella didn't remember much of the rest of the day, or the following morning, when Maribel came in to help her dress. In fact, Isabella stood unmoving while her lady's maid primped, prodded, and cinched. It was if her body was numb, her mind skimming the waves of the Atlantic while hanging precariously out over the bow of a ship.

Since disembarking in Savannah, everything had happened too fast. At the small chapel on the estate, time continued forward without her, as if she were outside her body observing the ceremony, standing beside a stranger to whom she heard herself promise to love, honor and obey.

Suddenly the vicar pronounced them man and wife. Mr. Schuyler, her husband, applied a hasty kiss to her lips and led her down the aisle and out into the sunshine, where he promptly clutched his chest and doubled over with the most horrific, pained bellow she'd ever heard.

Isabella threw her arm around his shoulders. "Good heavens, are you ill?"

Grunting, her husband collapsed, taking her to the ground with him.

"Mr. Schuyler!" On her knees, she clasped his face between her palms. "Arent!"

When he did not respond, she twisted in place, searching the stunned faces of the dozens of servants and laborers in attendance. "Help!"

Mr. Booker pushed through the crowd. "Doctor!" he shouted.

Isabella frantically searched the crowd for anyone who might be a physician. A young fellow kneeled beside her, placing two fingers on her husband's neck. "His pulse is weak. Quickly, we must take him to his bed."

At least a dozen men hosted Mr. Schuyler's unconscious body onto their shoulders and started for the house. As she followed, Isabella's hands trembled, especially the one now adorned by a shiny gold wedding band.

She was instructed to wait in the corridor while the doctor tended Arent inside his bedchamber—a room she was yet to see. Maribel brought a chair, upon which Isabella sat hour after hour while the doctor sent for and received his bag. There was no wedding feast. There would be no wedding night. And while the time ticked past, Isabella began to wonder if the wedding had actually happened at all.

It was dark when the doctor emerged, his expression sullen and drawn. He addressed her with hollow, unblinking eyes. "I am sorry to be the bearer of tragic news, but your husband suffered heart failure. I'm afraid I was unable to revive him."

A lone tear slid down her cheek and into the corner of her mouth, bringing with it a salty taste. Bleary-eyed, she peered through the open doorway at the lifeless form of Mr. Schuyler, a man she barely knew.

He had been kind, and she believed he would have treated her well.

Bursting into tears, Isabella bent forward and buried her face in her palms. "Dear God, what am I to do now?"

There came no reply to her question, the corridor filling with the sobs racking her body. Isabella had merely come to America to help her father. And along the way she had fallen in love with the only man who had ever given her a passionate kiss. But she had turned her back on him because of duty—not because he had said he would never marry, but because she was duty-bound to follow through with an agreement Papa had made with the gentleman who had just made her a widow.

By now, the *Prosperity* had set sail for England, and there she sat in a foreign land where she knew absolutely no one.

"Mrs. Schuyler. I'm sure this must have come as an awful shock." The doctor placed his hand on her shoulder. "Allow me to give you something to help you sleep."

SLEEP CAME WITHOUT DREAMS, as if someone had placed Isabella in a sealed tomb. She didn't want to wake, didn't want to do anything but succumb to the blackness surrounding her.

"Miss?" Maribel's voice cut through the fog. "Are you awake?"

Isabella rolled to her side. "Go 'way."

"But it is afternoon." The maid opened the drapes to vicious beams of light. "I'm ever so worried about you."

Isabella slung an arm across her eyes. Had she heard Maribel correctly? She must have, because the windows faced west and the sun had most definitely traversed to that side of the house. "Did you say afternoon?" Heavens, her mouth was sticky and dry. "What time is it?"

"Two o'clock."

Never in her life had she slept late, and Isabella still didn't believe it could possibly two until she raised her head enough to see the mantel clock. "Ugh," she muttered, promptly dropping back to the pillow. "The doctor's tonic must have been very powerful indeed."

"I came in several times to offer my condolences. I am so very, very sorry for your loss. You must be grieving something awful." Maribel moved to the side of the bed and held up Isabella's dressing gown. "How are you faring now?"

"I can hardly say." Isabella's head swam as she swung her legs over the side of the bed and slowly stood. "This entire charade from the time my father told me I had been promised to Mr. Schuyler has been an utter nightmare."

"Imagine becoming a widow only hours after taking your vows."

Isabella donned the dressing gown. Good Lord, she was indeed a widow.

*Mrs. Schuyler, the widow.*

"Let me help you to the table. I've brought up some tea and a bowl of porridge with honey and raisins." Maribel took her by the elbow. "It isn't too late in the day for porridge, is it?"

Isabella sat and reached for the teapot. She didn't feel like eating anything, though a spot of tea ought to clear the cotton out of her mouth. "Porridge is fine."

"Excellent." Maribel sat in the chair opposite. As a

servant, she didn't often make herself familiar, but Isabella didn't mind—actually, she never minded. She had been with the maid for so long that she looked at the woman as more of a friend than a servant. "I suppose it wouldn't come as a surprise if I said that the vicar and Mr. Booker have been waiting to see you?"

Sipping her tea, Isabella closed her eyes and let the liquid warm her. "Have they?"

"Yes—you must agree to the arrangements, you know."

She rubbed her temples to assuage the pounding in her head. "I suppose I must."

For the second time, Isabella went through the motions of dressing and preparing for the day while her mind seemed to be in an utter fog.

"I don't imagine you've given much thought to what you will do?" Maribel asked while she tucked in the laces.

"How could I possibly?" Isabella grasped her lady's maid by the hands. Though now she was a widow, she had no idea who might be Mr. Schuyler's heir, and the dread of what might become of her brought on a new queasiness. "Whatever may happen, you will always have a position with me." Though she had no grounds upon which to make such a promise, she felt compelled to put her faithful lady's maid at ease. After all, Maribel had chosen to disembark in Savannah, turning her back on Mr. Erskine.

Giving a nod, the maid's mouth puckered, then twisted as if she had more to say but couldn't find the words.

There was no use putting off the inevitable, and Isabella dropped Mirabel's hands, her fingers trembling as she smoothed out her skirts. "Where did you say Mr. Booker and the vicar are waiting?"

"The library."

Isabella started for the door but stopped abruptly and turned. "Where, exactly, in this manse is the library located?"

"First floor, off the entry."

"Of course." She pointed to the floor. "Down the enormous staircase...which is...?"

Maribel snorted good-naturedly. "Take a left, then keep going until you cannot help but notice it."

"Right." Isabella gave a quick bow. "Thank you. I do not believe I'd be able to survive this ordeal without you here."

~

Of course, Mr. Booker and the vicar needed to discuss the funeral arrangements, and the next few days were taken up with the morose duty of playing the deceased's grieving wife. After the undertaker prepared Mr. Schuyler's body, the corpse was placed upon a table in the drawing room, where Isabella sat with the curtains closed, wearing an old brocade mourning gown that she'd once worn to a funeral in West Sussex. So many people passed through to pay their respects, most dressed in working clothes, an inordinately large number being men, of course, since this was the site of the mine.

As planned with the vicar, the funeral was held on the third day. There were so many people in attendance that most of them could not fit into the chapel and stood outside. At the gravesite, every last one of them kissed her hand and expressed their sympathy before they took their leave.

It was late afternoon when the only person left

was Mr. Booker. "Would you care to take a stroll, madam?" he asked, offering his elbow.

She gladly placed her fingers in the crook of his arm. "I would truly love to, thank you."

"Did Arent show you the mine?"

"No, I'm afraid we didn't make it that far."

Mr. Booker headed off. "Of course, the men were given leave for the day, but I thought you might like to see what you've inherited."

She coughed out a sardonic laugh. "Inherited? I mustn't have heard you correctly, sir."

"On the contrary. You heard me quite clearly. Shortly after the War of Independence, the state of Georgia adopted a constitution in which the practice of primogeniture was abolished. The law clearly states that any person who dies without a will shall have his estate divided equally among their children, and the widow shall have a child's share or her dower at her option."

"But I had no dower."

"And no children, which means you inherit the entirety of the estate."

"The entirety? Did Mr. Schuyler not have a will?"

Mr. Booker sighed, his expression grim. "He did have one, though when he received word from your father agreeing to the terms of the marriage, he insisted upon adding a clause that all of the above was null and void upon taking his vows."

"He did so without meeting me first?"

"I think he was in love with you before you set sail from Britain. At least, he was in love with the *idea* of you."

With a grunt, she closed her eyes and admonished herself for not considering the man at all and completely losing her heart to Captain MacGalloway. She hadn't even considered giving her husband a chance. "He was a good man, was he not?"

"A generous, but demanding employer."

"How long did you work for him?"

"Two dozen years, give or take."

"Did he pay you fairly in that time?"

"Quite fairly."

"And I take it the mine is producing well?"

"Quite well. In fact, we've recently found a new vein of gold ore that I'm hoping will keep us occupied for some time to come."

Stopping, Isabella clapped her hands to her bonnet. "Did you say gold?"

A wry grin spread across the lawman's lips as he gave her a nod.

"But I thought this was a silver mine."

"It started out that way, but truth be told, silver is often found with gold—we just haven't made it known for security purposes. Arent was not only a good man, he was very shrewd. Though the mine employs an elite militia to keep the thieves at bay, he always treated his miners well, and, in turn, you'll not find a more loyal group of laborers."

"My heavens." She continued onward while thoughts bounced around her head as if they were tied to springs. "I take it with this new vein of ore, you anticipate the estate's wealth to grow exponentially?"

"Most definitely, ma'am."

Isabella glanced back to the house, realizing it was indeed palatial, especially when compared to anything she'd seen thus far. "Tell me, before my husband added the clause that put the entirety of his estate into my hands, who had he named in his will?"

Mr. Booker stood a bit taller and smoothed his hands down his lapels. "Me."

# 18

After delivering the shipment of cotton to the MacGalloway mill, Gibb was summoned to London by his mother. Actually, all eight of her children were summoned. Their presence was requested not only for the commencement of the Season but to celebrate Mama's forty-fifth birthday. Of course, his mother was English, and, with eight children, Her Grace was one of the *ton*'s most esteemed patronesses.

Gibb sat across from his elder brother, Martin, in the ducal library of the family's Mayfair town house.

"There you are." The duke beckoned a housemaid inside. "Place the tea service on the low table, if you please."

"Aye, Your Grace."

Gibb cringed. "Tea?"

To the question, Martin's resultant expression was one of elitist incredulity—tight lips, slightly upturned nose, wide blue eyes. It was a reflection of their father, affecting a practiced air that implied, *I do believe the drivel that just came out of your mouth is nonsense and I'll not stand for another word.*

However, the duke replied, "It is rather early yet.

Dunna tell me your years asea have turned you into a drunkard."

Regardless of if he was a duke, Martin was first and foremost Gibb's brother, and Gibb wasn't about to take the rebuke—he never had done so and never would. "Has marriage turned ye soft, ye bletherin' numpty?"

The maid's face turned scarlet, her lips disappearing into a thin line. She was obviously trying not to burst out with laughter while she poured and charged both cups of tea with dollops of milk.

Martin, however, didn't flinch. "If anything, marriage has made me smarter, ye sheep-shaggin' eejit." Regardless of his rank, Gibb's elder brother never failed when it came to returning insults.

Still not breaking into a smile, the duke reached for his cup and saucer. He raised his little finger as he drank, receiving a snort from his younger brother. "Tell me, did everything go as planned with Miss Harcourt?"

Gibb's gut twisted. This must be twist number five hundred and forty-three, because his gut had not stopped punishing him since the day the *Prosperity* left Savannah. Over and over he had chastised himself for letting her go—but he'd had no choice, had he? His orders were to ferry the woman to Savannah, not to fall in love with her. Besides, he absolutely was *not* in bloody love. That fact he'd repeated to himself every hour for the past two months. "Aye, I sent word from Norfolk, and Mr. Schuyler was there to meet us at the wharf. He seemed to be an affable chap."

Martin blew out a sigh through pursed lips. "I'm glad to hear it. During the lassie's brief visit to Newhailes, the lass endeared herself to the family. We've all been hoping she was marrying a decent fellow."

By the size of the hole in his chest, Gibb felt no relief. "Why did Sir Kingston sell her hand to a complete stranger?"

"He dinna say much about it, other than his daughter was getting on in years and needed to make a match whilst there was still time."

"Good God, she's only five and twenty."

"Old enough, I'd reckon." Martin pushed the cup and saucer toward Gibb. "Go on, have a wee sip. I've never seen you turn your nose up to one of Cook's shortbread biscuits, either."

Gibb glanced down to the tray, noticing the biscuits for the first time. Indeed, he'd never been able to resist them. He took one and shoved the whole thing into his mouth, just to watch Martin's expression. When he was rewarded with another air of elitist incredulity, he picked up his tea and drained the contents of the cup in one gulp, careful to keep his little finger curled into his fist.

He returned the cup to the saucer with a clank and belched for added emphasis. "Why has our mother decided to make her forty-fifth birthday a momentous occasion?"

With a grunt, the duke shifted his gaze away from Gibb. "She wants a bit of fun. Especially after Papa succumbed to dropsy, she feels she doesna have a great deal of time left."

"Our mother?" Gibb snatched another biscuit. "She'll live forever."

"I thought the same, but why not let her plan a grand affair? After all, the woman mourned for two bloody years. It is time she set her sights on...other things."

Gibb wasn't sure he liked the sound of his mother doing anything aside from mothering and duchessing

—definitely not flirting. No, absolutely not flirting. "Do you reckon she'll remarry?"

"With Grace and Modesty yet to come out? I doubt she'll have the time to entertain a courtship." Martin picked up a biscuit and took a bite. Damnation, not but three years past, he would have shoved the whole thing into his gob. "And her age is to remain a mystery. We're not to mention it to a soul."

"Truly?" Gibb asked. "She's a duchess. Half the members of the *ton* already ken her age."

"Not a word." At least Martin popped the remaining half of the shortbread into his mouth. "And she expects you to stay away from the card tables and dance. All night, mind you."

"Bloody hell, just me, or does the dancing edict apply to Philip, Andrew, and Frederick as well?"

"All of us."

"What of Grace and Modesty? Are they not too young to attend a ball?"

"'Tis a birthday party. Mama wants us all to celebrate with her, and so we shall. And she expects to have a full dance card." Martin finished his tea. "But enough of that. Tell me, how is the *Prosperity* faring?"

"Quite well." Gibb sat back, relieved to have the discussion moved away from family matters. "I've scheduled some needed repair work whilst I'm in London."

"Good, I was hoping you'd stay for a time." Martin gripped the velvet armrests of his chair. "Any thoughts about settling down?"

An image of Isabella on deck with her hair blowing like a sail in the wind came to mind. "None."

"I dunna see why you're so averse to the idea. I ken of many sea captains who marry and have families. They all seem to manage."

Lips curled into a flat line, chin down, eyes homing like an eagle's, Gibb made certain his expression was one his brother would not trifle with. "Not interested in marriage."

"Well then, what are you interested in? Philip tells me you willna need to sail for America again until spring."

Gibb sat back a tad. "Last we spoke, we discussed adding to the fleet—shipping MacGalloway cloth to every port in Europe."

"Right you are. Do you have a ship in mind? A crew?"

"It is a concept more than specifics. The journey to America is a long one and best sailed by a ship with a substantial hull."

"I thought the *Prosperity* was the largest of her class."

"She is. I'd be happy to keep her for the transatlantic voyages." Gibb picked at a bit of loose stitching on his chair's blue damask upholstery. "Though I'm thinking of cutters for the European shipments, as well as acquiring one like the *HMS Temeraire* that can sail anywhere she so desires—that ship is a colossal beasty."

"Och, I like the way you think, brother." Grinning, Martin drummed his fingertips together. "Whilst you're here, I reckon ye ought to look for a place to call home."

In truth, the idea of buying a house had crossed Gibb's mind—for about a quarter of an hour, and then he'd come to his senses. "A wee cottage does sound tempting, but nay. I'm content to let rooms whenever necessary."

"Oh, aye? Now who's the bloody numpty? Sooner or later you'll need a permanent domicile—a place to put all the treasure you're collecting in foreign ports. I ken ye think your heart is locked away in some sea chest at the bottom of the Atlantic, but mark me, one day a fair maid will capture your heart."

Gibb shifted in his seat. There was no chance he'd mention all the hours he spent beside Miss Harcourt piecing together her tablets. Or the kisses—*never* would he admit to the kisses. "Och, I'd rather take my crew on a voyage into the Caribbean and search for Spanish silver."

"Now you're sounding like a pirate."

"And you're sounding like Da." Gibb checked his pocket watch, noting the time was now three in the afternoon. "Do ye reckon it is late enough in the day for a wee dram?"

Martin pushed to his feet and started for the sideboard. "Ye twisted my arm. Mayhap we ought to raise a toast to your next adventure."

~

THE BALLROOM at the family's London town house was nowhere near as magnificent as the ancient great hall they used when hosting an affair at Stack Castle on the northeastern tip of Scotland's mainland, but it was close. Gibb's mother had outdone herself, from the dozen brand-new brilliant chandeliers overhead to the hardwood floor polished to a sheen as glassy as a Highland loch on a windless day.

Everywhere Gibb turned, he was met with an exquisite arrangement of exotic flowers, each more magnificent than the next. The one beside him was full of blooms in every shade of pink imaginable. Who knew pink flora could be represented in so many hues?

"Mama must have emptied all the hothouses in

the South of England," said Philip, sidling beside Gibb and handing him a glass of something that was as pink as the brightest yellow-centered cosmos flowers in the arrangement he'd just been admiring.

Gibb took the drink. "Have ye tried this?" he asked, his gaze shifting to the crown of his brother's head to ensure he hadn't mistaken Philip for his twin, Andrew. Though Philip's identifying cowlick was tamed by a practiced application of hair oil, it still popped up a bit right at the point where his crown started to arc downward.

Philip raised his glass and frowned. "Aye, 'tis a bit too sour, though it hasna gone without sugar. I reckon this syrupy brew is as sweet as the icing on a cake."

"Blech," Gibb said under his breath. "And I'll wager there's nary a drop of spirit in it."

"With Grace and Modesty present, I reckon you're right."

Gibb took a more robust drink and nearly gagged. The sweetness was almost overwhelming, followed by a biting tang that darted beneath either side of his jaw. "Bloody hell, this is enough to make a warrior's eyes cross."

"Aye, or send his ballocks into his throat."

Both attempted to suppress chuckles, which made them snort. As Gibb was growing up, he always strove to best Martin, and he was oft joined in camaraderie by Philip and Andrew. Philip was the more dogged of the twins, similar to Gibb. Often, Gibb and Philip saw eye to eye on things upon which everyone else disagreed.

The dowager duchess danced past, her hand atop that of the Earl of Sussex. Gibb raised his glass to both. "'Tis good to see Mama is enjoying herself."

"And not a one of her sons was wrangled into

signing her dance card." Philip winked. "I have it on good authority we're to thank Julia for her intervention."

"I kent I liked Martin's wife," Gibb agreed, spotting the duchess herself dancing with the Marquess of Northampton.

Philip regarded him with a pinch between his auburn eyebrows. "I thought you dinna approve of the match."

"Mayhap not at first—after all, I was initially introduced when she was parading about as Jules Smallwood, steward to our esteemed brother. I was a bit flabbergasted when I discovered he was actually a female. Nonetheless, now that I've come to know her, I have realized that aside from being a perfect match for Martin, she truly is quite enterprising."

Philip nodded to the duchess as she passed. "I'd have to agree. After all, there's most likely not another woman in all of Great Britain able to position herself as a steward to a duke without her ruse being exposed on the first day of her tenure."

Next, a stunning beauty danced by, greeting them with a brilliant smile. "Good God, is that Grace?" Gibb asked, staring after his sister, his chin nearly dropping to his chest.

"Heaven help us all," Philip mumbled under his breath. "She's too bloody young."

"She's too bloody bonny, if ye ask me."

"Aye, that as well. Martin will have to keep his dueling pistols primed when the lass comes of age."

Gibb tipped up his glass and realized that during this discourse he'd managed to empty its contents regardless of the cloying confection.

Philip beckoned a footman toting a silver tray filled with too much sloshing pink and replaced their glasses with a new pair. "Are ye man enough to tolerate a second?"

Without even taking a sip, Gibb winced at the anticipation of the sour aftertaste. "How about we slip into the library and add a dram of whisky to these?"

His brother waggled his auburn eyebrows. "Now why dinna I think of that?"

"Och, I have no idea. Has Marty been inviting you for tea of late, or are ye just plain addled?"

"The only thing addling my mind is this punch."

Gibb inclined his head toward the doorway behind them. "We ought not to be missed."

"Are you jesting? We have strict orders from Martin to be present at all times—I reckon he has spies posted at every refuge in the house."

Gibb tugged the sleeve of his brother's coat. "Then it is up to us to mutiny."

"Allow me to lead the way."

The two partners in crime had taken no more than two steps into the corridor when Modesty, the youngest MacGalloway sibling, blocked their path. "Phiiiiilip!" she cried, throwing her arms around the eldest twin. "I'm having a calamity, and I need your help immensely!"

With a groan, Gibb rolled his eyes to the ceiling while his younger brother planted a hand upon the lassie's shoulder. "Och, ye look so bonny, how could anything worry ye this eve, lass?"

Modesty scrunched her face, making her spotty freckles stand out more, if that was possible. The lass looked nothing like Grace. Modesty was cursed with flaming red hair and more freckles than Philip and Andrew combined. "Miss Annabel untied my ribbons. She's a shrew, I say."

Philip tapped the gel's nose. "I'll agree with ye there, but have you no lady's maid to set ye to rights?"

"Nay." Modesty swung her shoulders to and fro, making those bright red curls bounce. "My governess helped me dress, but she's all the way up in the nursery."

"And your sisters?" Philip asked.

"They're both dancing."

Gibb took the glass of punch from Philip's grasp. "I'll take care of these whilst you retie our wee sister's ribbons."

He didn't wait for a reply before he quickly slipped up the stairs and into the library. Except the crystal decanter had been removed from the sideboard. Blast Martin and blast Mama or Julia. One of the two women had put Martin up to hiding the liquor for certain.

After setting the glasses on the empty silver tray, Gibb strode to the writing table and opened the bottom drawer. Blast, blast, and double blast, it was empty as well.

*Good God, Marty, next they'll be sainting you, ye blathering numpty.*

He tapped his lip, a leather-bound book catching his eye while a memory sparked—one from his boyhood. He strode directly to the book and removed it from the shelf. Years ago, when he was a wee laddie, he'd been playing a game of hide-and-seek and hidden behind the library curtains. While he was concealed, his father came in, removed that very book, opened it, and pulled out a key. With it, Da pushed one of the far curtains aside and, after a few clicks and clunks, returned into view carrying a box of snuff.

"There you are," Gibb said, finding the key hidden in an envelope adhered to the back cover of the volume. "Let us see if Da's booty includes more than tobacco."

Gibb pulled aside the curtain and located a tiny keyhole about waist-high, so concealed that it could easily be mistaken as a flaw. He smoothed his hand over the wood paneling, his fingertips sensing only a hint of a gap. Whoever installed this hidey-hole had done so with superb craftmanship. "What did you stow in here, dear father?"

He glanced over his shoulder as a shiver coursed across his skin. Was Martin aware of Da's hiding place? Gibb highly doubted Mama would be. After sliding in the key and opening the hidden door, he indeed found a wooden box of Imperial Snuff. Farther back, however, he caught a glint from a glass bottle.

"What have we here?" he asked, pulling it out and examining the label—MacGalloway Whisky, bottled 1745. "My thanks, Da. I kent ye'd stash away only the very best."

Gibb made quick work of charging the glasses with two drams each, then replaced everything exactly as he'd found it. One day, he might inform Martin about the hidey-hole, but not today.

It was only after he exited the library that he heard the shriek of a hysterical voice—a mature female voice that was decidedly not Modesty's, nor that of any woman Gibb knew.

"This is a scandal of magnanimous proportions!" the voice squawked.

*What the devil?*

With haste, Gibb dashed down the corridor to the stairs, sloshing his punch concoction over his fingers. When he reached the landing, he could not believe what he was seeing.

"It is my fault," said a young woman as she pushed

away from Philip's arms. Good God, from his bloody arms! "I tripped on my hem," she said, appearing horror-struck. "I'm ever so clumsy."

"You tripped?" The older woman scoffed, flipping open her fan and vigorously cooling her face. "I do not believe it for an instant. You were out of the ballroom for ages. When I set out in search of your whereabouts, I discovered you in the arms of this man. Do not try to tell me Lord Philip MacGalloway has not compromised you. This is *scandalous*, I say, and by morning on the morrow, all of polite society will know you have been ruined."

"I beg your pardon?" Gibb descended the remaining stairs and stepped between the woman and his brother. "Why does anyone need to ken what happened here?" He looked from one end of the corridor to the other, thankful not to see any bystanders, aside from Philip's twin Andrew, who stood blocking the doorway to the ballroom, most likely having overheard the exchange.

"*I* know," the woman insisted. "And everyone present who has a pair of ears knows. I demand you make an offer of marriage to my daughter at once, or I'll have no recourse but to inform her father of this impropriety!"

The lass grasped her mother's arm. "Please, Mama, it was not His Lordship's fault."

The woman's eely-eyed stare did not shift from Philip's face. "Balderdash!"

Gibb had heard enough. Holding both glasses perfectly level, he considered dumping the contents of both on the woman, except it was a damned waste of vintage 1745. "Excuse me, m'lady, but I reckon you're—"

Philip firmly grasped Gibb's shoulder, ushered

him aside, and cleared his throat. "Miss Radcliffe, it would be my esteemed honor if you would take into consideration my heartfelt offer of marriage."

"What?" Gibb boomed, earning an elbow in the ribs from the eldest twin, making the punch again slosh over his fingers and unfortunately not on Mrs. Radcliffe.

The woman smiled with a haughty air of triumph. "Respond to him at once, Eugenia."

The lass's gaze slowly meandered upward and met Philip's stony stare. In truth, she was quite a comely gel, with blonde hair and azure eyes—a face of an angel, accompanied by a woman how could only be described as the spawn of Bloody Mary. "If it is truly what you want, my lord, then I accept."

Philip took her hand and applied a kiss that imparted no more emotion than a carp gasping for air on the shore. "Thank you, miss. I shall call upon you in the morning."

Witnessing the farce play out before him, Gibb stood dumbstruck. It wasn't until the woman and her daughter took their leave and returned to the ballroom that he handed Philip the glass of punch. "What the devil happened? I left you to tie Modesty's ribbons, and when I returned, you were in the midst of being *tricked* into making an offer of marriage."

Philip drank the entire contents of the glass, belched, and shoved the empty into Gibb's belly. "I need a wife, and Lord kens I'm too busy to search for one. Besides, Miss Radcliffe is bonny. I reckon she'll do."

"She might be Aphrodite incarnate, but her mother's a dragon-hearted shrew. I'd rather take my chances with a duel than marry into that family."

"Mayhap, but my future mother-in-law will have

to come to Scotland when she wants to see her daughter. If she's overbearing when she visits, then the pair of them will never be able to find me."

"Good God, man. Marriage is nay that simple. You are not thinking this through."

Philip gave the captain's shoulder a shove. "What do you ken about it? You're asea more than you're ashore. Give it a rest. I've made up my mind."

Gibb moved the glass toward his lips. "At least I hope you're planning for a long engagement."

Philip took Gibb's concoction and drained it as well. "Believe me, it might be the longest engagement in Scotland's history."

# 19

Regardless of how much she wanted to race back to England, Isabella didn't leave Georgia right away. No matter what her heart told her, over and over again, she had thought about her last weeks aboard the *Prosperity* and had no idea if Gibb MacGalloway might desire to take up where they left off or not. It wasn't as though the captain had given her any indication that he might one day entertain the idea of marriage. In fact, he had been clear about being married to the sea and most passionate about never taking a wife.

His words, *"I've known many married seamen, and not a one was happy,"* repeated in her thoughts time and time again.

Though once Isabella allowed herself to feel strongly about anything, she wasn't keen to let it lie. Her will had a way of making her do things she didn't necessarily agree with. Well, she agreed, because it was *her will*. It was just that society always had different ideas, and she oft found herself pulled in one direction while yearning to go in the other.

However, since Captain MacGalloway had escorted her off the ship, delivered her into the hands of

Mr. Schuyler, and sailed away from Savannah and America, she could come up with no logical excuse to flee immediately following Arent's funeral—at least not after Mr. Booker had explained the particulars of her inheritance.

The details had all been incredibly overwhelming, from the mansion in Lockhart, to the mine, to the town house Arent kept in Savannah. Then there were his numerous bank accounts, including money held in England, France, and Italy, all amounting to a blindingly large fortune. The man could have married a princess if he so desired, but according to Mr. Booker, Arent Schuyler had no intention of ever leaving Georgia. It wasn't until the doctor told him his heart was failing that he realized he'd best marry. Though he didn't seek out a princess, he also did not want to settle for a colonial woman. His dream had always been to wed an English rose.

In short, there was a great deal to set to rights, and she felt responsible to do so. Isabella had remained in Lockhart while Mr. Booker gave her a detailed overview of the inner workings of the entire estate, from the lowest scullery maid to the mine's overseer, and finally explained his own compensation.

Two months and three days after she had taken her vows, Isabella devised a plan. She'd knocked on Mr. Booker's office door and presented him with the details of how she wanted the estate to be managed. Because the lawman had been forthright and honest with her when he could have lied, falsifying documents and keeping everything for himself, she realized that Arent could not have chosen a more suitable successor to run his affairs.

After all the legal agreements had been completed, she sailed to London, having appointed Mr.

Booker as the president and partial owner of the Schuyler mine. She had planned to give him a controlling interest, but he once more had proven to be honest to the detriment of his own fortune. His advice was for Isabella to retain a majority ownership in the mine, thus making her wealthy beyond her dreams.

Of course, it didn't take long for her to realize living in a remote area of northeastern Georgia wasn't the life for her. And though she told Maribel she wished to return home, Isabella hoped that by returning to England, and especially London when the Season was to be in full swing, she might happen upon Lord Gibb MacGalloway—or at least a member of his family.

Isabella decided against first stopping in West Sussex to call on her father. Papa's house was no longer her *home*, and in truth, she wasn't especially anxious to see her father, or to let him know she was back in the kingdom for that matter. Her whereabouts were no longer her father's concern, just as her fortune was most decidedly not his concern.

*One day soon I'll write to him. Just not yet.*

Today, Isabella sat in the parlor of the suite of rooms she had let at Lady Blanche's Boarding House in the center of Mayfair. Her Ladyship catered only to affluent women, and had very strict rules prohibiting men on the premises. This suited Isabella ideally, at least for the time being. She was highly doubtful that she would settle in London, and it seemed a bit excessive to rent an entire town house and bring on a great number of servants when one was searching for a sea captain.

Maribel appeared with a tea service. "Shall I pour, miss?"

Isabella gestured to the seat across. "Please do. Will you join me?"

"Oh, I couldn't."

"Why? You never join me, and after all that we've been through together, I believe it is high time that you did."

"No, Miss Isabella. I am a servant. I mustn't become accustomed to being treated equally with ladies of quality."

"Balderdash." Isabella thrust her finger at the chair. "I insist that you join me."

"Perhaps this once." Maribel dropped to her seat and pushed the *Gazette* forward. "I thought you would want to read the newspaper straight away."

"Thank you." Isabella reached for it, noting the headline as she took it into her hand: *Brother of the Duke of Dunscaby Engaged.*

Her face grew hot, her hands trembled, and her stomach shrank into a tiny ball as she forced herself to read the next line: *The match of the Season has been announced, subverting what might have been a disgraceful scandal. The editor of the* Gazette *has received a firsthand account that whilst attending the Dowager Duchess of Dunscaby's birthday celebration, Miss Eugenia Radcliffe was discovered in the embrace of none other than Lord Gibb MacGalloway...*

Hardly able to breathe, Isabella folded the paper and set it aside. She didn't want to read another word.

Maribel finished pouring and looked up, teapot in hand. "Goodness, are you unwell? You suddenly look awfully pale."

"I am quite well," Isabella said, taking her cup and sipping while inside she grew hotter than the steamy liquid. She couldn't tell Maribel about the news article, and thank goodness the maid didn't read. "However..."

"Hmm?" Maribel asked, replacing the pot on the tray.

"I've suddenly realized that I have absolutely no idea what I am doing in London."

"I thought we were here because it is the Season. And since you are an heiress, this is the best place for you to find a match."

Well, yes, that was the story Isabella had given just about everyone, including her lady's maid. But there was only one match that interested her, and it seemed the gentleman in question had wasted no time in moving on.

"Who am I fooling?" Isabella added a bit of extra milk to her tea. "I failed miserably to find a husband when I came out, and now I am too old and too seasoned for anyone to find me appealing."

"I disagree. You are lovely, and anyone who doesn't see it is blind. Even Mr. Erskine commented on how comely you are."

Isabella picked up her cup and saucer, not believing a word. "Oh, did he?"

"Yes, most definitely. And do not forget Captain MacGalloway. He's such a handsome man, and he spent hour upon hour helping you piece together your tablets. I know it is not my place to say so, but I do think he was quite fond of you. Quite fond."

If the color had drained from her face before, Isabella imagined she had now completely blanched. Rumors had always been to steer clear of sailors, and now she knew why. The louts had wandering hearts. Why was it that every man in her life abandoned her? And why, in all that was holy, did she believe she needed any man at all?

"I think it is time to spread our wings. And in order to do so, one most definitely does not need a husband," Isabella said, diverting the subject elsewhere because she didn't want to hear another word about the *Prosperity* or any member of the vile captain's crew. Besides, she had another idea—one she should have acted upon years ago. "Maribel, since you are so reluctant to join me for tea, I hereby promote you to companion."

"Madam?"

"You've been acting as my companion for years, have you not?"

Maribel's eyebrows pinched together. "Yes, I suppose I have, though aside from accompanying you to America and back, I have merely performed the role of lady's maid."

"Well, things change, and you have proven to be not only an exemplary lady's maid, but a trusted companion."

A bit dazed, Maribel sat back. "Thank you."

"That said, as soon as you finish your tea, please begin packing our things. I have decided we've been in London long enough."

"But it has only been a matter of weeks. And did you not tell me you had compiled a list of old friends upon whom you wanted to call whilst in Town?"

"I suppose they may as well remain old friends a bit longer." Isabella pushed to her feet. "I must settle my account with Lady Blanche straight away."

# 20

Platja de la Garrofera was a very long, narrow beach with the sea on one side, and no more than a half-mile inland, a freshwater lagoon seeped into the shores of marshland. Duncan ran ahead of the captain and picked up a long piece of driftwood ideally suited for a walking stick. "I reckon snakes like it here."

Gibb bit back a shiver. None of God's creatures gave him a chill as much as the thought of a slithering asp. His instincts as a boy had been to give snakes a wide berth, and the conviction had carried into adulthood. "At least the wee beasties are skittish. I doubt we'll see any."

Duncan poked the stick into a bit of brush and lifted it up, peering beneath. "I'd like to find one."

Gibb took a cautious step aside, squinting into the dark cavern. "Aye? What would you do with a snake if you found one of the beasties?"

The lad reached in, pulled out a frog, and examined the amphibian. "Mayhap I'd play with him."

"I dunna recommend toying with snakes. Asps can be poisonous, especially in warmer climes." Gibb regarded the little fellow, its eyes filled with trepidation. "Ye may fare better with frogs."

Moving to the edge of the lagoon, Duncan bent down to the water and let the fella swim away.

"Come along. The ground is too marshy here. We'll be more likely to find Roman ruins where it is dry."

"I dunna think I would build a house here."

"No? What about a temple?"

"What kind of temple?"

"Well, the Romans had a lot of gods. One in particular that Miss Harcourt's tablets mentioned was Mars. I got the impression there was a temple on or near the beach."

"Did they think Mars was a god?"

"Not the planet, I suppose. Mars was the god of war and the guardian of agriculture."

"Aye? I reckon those two duties seem a wee bit contrary."

"Why?"

"Because war destroys things and agriculture—well, it doesna exactly build things like houses, but it grows things so people can eat."

Gibb slung his arm around the lad's shoulders and gave a squeeze. "I am impressed with your reasoning."

Duncan dragged his feet through the sand. "I'm nay so certain about that."

"Because..."

"Well, I've been reading the book you gave me, *Robinson Crusoe*, and I canna understand why Friday became his slave. Isna slavery wrong?"

"It is, and that's why the MacGalloways buy cotton from the Irish sharecroppers. They dunna believe in the use of slaves." Gibb rubbed his knuckles through the boy's thick brown hair. "Keep in mind the book was written before King George began taking steps to abolish slavery."

Duncan kicked a stone. "Verra well, but if I were Friday, I'd tell Crusoe that I'm my own man."

"I would expect no less. You are a very enterprising laddie, and if ye keep up with your lessons and your duties aboard ship, there'll be nothing ye canna achieve."

Gibb panned his gaze across the terrain. It was too flat, and there was nothing whatsoever that looked as if it might be from a previous civilization—nothing like a wall or steps or a pile of rubble for that matter. The sand was strewn with clumps of sea grass and peppered with driftwood and a few rocks. Perhaps he and Isabella had been too hasty to pinpoint this beach as the one near Marcus and Flavia's home. After all, nearly seventeen hundred years had passed since the tablets were written.

Duncan set to prodding every molehill-sized mound with his newfound walking stick. "Do ye ken what I canna understand?"

Gibb could rattle off hundreds of quandaries—why the moon controlled the tides, why the earth was round, why women wore stays... "I have no idea," he replied.

"Why did ye let Miss Harcourt marry that American? I liked her, and I ken ye fancied her as well. I even saw ye kiss her when you were standing near the bowsprit."

Quickly looking away, Gibb swiped his hand across his face. He'd been so damned careful to ensure no one saw them when he stole kisses. But if anyone was crafty enough to spy, it was this wee blighter. "Ah...I most likely shouldna have done that. 'Twas a moment of weakness."

"I dunno 'bout that, Cap'n. She was awfully bonny. Friendly, as well."

"I agree with all those things, but her hand was promised in marriage."

"Aye, but it doesna seem fair, does it? She was promised to an old man—a fella she'd never met."

"Many things in this life are not fair, but we have to accept them all the same."

"Well, I reckon you should have told that man on the wharf that you wanted to court the lady and that he needed to find someone his own age to marry."

Clenching his jaw, Gibb looked southward without responding. What the hell was he doing in Spain on this godforsaken beach? He'd spent some time with a pleasant woman, piecing together some ancient tablets, and that was the end of it. He should have taken the *Prosperity* up to Scotland and found a seaside cottage that he could call home—a place where he and Duncan could stay when they weren't at sea, as Martin had suggested. No, Gibb didn't want a manor or a castle, just a little place of his own.

Archie and Gowan approached, their expressions glum.

"I dunna reckon there's anything to find for twenty miles or more," said the quartermaster, pointing his thumb over his shoulder.

Gibb raked his fingers through his hair. "Och, coming here was a harebrained idea if I've ever had one."

"I want to find a real treasure," said Duncan.

"Ye're dreaming if you think we might find treasure here," said Gowan. "The Spaniards wouldna leave a wrecked ship laden with silver on their own beach."

Looking to his quartermaster, Gibb asked, "Shall we keep searching, or shall we head for home?"

"I reckon we ought to weigh anchor and head for Scotland. I've a hankering for a meaty Scots ale and a wench to match."

IT TOOK a fortnight to sail to Valencia, and once Isabella arrived, it took another fortnight to find a guide and laborers, and to purchase mules, horses, and all the supplies needed for a proper excavation. Now, for the first time in all her days, she was following her dreams. For the first time in her life, she was in charge of her destiny. In fact, the only person who knew of her whereabouts was Maribel—be it folly or nay, Isabella was thrilled to have finally taken her destiny into her hands and followed her heart.

As the caravan headed south and away from the city of Valencia, the wind made the straw brim of her bonnet flip backward. She clapped her hand atop. "My, there's quite a breeze today."

Riding beside Isabella, the guide, Luis, gave her a gap-toothed grin. "It is always windy here, *señora*."

"I don't mind," she replied, easing the tension on her reins to allow her mount to amble freely. Nothing could detract from the excitement of setting out on her first expedition. Things may not have turned out exactly as she had dreamed, but if anyone had given her choices, Isabella could not have chosen a better path. She was wealthy beyond her dreams and able to finance her very own expedition.

Sometime after they'd stopped for their luncheon, they passed a freshwater lagoon and continued toward Platja de la Devesa, a beach south of Platja de la Garrofera. It wasn't until Isabella had pieced together a tablet during the return voyage from America where

Marcus had written about his home and mentioned that the villa was built upon a hill overlooking the sands of Platja de la Devesa. And now she knew exactly why. Platja de la Garrofera was only a narrow tract of beach between the lagoon and the Mediterranean. It was marshy and sandy, and the ground was far too unstable to support the foundations for a house.

The sun had moved low on the western horizon when Luis reined his horse to a stop on an expansive beach. The guide swept his arm in a grandiose arcing gesture. "This is Platja de la Devesa, *señora*. Are you sure this is where you want to stop?"

"Up there." Isabella tapped her heels, urging her horse to climb the dunes until they were atop a grassy plateau shaded by stout trees. She turned in her saddle and beckoned the guide. "Have the men make camp here."

"This is the spot?" asked Maribel, sounding uncertain.

"At least it is a promising place to begin." Isabella slipped her knee off the upper pommel of her sidesaddle and dismounted without assistance. "Come, let us stretch our legs and have a look about."

At a brisk pace, Isabella led the way across the rugged terrain, looking to the hills. Farther inland, grass was greener, with far more trees and shrubs than there were near the shore.

Maribel held her skirts high enough to keep them from dragging in the sand. "I'm going to have to empty my boots of sand every day."

Glancing over her shoulder, Isabella grinned. "I'll be happy to empty the sand out of my boots because I know we are enjoying the adventure of our lives."

"It is nice to see you so happy, but..."

"Hmm?"

"What do you think of Luis and his men? We hardly know them."

When their ship arrived in Valencia, Luis had been on the pier, as had several other translators, but Luis was the only one interested in accompanying her on an expedition. His English was good and he knew exactly where to find everything they needed, and though his fees were rather exorbitant, Isabella had gladly paid. "I think he's endearing, and he's eager to help us."

"I suppose you're right."

"Why do you ask?"

"It isn't Luis so much as the two men who were riding behind us. Every time I glanced back at them, I felt as though if I were alone in a dark alley, they might take advantage."

"I'll admit that pair have rather leery eyes, but Luis assured me that all seven of his men are hardworking and trustworthy." Isabella reached back and looped her arm through Maribel's elbow. "However, that is exactly why we will be sharing a tent. We shall be far safer that way. Besides, I shall be sleeping with a pistol under my pallet."

## 21

Isabella awoke to the sound of the surf and seabirds, which she normally would enjoy. However, today the noise made the back of her head throb and her stomach roil. Stretching, she rolled to her side, finding Maribel on her pallet across the tent, still sound asleep. Daylight shone through the canvas, casting rays of light that made her head pound all the more.

What was the time? Isabella never slept late, and nor did Maribel, who was always up at dawn.

"Time to wake," she said, giving her companion's shoulder a tap.

Maribel moaned and draped an arm over her head. "I feel as if I drank a flagon of gin."

Isabella felt the same. She crawled off her pallet to the bowl and splashed some water in her face. "I allowed myself one glass of wine and that was all."

The maid pushed herself up. "As did I. What did they put in it, I wonder?"

"Our fatigue is most likely from the change of pace. We did a great deal of riding yesterday. I'm sure we'll feel better after we've had a bite to eat."

Both women had slept in their clothes, and it took little time to tighten their laces and don their boots.

Maribel stepped out of the tent first, her sharp gasp giving Isabella pause. The maid hastened outside. "What—?"

As Isabella followed, the sight before her robbed the air from her lungs. "Everything is gone."

"*Everyone* is gone."

The food, the horses, the mules, the brand-new tools she had paid for.

Good glory, she felt so lousy when she awoke that she hadn't paid much attention to her belongings in the tent—but now that she thought about it, things seemed to be out of place. Isabella dashed back inside, clapped her hands over her mouth, and screamed. Not only had Luis and his band of thieves disappeared with the tools and the animals she and Maribel needed for the journey back to Valencia, the fiends had stolen her money chest.

"Oh, dear God in heaven help us!" said Maribel, stepping beside her. "We have no food, no horses, and no coin."

Clutching her chest and trying to force herself to breathe, Isabella turned full circle. Not seeing what she was looking for, she pulled away her blankets and bed linens, tossing them onto Maribel's pallet. "They took my journal, the louts!"

"Truly?" Maribel checked beneath her pallet as well. "What use would a journal written in English be to them?"

"I have no idea, not that anyone would care to read it, especially a band of thieves. Obviously, Luis and those scoundrels couldn't give a fig about Marcus or antiquity in general."

Maribel picked up a blanket and looked beneath.

"Perhaps they thought it might be of value when they saw you reading it as we were sitting by the fire last eve."

Isabella smacked her forehead. "Yes, that and I referred to it a number of times. I'll wager they'll be searching for treasure after we're gone."

After folding the blanket, Maribel picked up a sheet and set to folding it. "And now we know why we slept so late and feel so badly. Those miscreants poisoned us."

By the swimming of Isabella's head, she had no doubt her companion was correct. "Thank the stars the poison wasn't lethal."

"I knew this trip was a bad idea from the outset. With all due respect, we were better off staying in America—or better yet, remaining on the *Prosperity* and sailing back to England before you became an heiress."

Though she heard Maribel's every word, Isabella turned numb. All her life she'd done what others expected of her. For once, she had taken a risk and chased her dreams. She'd trusted a stranger—a man who seemed quite respectable, but who turned out to be a scoundrel—and now she was not only stranded, she'd brought Maribel into this mess as well.

Dropping back to her haunches, she pressed her head into her hands. "How much water do we have?"

Maribel held up two goatskin bota bags. "Just these, and one's half-full."

"Well, those ought to keep us alive until we can make it back to Valencia."

"On foot?"

"Have you a better idea?"

"But we've nothing to eat."

Isabella spotted the shoulder strap of her satchel

beneath her pallet, pulled it out, and looked inside. "At least we have a few coins, and the pistol I purchased in London."

"If only we'd had our wits when they robbed us, you could have shot the miserable fiends."

"If only," she replied, closing the satchel and standing. "Then we mustn't tarry. The longer we remain here, the longer we'll have to go without food."

~

ARCHIE POPPED his head into Gibb's cabin. "Come ashore, Cap'n, and have a wee dram whilst Cookie replenishes supplies."

Though he had intended to sail for Scotland straight away, the ship's biscuits not only were full of weevils, a barrel of vinegar had spilled on them and rendered them completely useless. Since the *Prosperity's* stores were nearly out of flour and their fresh water was turning green, they'd had no choice but to drop anchor in Valencia. Of course, the cook had asked to bring aboard some additional food stores, as he always did when they moored off a port city. And Gibb rarely argued with him. He liked fresh meat, fruits, and vegetables as much as any man.

Gibb glanced up from his writing desk, quill in hand. "I'd rather stay here."

"Och, suit yourself. But ye havena long to change your mind. The men are lowering the skiff now. Think on it, Cap'n. Ye canna visit a city in Spain without having a wee dram of orujo."

"Orujo? If you drink too much of that, you'll not be able to find the horizon for days."

Archie thumped his chest. "Ye ken I can hold my liquor with the best of them."

Gibb placed his pen in the holder. "Aye, ye can fight with the best of them as well."

"So, are ye coming?"

"Mayhap—just to keep your nose out of trouble, mind you. The last thing I need is to be forced to stay here a day longer whilst pleading with the magistrate for your release from a Spanish jail."

"Och, I havena been hauled off to the pen for over three years now."

"Which is exactly why I'm going with you. I'd prefer to keep your streak going."

A big grin stretched across Archie's lips as he waggled his ruddy eyebrows. Aye, the man knew if he mentioned orujo, Gibb would opt to come along. Because when it came to sweet and potent liquor, the quartermaster was likely to end up blootered.

Mac and Gowan joined them on deck, and they all used the boatswain's chair to wench down to the skiff. Within a half-hour, the crewmen had tied the boat to the pier. Gibb checked his pocket watch and turned toward the cook. "An hour?"

Cookie blew a snort through his inordinately large nose. "Sir? Do you speak bloody Spanish?"

Gibb might know a bit of Latin, but his Spanish was limited to a few words. "Two hours. And if you havena returned by then, we'll set sail without you."

"I reckon ye'll all starve on the voyage home."

Gibb gave the cook a level stare. "Two hours is plenty of time."

"But hardly enough to enjoy a bottle of orujo," Archie added, the numpty.

"We're not drinking an entire bottle of sickly-sweet poison."

"Is it really poison, sir?" asked Mac, the youngster.

Gibb clapped the first mate on the shoulder. "Aye, at least in the quantities Mr. MacLean consumes."

With a devious chuckle, Archie headed onward, pointing toward a tavern. "It never fails—there's always a watering hole at the end of every pier."

Gibb licked his lips. In truth, he enjoyed a drink as much as any sailor, but his taste was more refined. Whisky was always his first choice, brandy next, and ale also suited him any time of the day or night, especially when the water aboard ship was suspect.

Along the busy road, vendors had their tables set up, selling everything from bread, to fruit, to pre-made shirts and tools. Gibb took an apple and tossed the vendor a coin. "Cookie ought to find everything he needs right here."

Archie started to cross the street. "Then we'd best make haste—"

"A moment, lads." Gibb stopped, something familiar catching his eye. "Come with me."

"What have ye found?" asked the quartermaster. "Whisky, perchance?"

Without answering, Gibb sauntered toward a man who was holding a shovel. "*Te vendo esta pala a buen precio*," the man said, holding up a spade.

"No. That." Gibb pointed to a worn leather volume atop the table. "I want to see the book...*libro*."

The vendor shifted the shovel to one hand and held up the journal. "*Esto?*"

Gibb's knees buckled. God save him, he'd only seen one leather-bound journal embossed with the name Issy, and it belonged to Isabella Harcourt. But her name was most likely Isabella Schuyler by now, and the woman was in America. How in the blazes did the damned book end up in Spain? He snatched it from the man's hand. "Where did you find this?"

Sputtering a staccato string in incomprehensible Spanish, the man gripped the shovel across his chest, his eyes wide and shifting from side to side.

Gibb tucked the journal under his arm while sliding his fingers over the pommel of his dirk.

"We can take 'em, Cap'n," Archie growled beside Gibb's ear.

At the mention of "'em," Gibb realized nearly a dozen scrappers had moved in behind the bastard, rendering him and his officers greatly outnumbered.

"Gowan, how's your Spanish?" he asked. Gibb would be more than happy to engage the blackguard in a brawl, but they hadn't stepped ashore to fight, and who knew how many more Valencians would join in a tussle with a handful of Scots?

"French is better," replied the boatswain.

Though his blood was thrumming with fire, Gibb figured he'd best make an attempt at civility. "Ask this man if he kens where the woman is."

Gowan moved beside Gibb's elbow. "Do you reckon that's Miss Harcourt's journal?"

Just to be certain, Gibb looked inside, and on the first page found her notes about the excavation on her father's property in West Sussex. "It's hers."

"Good God," mumbled Mac.

Gowan stepped forward and engaged in a conversation spoken too fast for Gibb to follow. Regardless, the exchange lasted too long, and by the way the man shrugged, no one needed to speak Spanish to realize he was playing dumb.

"The crew from the skiff have arrived behind us," Archie mumbled.

Gibb glanced over his shoulder, relieved to find six of his best fighting men. The odds were getting better. He stepped between Gowan and the vendor's table and looked the man dead in the eyes. "Where. Is. She?"

"He told me he found the journal," said the boatswain.

Gibb didn't believe it. "Where?"

*"¿Donde?"* Gowan asked.

The man launched into another string of rapid Spanish.

Gowan turned his lips toward the captain's ear and cupped his hand beside it. "He's trying to say he found the book, but if you ask me, the bastard's about to soil his breeches."

"Platja de la Garrofera?" Gibb asked.

The man's eyes flashed wide before he backed away.

Dear God, if there was any skullduggery afoot, Gibb would tear the entire pier apart to uncover it.

Gibb upended the table and grabbed the man by the throat to the tune of at least a dozen hissing swords being drawn from their scabbards. "Is. She. Here?"

The point of a cutlass was level with his eyeball. He glanced at the bastard threatening him, then pushed the man holding the shovel toward the attacker. Quickly, Gibb shuffled backward and held up his hands along with Isabella's journal and glared directly into the lout's eyes. "I'm keeping this, and if I hear of any lawlessness, I ken where to find you."

Archie and the men flanked him while the scoundrel backed into a mob of his friends. Slowly, Gibb urged his men away from the upended table. "She's on the beach. I can feel in in my bones."

"With Miss Hatch?" Gowan asked, his tone hopeful.

A shiver thrummed across Gibb's skin. Was she hurt...or worse? "I pray she's not alone."

As soon as they had moved far enough away from the skirmish, Gibb gathered his men around him. "Sorry, Archie, but there will be no orujo. Find Cookie and get him back aboard the ship as quickly as possible. Sail the *Prosperity* down to Platja de la Garrofera and drop anchor off the coast. We'll meet you there." He turned to the boatswain and first mate. "Gowan, Mac, come with me."

# 22

In the shade of a juniper tree, Maribel grasped Isabella's arm. "Look there, are those riders ahead?"

While shoving the cork stopper into the bota bag, Isabella squinted, seeing nothing but an endless stretch of beach, the sands being blown in clouds out to sea. Above, a handful of seabirds squawked in the sky, their song jeering, as if to say, "Fool, fool, look at the silly fool." Moreover, this place was uninhabitable, proven by the fact that they had seen nary a traveler in the hours since they'd started out, and now it seemed her companion was on the verge of going mad. "I think you are so hungry you're seeing things."

"Perhaps you're right, but it would surely be nice to be rescued by a gallant knight riding a white horse. I already have dozens of blisters on my feet from these new boots you purchased for me. I might have been better off had I worn my old ones."

Isabella tugged on her companion's sleeve. "I'd be happy to be rescued by anyone as long as he isn't a salacious fiend. And my feet are blistered and sore as well." She groaned. "I was a dolt to believe the new boots were necessary for an expedition."

Limping, Maribel fell in step beside her. "I wish we could order them already broken in."

"Perhaps we ought to invent a line of worn-in boots for ladies. I can see the placard now: *Boots for the foolish, nonsensical, dreamy-eyed bluestocking*."

Maribel snorted. "That might be funny if we ever make it home."

"We will. Mark me, the only regret I have, aside from trusting that scoundrel Luis, is that you have had to suffer so much because of my inexperience."

"I shudder to think of what might have happened had I not been here."

"Well, I thank you for being my companion. The execution of your duty has been above and beyond."

They continued northward, saying nothing for a time as they endured the constant gnawing pain from their blisters and the trudging agony of walking in hot sand to an overture of growling stomachs.

"Will you buy a home when we return to England?" Maribel asked after a time.

"I think that makes the most sense. I need a place of my own that is not hundreds of miles away in the wilderness of America."

"I agree. Do you think you might settle in West Sussex?"

Isabella bit down her bottom lip. She did have friends in West Sussex, but still hadn't come to terms with the way Papa had sold her hand in marriage. Even if he needed the coin, he'd been rather clandestine about the whole ordeal—not telling her what he was doing until an agreement with Mr. Schuyler had been reached.

*Where do I want to settle?*

Most of her childhood friends were married now and had moved away. She knew a few ladies in

London who had been fellow wallflowers during her Season—they exchanged letters from time to time. But in all honesty, those women weren't exactly close friends. Moreover, Isabella didn't want to live in London. The few weeks she spent there had reminded her of how much she detested the snobbery of the *ton.*

*As well as deceitful, lying sons of dukes who were wealthy enough to buy their own ships.*

But as they continued northward, Isabella doubled back on her last thought. She was now wealthy enough to purchase a ship of her own if she so desired. "Mayhap I'll buy a Scottish castle," she blurted, having no idea where that notion had come from.

Maribel stumbled over a stick of driftwood and quickly regained her balance. "A drafty old castle?"

Isabella huffed. Of course the maid had to bring logic into the conversation. "Perhaps a *little* castle?"

"If that is what you want, of course I'll follow you. However, I would be remiss if I didn't remind you that my parents worked at Durham Castle, and in winter the chambers were forever cold. I think that's why so many of those old fortresses have been left to ruin."

Isabella wasn't fond of icy-cold winters or of fireplaces that sent all the heat upward. "Perhaps a cottage would suit us better? A cottage with an expansive library."

"A library in a cottage?" Maribel asked, showing no imagination whatsoever.

"A manor, then."

"Newhailes would be nice. Did you see the duke's library when we were there?"

Of course Isabella had seen it. She and her father had met with the Duke of Dunscaby in his monumental library—not long before they boarded the

*Prosperity*—and not long before Gibb MacGalloway tricked her into kissing him. "The fiend."

"I beg your pardon?"

Had Isabella cursed the man aloud? "Never—" She clutched Maribel's arm. "Oh my heavens, you did see riders!"

"Look there!" The maid clapped her hands and then cringed. "What if they're not friendly?"

"But what if they are?"

"I say, after our last encounter with the Spaniards, I'm not feeling very lucky."

Isabella looked back from whence they'd come. The last tree they'd seen was the one that provided them with shade. Now they were surrounded by sand, scrubby bushes, and water with no place to hide.

Maribel pointed to the satchel across Isabella's shoulder. "The pistol."

"Oh, right you are." she agreed, dropping her leather bag on the sand and pulling out the flintlock, along with the powder flask.

"They'll be here by the time you manage to get it charged."

Isabella glanced to the items in her hands, realizing she'd never charged a pistol in her life, though she'd seen her father do it. "Are you adept with flintlocks?"

Maribel snorted out a guffaw. "Me? I was raised to be a servant, mind you."

"Right." Isabella cocked the hammer. "At least they won't know if the gun is loaded or not. Now stand behind me."

"Wonderful. Your Spanish is as good as mine, which amounts to nil." Maribel threw out her hands and didn't budge. "I can see the news headlines now:

*Two lost British women arrested after attempting to steal horses in Spain.*"

"But we're not stealing horses."

"Are you certain the approaching riders won't misunderstand our intentions when you point that weapon at them?"

"But you were the one who suggested it in the first place!" Heaving an exasperated huff, Isabella shifted the pistol behind her back. "Perhaps we should ask for help first, though I do wish I had taken Spanish rather than Latin. It would have come in quite handy."

"Oh, my good glory!" the maid squealed, clapping her hands over her mouth.

"What is it now?"

"'Tis Gowan, Mr. Lyall, and Captain MacGalloway!"

Isabella blinked. Now that the riders had come close enough for her to see their faces, they were definitely not Spanish, and most decidedly were the captain and two of his officers. Her stomach squeezed and somersaulted while several butterflies chose this moment to take flight.

*I mustn't forget that the man left me in America, and when he returned home, he proposed to some woman. I cannot and will not allow myself feelings for Gibb MacGalloway ever again!*

But there Isabella stood, dumbfounded while the men headed toward them. She clenched her hand around the pistol's handle, unable to ignore the relief flooding through her. "What the devil are *they* doing in Spain?"

As he reined his horse to a stop, Gibb still couldn't believe what he was seeing. Right there on the expanse of deserted beach, Isabella stood like a queen, wisps of black hair whipping in the wind. She held a pistol at her side. Oddly, her expression was not of surprise but of fear...or was it defiance?

Gibb dismounted and stared at the woman while everything else on the beach faded into oblivion. "You're here," he muttered—not exactly a long-winded greeting that articulated the relief presently flooding throughout his chest, but it was a start.

As he approached, she took a backward step. "What I don't understand is why *you* are here," she said rather curtly. Quite a curious response from a lass who was obviously stranded and in need of being rescued.

Gibb pulled the journal from the inside of his doublet. "We stopped in Valencia for supplies, and I spotted this wee book on a vendor's table."

"My journal!" She shoved the pistol into a satchel and took the book. "I thought it was lost forever."

"When I got close enough to see your name, I feared *you* were lost forever. What happened here? How did that man end up with your book? Did something untoward happen in America? Why are you here?"

She gulped, clutching the book to her chest while a tempest brewed behind those fathomless dark eyes.

"A moment." He held up his palms in surrender. Perhaps he'd been too forward with his outpouring of questions. "Let us take one thing at a time, shall we?"

Isabella nodded. "I-I wanted to do more research about Marcus and Flavia."

"I see." Gibb didn't see anything aside from the

fact that she was standing before him in the flesh and looking at him as if he were the one who was a wee bit daft in the head. "And Mr. Schuyler was amenable to sending you to Spain for an expedition...?" Which obviously had failed, and she was left with little more than the satchel across one shoulder and the bota bag across the other. "Did those blackguards ravi—ah... raise a hand against you?"

"I am unharmed, though they took everything including a chest full of coin."

So, the silver miner did send her off, the bastard. How could a man give his new wife a chest full of money and let her sail to Spain? "And they left you stranded?" Gibb asked, unable to calm the boom of exasperation in his voice.

"Yes, and a bit ill. Maribel and I believe the men we hired must have put something in our wine to make us sleep rather soundly."

"Good God, you could have been killed. What was your husband thinking allowing you to sail all the way to Spain alone?"

Isabella glanced to Maribel, who stood holding Gowan's hand, paying no attention to them. "It seems Mr. Schuyler made me a widow shortly after we took our vows."

Damnation, the man had died? Gibb's first impulse was to pull her into an embrace, but something told him she wouldn't want that. Instead, he looked to Mac, who stood dutifully holding the horses. "We ought to go back to Valencia and teach those miscreants a lesson."

"I'll reckon they're long gone by now," said the first mate.

"Aye," Gowan agreed. "Besides, we're already at

war with the French. We might lose favor with the Spaniards if we attack."

"Where is the *Prosperity*?" asked Maribel, her voice high-pitched and winsome.

Gibb cast his gaze out to the blue Mediterranean Sea. "Mr. MacLean is sailing her down from Valencia —we ought to see her drop anchor soon."

"Here?" asked Isabella.

"Aye. This is Marcus' beach, is it not?"

"This is Platja de la Garrofera, but after we parted ways, I translated another text that made me believe he and Flavia lived farther south—not far from Platja de la Devesa."

"That sounds more plausible. After scouting about for a few days and finding nothing, I figured Platja de la Garrofera couldna have been the right location, unless Marcus made his living trapping waterfowl in the lagoon."

Isabella chuckled—a nervous titter filled with apprehension. There were still so many questions to ask, yet by the current of tension darting between them, he was damned if he couldn't put a one into words.

"Why—" the lass started, but stopped abruptly and bit down on her bottom lip. Evidently Isabella was having difficulty as well.

Gibb arched his eyebrows. "Was there something you wished to ask me?"

"Why are *you* here?" He opened his mouth to reply, but she continued, "In Spain. Surely you weren't delivering whisky to Valencia, of all places?"

"No." He wanted to take her hand. He wanted to drop to his knees and beg her forgiveness, even though he wasn't quite certain what he needed to be forgiven for. But all his feelings aside, Gibb couldn't deny her the truth. "I, too, was curious about Marcus and Flavia..." *And being on this beach made me feel closer to you.* "I thought it might be diverting for the men to do a bit of hunting around to see if we could find some trace of them."

# 23

When the *Prosperity* sailed into sight and was moored off the shore where they stood, Isabella hadn't been able to think of a good reason why she oughtn't go aboard. Of course, all the obvious reasons to embark were undeniable—she and Maribel had been robbed and abandoned on a deserted beach in a foreign land. Her feet hurt, she was hungry and thirsty, and she still had a nasty ache pounding inside her head. Atop all of that, dusk had fallen, and with it, the November wind brought a chill.

Once they'd been hoisted aboard via the familiar boatswain's chair, she had been given the same cabin, but other than that, nothing was the same at all. She and Maribel had left their clothing behind in the tent, aside from a clean shift and a few necessaries she'd stowed in her satchel.

As usual, Gibb had been hospitable and courteous, though it was still unbelievable that he was there at all. It was beyond Isabella's comprehension that he would been wiling away his time in eastern Spain so soon after announcing his engagement.

Also as usual, Cookie had prepared a delicious meal, but this time, since the lady's maid had been promoted to companion, Maribel had agreed to join the captain's table for dinner.

"So, you believe Marcus and Flavia lived near Platja de la Devesa?" asked Gibb.

"Yes." Isabella finished her last sip of wine. "I pieced together a tablet that mentioned Platja de la Devesa. Our camp is there, or it was there. I imagine the wind has blown our tent away. That is, if it wasn't looted beforehand."

"Then we ought to have a look for it on the morrow. Did you do any excavating?"

Isabella paused for a moment. The captain was planning to go ashore tomorrow rather than sail home to his fiancée? "No, I wasn't there long enough to survey the grounds, let alone start digging."

Gibb pushed his chair way from the table. "I have the map open on my writing table. Why dunna ye show me where you set up camp?"

Gowan, Archie, and Mac all stood with Isabella.

"Would you mind if I took Miss Hatch on a turn about the deck?" asked Gowan.

Gibb waved them off. "Go on, then."

Isabella wasn't surprised that the other two men took their leave as well. Rather than move beside the captain, she opted to stand on the opposite side of his desk. "I had initially planned to establish an excavation and stay for a time. You are aware the weather here is temperate?"

"It is," he said, sliding his finger from Valencia down the long expanse of shoreline.

Deciding now was the time to press him about his engagement, she cleared her throat. "I am not one to pry, but I'd imagine you are most anxious to return home."

"Not especially," he said as if he were talking about

the weather. "I'm not planning another voyage to America until spring, though I may start transporting whisky and cotton cloth to the continent."

"How long were you planning to stay here?" she asked.

"Initially a month or so—mayhap surprise my kin with a visit to Stack Castle on Christmas."

Good Lord, she had misjudged this man considerably. "How can you do such a thing to your poor fiancée?"

The captain straightened, his expression utterly baffled. "I beg your pardon?"

"It was only in the headlines of the *Gazette* —*Brother of the Duke of Dunscaby Engaged*."

"Engaged?" Gibb threw his head back and laughed from his belly. "Och, what a bleeding mess that was— however, I wasna the one cornered into making a proposal."

Isabella drilled her finger onto the map. "But the newspaper reported that you had spared some poor woman from scandal because you were found alone with her at the duke's town house in London."

"I was there for my mother's birthday celebration, and ye're right about one thing. There was such a newspaper article released by the *Gazette* the following day. However, they got it wrong—and Marty made certain the eejits published an apology in the very next issue."

The fact that the duke had forced the newspaper to issue a retraction gave her no peace of mind whatsoever. "Excuse me, but what happened to the poor lady who was scandalized?"

"My brother Philip was the man who offered marriage."

She blinked. Twice. "So, why not you?"

Those thick blond eyebrows shifted outward with the widening of his eyes. "There are several reasons, the first being it was Philip who caught Miss Radcliffe after she stumbled into his arms."

"Oh," she replied, somewhat baffled. "And the other reasons?"

"The situation at the time appeared very suspicious to me, and I was convinced it was a marriage trap. Aye, Miss Radcliffe acted as if she dinna intend to walk into a corridor without a chaperone, trip, and happen to fall into Philip's arms. But the lassie's mother was too fast on her heels, pointing her finger and accusing my brother of compromising her daughter."

Shaking her head, Isabella clutched her hands over her chest. "Good Lord."

"So, Philip did the right thing." Gibb rested his hip against the writing table. "I canna say that I would have acted with such haste had it been me."

"How awful for him."

"That's what I thought, until Philip admitted it was a relief."

"Truly? Did he know Miss Radcliffe? Was she a friend of the family?"

Gibb shrugged. "He kent her name."

Even though this news changed things considerably, Isabella wasn't content to let it lie—not yet. "You mentioned that you wouldn't have acted with such haste. What would you have done if the woman had tripped into *your* arms?"

The captain casually rested his hand on the hilt of his dirk. "Aside from let her fall?"

"You wouldn't have let her fall. I know you better than that."

The big Scot's lips twitched slightly upward with a

wry grin. "Mayhap not, but I would have put forth an argument. The mother who made such a fuss was the lassie's chaperone, after all. I'll reckon she witnessed the entire incident."

"How horrible for your brother."

"I dunna think Philip cares overmuch. He said he needed to marry one day, and dinna have the time nor the inclination to look for a wife."

"He said that?"

"Aye, he figured Miss Radcliffe was bonny and would fit the bill."

The story grew odder by the moment. Isabella felt a bit sorry for Miss Radcliffe—after all, she must be rather clumsy, and then to have a mother who behaved like a dragon must be unbearable. "Did you not to stop Lord Philip from making a grave error?"

"Bloody oath I did. But once the eldest of the twins sets his mind on something, 'tis difficult to change it. Though he did say he intended to enjoy a verra long engagement." Gibb tapped the map. "So, now that we have that sorted out, would ye mind pointing out where you set up camp?"

Isabella reverted her attention to the writing table and moved her pointer finger down the map's coastline. "There."

"'Tis close, then."

"Yes—with luck, our clothing is still there. But—"

"Hmm?"

She gave him a hopeful grin, even going so far as to flutter her eyelashes. "While we are here, it would be a folly if we didn't do at least a little bit of investigating."

"Agreed."

"I didn't think you'd concur so easily. Were you not

in Valencia purchasing supplies for the return trip home?"

"We were." Gibb pointed to the beach where they had found each other. "After discovering Platja de la Garrofera to be nothing but a wasteland, there seemed no reason to stay. Besides, Archie and the men were convinced they had no chance at finding treasure."

"I doubt there will be a treasure chest anywhere."

"I ken, but the fellas like to dream."

"Ah...how long do you intend to stay—here—ah —with me?"

"Well, I reckon we ought to decide that after we have a wee peek at Platja de la Devesa on the morrow. But there's one thing for certain..."

"Which is?"

"The *Prosperity* is not sailing back home without ye." He thrust his fists onto his hips. "You shouldna have come here alone. I nearly lost my mind when I saw your journal in that man's possession, and I'm sure as hell not going to allow ye to stay."

"*Allow* me?" she asked, ignoring the flutter in the pit of her stomach that was on the verge of performing pirouettes because he'd just told her he'd nearly lost his mind and he'd hastened to her rescue. But she wasn't about to let the captain suddenly take charge of her independence. "I may be grateful to you for coming to my aid, and I may owe you a debt of gratitude. However, I am no longer a meek maiden beholden to the decisions of the men around me. I am a widow and free to do whatever I may so choose."

"Is that right?" Gibb stepped nearer, his deep blue eyes growing darker. "If you are so able to protect yourself from scoundrels like the one I saw in the market, then tell me, why was it I found you hungry and windblown on the beach like a castaway?"

GIBB STOOD ROOTED to the floor while Mrs. Schuyler stormed out of his cabin.

God on the bloody cross, his temper had reached its boiling point, and he had naught to do but slam his fist on the table. "Fie!"

What the devil was she thinking? Had the woman completely lost her mind? She was married for all of a day and had suddenly developed a misplaced sense of independence. She might be a widow, but she was still a woman. Isabella was fortunate not to have been ravished while she so blindly hired a scout to take her to a deserted beach.

And once Gibb found her, she'd acted as if they'd never shared an embrace or a passionate kiss. Though now he had a good idea why she'd been so standoffish. The woman had thought him daft enough to make a proposal of marriage to Miss Radcliffe. Well, even though the papers had cocked up their report, Isabella of all people knew him better than that. And Philip didn't need to propose either. Had the lassie's mother held her tongue, there would have been no scandal at all. Lord knew Philip wasn't the first wealthy gentleman who had been hoodwinked by a fortune-hunting mama.

Nonetheless, Isabella didn't appear terribly happy that Gibb had not been the one to propose to Miss Radcliffe. What did she expect him to do, fight Philip for the right to marry the wee imp?

Gibb paced his cabin, shooting glares at the latch on the door. She had been the one to storm away, not he. There was no chance in hell that he would swallow his pride and knock on her door. If she desired privacy, then he'd let her have it.

Blast it all, he hadn't expected to see her here. She knew he wasn't one to dish out marriage proposals—he'd confessed that fact more than once when they were sailing to America.

Why did he feel as if he was the heel in all this? Aye, he'd feared the worst when he found her journal. Who wouldn't want to find a woman—a *friend* in distress? But she wasn't supposed to be here.

Truth be told, she most likely found it a bit out of the ordinary to learn he'd been doing a bit of poking around as well. But Marcus and Flavia's story had interested him—at least, that was what he'd told himself and the men.

He faced the door and crossed his arms, trying to not to admit that he was smitten, but the bald truth kept forcing its way into his thoughts. When he was on the beach looking for signs of Marcus, he'd felt closer to Isabella. He'd dreamed about finding something to prove Marcus had lived near the beach, and when he did, he planned to write to Mrs. Schuyler and tell her all about his adventure.

But now she was here.

And that terrified him.

# 24

The next morning, Isabella appeared to have enjoyed a reasonable night's sleep, even though she was still wearing the same traveling dress. Her hair was pinned up in a tidy chignon—at least, Gibb imagined it had been. There wasn't much of her hair to be seen beneath her bonnet. He, on the other hand, had spent countless hours tossing and turning and wondering how he had ended up on the wrong end of the woman's ire after having nearly incited a war for her sake.

She gazed to the shore expectantly while the men rowed the skiff. Miss Hatch had opted to stay behind, since Gowan was remaining aboard as officer of the watch. "Look there," Isabella said, pointing. "I can see the canvas of our tent flapping in the wind."

Gibb clenched his fists, fuming about how much danger she'd placed herself in—and how little remorse she seemed to harbor about it. He never would have been able to live with himself if she'd been hurt.

After they arrived on the beach, he led her to the campsite while the men followed with a few tools they might need for an excavation. The tent sagged, its stakes nearly wrenched from their moorings—that or they hadn't been properly driven into the ground in the first place. It didn't matter. The tent looked as sorry and abandoned as Isabella had when he first found her.

Together they climbed the sand dune and crossed to the campsite.

"Good gracious." Isabella clapped her hands over her mouth. "I feel so foolish."

No matter how much he agreed with those words, Gibb wanted nothing more than to wrap her in his arms and kiss her. But gone was the doe-eyed lass who had kissed him on the deck of the *Prosperity*. Circumstances had changed her, and he sensed she still would not welcome his affection. Besides, it was broad daylight and they were accompanied by a half-dozen sailors.

Given the situation, Gibb did the only suitable thing he could think of. He placed his hand on her arm and held it firm, praying it imparted a modicum of the tenderness in his heart. "You were following your dreams. Most men would never muster the fortitude or determination to set out on a journey as perilous as this. And ye ken most women sit beside their hearths content with their embroidery—very few could even imagine traveling to a remote beach in Spain."

A sad smile turned up her lips. But as her dark gaze gradually meandered upward and met his, a spark ignited deep in his heart. Taking in a deep breath, he summoned a smile as well, and patted her arm. "I'll have a wee peek inside."

"I doubt you'll find anything."

Regardless, he parted the flap and popped his head in. "Perhaps I do believe in miracles," he said with a grin, holding the canvas wide to reveal her trunk. "It looks as if you'll have a change of clothes whilst we conduct our survey."

"Thank heavens."

Gibb turned to the crewmen and took one of their shovels. "Lads, take Mrs. Schuyler's things aboard the ship and return anon. The lady and I have some exploring to do."

"What about the tent, Cap'n?" asked Duncan.

"Reseat the spikes. We'll leave it be for now." Spreading his palms wide, Gibb regarded Isabella. "So, this is where we ought to start searching?"

"I think so. Aside from Platja de la Devesa, Marcus mentioned goats and chickens and a house upon a knoll."

"Hopefully you've pinpointed the spot. There's about sixty miles between Valencia and the promontory at Xàbia. It would take a thousand men years to excavate that much land."

"Then let us not delay."

Gibb offered his elbow. "Shall we, madam?"

She pointed to a hillock. "Perhaps we ought to begin there," she said, placing her fingers on his arm, her mere touch making his heart race.

He drew in a deep breath, willing his heart to slow, though it did little good. "It seems you have endured your share of calamity over the past few months."

"I must admit, I didn't expect any of it, starting with my father coming into my bedchamber and telling me he had agreed to Mr. Schuyler's suit of marriage."

"The miner seemed like a fit man—agreeable as well, which is why I resolved to leave you in his care. I hope my impression of him was not misguided."

"No. I think he was kind—very kind to be forthright."

"Oh?" Gibb asked, shifting her hand to his as they negotiated the craggy ground on the slope.

"Were you aware that the state of Georgia abolished primogeniture in seventeen seventy-seven?"

"Truly? I had no idea."

"They did. And furthermore, prior to my arrival, Mr. Schuyler took steps to ensure I would live in luxury after his death—though the poor man had no idea that he wouldn't live long enough to..."

"Hmm?" Gibb asked, but, noticing her blush, he knew better than to ask her to explain. She had already said the man had collapsed just as they walked out of the church. There was no chance the miner would have been able to consummate the marriage. "So, once you received your inheritance, you decided to stage an expedition?"

"Yes." After cresting the hill, they stopped at an outcropping. Isabella released his hand and took a few steps away, sweeping her gaze across the sea. "The view from here is astonishing."

Gibb rested the shovel against the rock, then also looked across the scene. From this point, the beach stretched north and south as far as the eye could see. And beyond were the deep blue waters of the Mediterranean Sea, with the *Prosperity* waiting at anchor. In the vast expanse, the ship seemed so small.

"I owe you an apology," Isabella whispered beside him.

Gibb's attention reverted to her lovely face, framed by a wind-blown curls beneath the brim of her bonnet. As he looked into Isabella's eyes, nothing mattered except for this woman here, at this moment. "Oh?" he asked, wanting to know more, his heart hammering with the thread of hope that she might still harbor a modicum of fondness for him.

"The newspaper article tainted my impression of you, and once I learned the truth, it took me some time to sort out my emotions."

He placed a hand on the stone beside her ear while tucking a black curl into her hat. "If it helps at all, I never once stopped thinking of you, no matter how much I tried."

"Which is why you came here?"

"Aye." Gibb's gaze slipped to her lips, and she rewarded him by licking that sensual mouth, bringing a moist sparkle to her lips. "Dunna ask me why. Mayhap I felt standing here would somehow make me feel closer to you."

She placed her palm atop his thundering heart. "Leaving you in Savannah was the most difficult thing I've ever done—but you are aware I had no choice."

He dipped his chin and shifted his head to the side, moving so close that her breath skimmed his chin. "I ken."

With Gibb's next heartbeat, she rose and closed the distance, sealing her lips to his, timidly at first. But the word *timid* seemed to slip from Gibb's vocabulary. He wanted to taste her. He wanted to devour her. He crooked his finger beneath her chin and tilted her face up just enough, sealing his lips over hers, demanding that she match his fervor.

It took but a tiny sigh before desire consumed him, and as the kiss grew in intensity, she slid her hands around his waist and clung to him. Lush breasts molded perfectly into his chest while he continued with his plunder, challenging her to match him stroke for stroke.

And she did.

Their bodies fused together, his harder than he'd ever been in all his days.

When finally he eased his lips away and met her heavy-lidded gaze, Gibb knew this woman had claimed his heart as well as his soul. He just had no idea what he was to do about it. Turn against his hard and fast rule to remain a bachelor and propose?

*Have I lost my bloody mind?*

But the answer drifted out to sea while Gibb's gaze settled upon the stone beneath his palm. "Isabella, I believe you are positively brilliant."

She giggled. "Though no one dislikes being told they are brilliant, it is rather an unusual endearment after imparting such a passionate kiss."

"Might I rephrase: your kisses make my knees melt into liquid honey, and your brilliance surpasses that of every scholar I've ever met." He gripped a handful of vines and pulled them away. "This stone wasna put here by God. 'Tis man-made for certain."

With a sharp gasp, Isabella turned and traced her finger along a crack in the white rock. "This is marble."

Gibb drew his dirk and cut away vines and brush.

Isabella helped to pull the debris away. "It is the top of a pillar."

With the shovel, Gibb cleared a bit of dirt around it. "I reckon most of it is buried."

"The ruins we discovered on Papa's lands were as well. The excavation took over a year."

"Once I have the crew working on it, we ought to go quickly enough." He dug down about three feet and hit something hard, making the shovel clang.

"What was that?" Isabella asked, bending over the hole.

"A stone." He tapped it with the toe of his boot. "A big one."

"Wait a moment. Let me see it."

Gibb made the hole wider, then helped the lady down. Isabella took out a handkerchief and brushed away the moist dirt. "This is marble as well—it must be part of the pillar." She straightened and clapped her hands. "Oh my heavens, we truly are onto something!"

Gibb lifted her up and into his arms, twirling in a circle. "I kent you were brilliant!"

# 25

After a delicious dinner of mutton, and a stroll around the deck with Gibb, Isabella retired to her cabin. He'd kissed her at the door—his magical lips claimed her mouth, and she did her best to match his fervor, not wanting the kiss to end, wishing to remain in his arms forever. This day had been one of the best she'd ever had, and it was ever so difficult to say goodnight at her door, but as always, she had acted the proper Englishwoman and done so.

Earlier today, it had taken nerves of steel to summon the courage to apologize for misjudging the captain. She'd spent hours contemplating what he might do or say or how he might judge her. After enduring years of being criticized by her father, combined with Papa's frequent departures due to his tenure in the army, she was lacking in the skills a young lady needed to endear herself to a man. It had been so much easier to be charming when she was engaged to be married and traveling across the seas to meet her betrothed.

At least she didn't seem as worried about how and when to say things back then. Even though they had kissed and formed a semblance of a romance, they both knew it couldn't last. They both knew they couldn't lose their hearts—regardless of whether she had lost hers all the same.

But today she'd summoned the courage to apologize, and he rewarded her with a kiss that trumped all other kisses they'd shared. As their lips fused, it was as if he'd opened a window into his soul. And in the very next moment, they realized the rock against which she had been standing was actually an ancient Roman pillar! To their astonishment, once the men arrived, they dug down far enough for her to be relatively certain that the marble stone Gibb had clonked with his shovel was the head of the statue of Mars that Marcus referred to in one of his tablets.

It might be late, but the very last thing Isabella was capable of was sleep. They had found Mars. Furthermore, she'd done it with Captain Gibb MacGalloway, the only man who had ever captured her heart. And together they'd found the statue as they were kissing.

If Isabella were a hopeless romantic, she would have swooned on the spot only to have been revived with smelling salts.

And she'd be lying to herself if she said her weak-kneed reaction wasn't caused by the captain. The fact that he was there in Spain—that he'd rescued her and Maribel on the beach, and he'd agreed to stay...that he admitted standing on the beach in Spain somehow made him feel closer to her.

Raindrops pattered on the small windowpane.

*He wanted to be closer to me. That has to account for something—mayhap not love, but certainly a deep fondness.*

Shoving the bedclothes aside, Isabella rose and peered out the window. Rivulets of water streaked downward, and beyond, the sea was as dark as ink.

When they were sailing, she'd oft seen the white foam from the ship's wake at night, but the *Prosperity* was moored. The sounds were more vivid when the ship was at anchor. When she was sailing, the flap of the sails, the intermittent groan of the hull, even the ship cutting through the water were sounds that made it nearly impossible to hear little raindrops tap the glass.

Something scraped the floor in the chamber next door—as if the captain had pushed his chair away from his writing desk. Was he writing in the ship's log? Two footsteps sounded.

Isabella glanced toward the door and grazed her teeth over her bottom lip.

*He oft told me that he doesn't sleep well.*

She donned her dressing gown, tiptoed across the floor, and rested her hand on the latch. Dare she go to him? Lord knew she wanted to. Lord knew she'd dreamed of him enough. She had even dreamed of Gibb MacGalloway when she should have been mourning Arent's death. Of course she mourned for the man, but not as a bereft wife would have done. How could she grieve at length for someone she hardly knew?

Drawing a deep breath, she placed her hand on the latch of her cabin door, her fingers slipping from perspiration. She wanted him, but didn't quite know what to do.

*What if he rejects me? What if he sees me as a woman of easy virtue?*

She gulped, knowing full well she would be devastated if he did. She'd never be able to look him in the face.

*I ought to go back to bed.*

Instead, Isabella pulled down on the latch, the resounding click loud enough to wake the dead. She stood with the door open for a moment, staring into the dark corridor, scarcely able to breathe.

*Have I gone completely daft?*

Her inner warnings served no purpose as she turned left and took the three steps to the captain's door. She raised her fist to knock, but trepidation finally took hold, and she gently placed her palm on the timbers.

*I am being incredibly audacious and irresponsible. I will turn around this instant.*

Except the door opened.

And Isabella hadn't budged.

Gibb stood as still as the statue of Mars, towering over her like a Highland king while the amber light from a lantern glowed around him. His eyes were nearly as black as hers, his hair mussed, his doublet off and his shirt sleeves rolled to his elbows. "Bella," he whispered, still not moving.

"I—"

As her mind whirred with a dozen excuses as to why she might knock on a captain's door wearing her nightclothes, his lips sealed over hers. Soft, masculine lips hungrily plied her mouth, and in a maelstrom of emotion, he ushered her inside without pulling his lips away. The door shut while he gathered her tightly against him, sliding his hands up her back and down again. Isabella clung to him, her trembling fingers roving frantically and nowhere near as expertly as Gibb's seemed to be.

He left her mouth, searching across her jawbone until his delectable nibbles stopped at her ear. "I canna help myself. I want ye."

"Then take me," she breathlessly replied, arching her back against him, shivering with every kiss.

"I've wanted to hear you speak those words ever

since the day you stepped aboard the *Prosperity*." But rather than ravish her against the door, he gripped her shoulders and took one step away. "Is this truly what you want, lass? To share a bed with a sea captain?"

She tried to lean forward and hide her face in his shoulder, but he held her firmly in place. She knew what he meant, and she didn't care. She wanted him, and damn the consequences. She'd been cosseted all her life, never once allowed to make her own decisions or follow her heart. "I, too, have dreamed of being in your bed since I came aboard. I want to lie with you as man and woman."

Taking Isabella's hand, Gibb pulled her deeper into the cabin. Those deep blue eyes focused on her. The corner of his mouth twitched up as he unfastened the brooch at his shoulder and tossed it on the table behind. He watched her while he let loose his belt buckle, hesitating for an instant before he let it fall away, sending his kilt billowing to the floorboards. She tapped her tongue to the corner of her mouth as her gaze traveled down the length of his shirt and to his well-muscled thighs—peppered with curls of blond hair.

No words were needed when he gave her a nod. Instinctively, she unfastened her sash and let her robe fall away. "Now you," she said boldly, her thighs quivering with the need to see all of him.

With a wry grin, Gibb whipped the shirt over his head, cast it aside, and stood with his hands relaxed at his sides as if inviting her inspection. Unable to turn away, Isabella looked over his naked body, lingering at his loins, her eyes growing wider, while the intense yearning deep inside her core demanded to be touched, to be bedded.

Again he nodded, this time to her shift.

She grasped the linen skirt. "Off?"

"Aye."

Isabella watched him as she slowly inched the hem to her ankles and then to her knees. When she reached her thighs, she could have sworn his member twitched. And she could take no more. In one motion, she pulled the shift over her head and flung it to the floorboards.

And then she was in his arms, his mouth exploring hers, their bodies melding together. He carried her to the bed and climbed in beside her. "Ye are so fine to me, Issy, Bella, my Belle. What pet name shall I call you?"

"I've always been fond of Bella," she whispered into his ear as she pulled him closer. "I—ah—hope you won't mind navigating these uncharted waters."

GIBB COULD HAVE COME with those words. He didn't have to ask to know she was still a virgin. Hell, it might make things a tad easier if she weren't. But if he understood nothing else about his attraction to this woman, he knew he must have her, but not in the usual way, not a fast hump and done. He wanted this night to last forever. He wanted Isabella to lock this night away in her heart and dream about it for years to come.

"You are the bonniest woman I've ever had the honor of setting eyes upon," he said, meaning every word. How he could have ever thought this woman plain, he would never fathom. Perhaps it was her frumpy bonnet when they first met; perhaps his eyes were dimmed by a sailor's rigidity. Isabella was an iconic beauty, a woman to be worshipped and adored.

"You steal my breath from my verra lungs," he added, cupping a shapely breast and teasing its tender peak with his thumb. Even her breasts were perfectly formed—not too small and not too large. Transfixed, he inched downward until he caught her nipple with a slow, succulent kiss.

Isabella gasped, arching into him, sliding her fingers into his hair.

"That's it, lass, close your eyes and allow yourself to feel."

With both hands, he framed her breasts, feasting on the luxurious curves, kissing, tasting, and nibbling as he adored her.

Gooseflesh pebbled along her skin, following his lips as he kneaded and kissed his way down to the nest of curls between her thighs. He traced the dewy slit with his finger while watching her lips part, her breathing become labored. And as Isabella's midnight eyes grew even darker, he knew she was ready for him.

"Easy, lass," he purred. "This is not a race with sails at full tilt, but a marathon across the oceans of the globe."

He met her trusting gaze and winked, right before he parted her sex and stroked down to her entrance, sliding his finger inside, only the tip at first, gradually increasing its depth as she moved and sighed in tandem with his touch.

With a moan, she gripped his shoulders, as if trying to drive him deeper, her walls opening for him as he found a pool of moisture. Isabella sighed and cooed, the sounds she made ushering him to the edge of madness. He held his hand still while he bent to kiss her belly, skimming his lips downward until he reached her black triangle.

She arched up as if to stop him, but he placed a reassuring hand on her abdomen. "Allow me to taste you, *mo leannan.*"

Her thighs quivered. "With your mouth?"

He grinned. "Your taste, your scent, is pure nectar from the gods. Lie back and feel."

After she dropped to the pillows, he settled himself between her legs, opening them with his shoulders and parted her with his tongue. She quivered beneath him, her flesh hot and searing. He flicked his tongue over her, then blew cool air, flicked, blew, flicked, blew.

At her sigh, he licked her fully, exploring the salty, feminine flesh with long licks and soft tongue taps, centering on the tiny button that could send her to the stars.

Isabella's fingers found his hair. "I think it is time now. I must have you!"

"You will, my sweeting, but not yet. I'm in command of this ship, and I say you're not quite ready, lass." Gibb entered her with two fingers and, finding resistance, further shouldered between her thighs and drove his tongue into the heat of her core.

Her hips swirled, her body jerked, and she nearly pulled his hair from its roots. "Pleaaaaase!"

But Gibb refused to let up. He moved to the little bud and suckled her until she was shaking and gasping and pleading for more. He slid a finger inside, and as she writhed, he managed a second and nearly a third.

With her sharp gasp, the edge of the world seemed to stop on a precipice of oblivion. She arched off the mattress, drew in a breath, and shattered around his finger.

At the sight of the ecstasy written on her face, Gibb was filled with an indescribably primal satisfaction. He drew out her climax, extending his own fulfillment by continuing to lick and love her until the last of her quivers subsided.

She toyed with his hair. "I have no words."

"The English language is deficient when it comes to making love." He lapped her again. "But I'll reckon you're ready to sail into stormier seas, lass."

Isabella might be far outmatched by the captain, but she was a fast learner. So much of the night was a blur of passion, but some things would remain with her for the rest of her days—Gibb's spicy scent mixed with rain—the salty and mellow taste of his skin. She'd driven her fingers into his hair, surprised at the silkiness of it.

But most of all, she would cherish in her heart the very moment when they joined. Though he was a large man, her body had adjusted with his patience. Never once did he push or rush. He touched her with a gentle reverence, his voice low as he murmured about how good she felt and how long he had wanted her. And she'd quivered and spread her legs wider while he sank deeper and deeper inside her.

Once he'd completely filled her, she was again writhing beneath him. Still, Gibb didn't rush, drawing out the ecstasy, kissing her, praising her, loving her. It was the most magical night of her life.

# 26

Gibb watched Isabella sleep as he wove her hair through his fingers. She lay on her side facing him, her mouth slightly parted, the crescents of her black eyelashes skimming creamy cheeks. He still couldn't believe she was there. A hint of trepidation entered his thoughts, but he quickly pushed it away. She had asked him to make love to her—the first and only gentlewoman he had ever lain with. Of course, he now needed to marry Isabella...*in time*. Presently, he was thankful to be moored of the coast of a remote beach in a foreign land. There would be plenty of time to think about their future on the voyage back to Scotland.

But presently, this magical night had come to an end. Gibb always stirred when the sky turned from black to cobalt, bringing the promise of dawn. This was his favorite time of day—the wee hours when night transitioned to morn. The hour always began in eerie silence, but by the time the sand fell through the hourglass, birds were busy and the ship bustled with the sound of sailors' boots pounding the timbers.

Not planning to encounter any able seamen, he

kissed her temple. "I'd best take you back to your own bed, lass."

She stirred a bit but didn't wake. Carefully, Gibb lifted her into his arms and carried Isabella to her cabin, tucking her in and giving her one last kiss before he slipped away. He rarely slept more than a few hours at a stretch, often awakened by the night terrors that had begun while he was serving his naval commission. It seemed a common malady for men who had fought during the wars—one he was unfortunate not to have escaped. But he'd sleep later. Presently he could barely feel his feet as he pattered about his cabin, preparing for the day as if he were on a cloud.

As the sun rose, Duncan brought in breakfast right on schedule. "Good morn, Cap'n."

Gibb sat at the table and breathed in the scent of salted pork, fried eggs, and warmed ship's biscuits. "A fine day it is, lad."

"Will we be going ashore for the excavation?"

"Indeed we will, just as soon as the ladies are ready." Gibb picked up the salt cellar's tiny spoon and sprinkled his food. "Will you be stepping ashore with us, or has Thane assigned you lessons?"

"I'm stepping ashore, sir. Thane believes the excavation is a good lesson in Roman antiquity, and I agree. I'd far rather dig in the dirt and uncover ancient relics than sit in the shadowy mizzen deck reading about it."

Gibb reached for his knife and fork. "I must agree. You'd best see to your chores, then. The ladies will need a good breakfast before they're ready to disembark."

"Straight away, sir." Duncan headed to the door, tray in hand, but stopped halfway. "Cap'n?"

"Aye?"

"I'm glad we found Miss Harcourt...I mean Mrs. Schuyler."

"As am I."

"It's odd, though, the way women must change their names."

"How so?"

"Well, I reckon it is difficult to keep it straight. And I canna imagine living all my life with one name, and then having to change it all of a sudden."

Gibb raised his pint of ale and did his best not to laugh aloud. "Then be glad you were born a man, laddie."

After breaking his fast, he took a turn around the decks as he always did—meeting with his officers and ensuring the watch would be adequately manned during the hours of excavation. When he headed back to his cabin, he paused outside Isabella's door.

Maribel's voice resonated through the timbers. "You seem in bright spirits, madam."

"Why wouldn't I be?" There was a bit of a pause before Isabella continued. "We have found the statue of Mars, for heaven's sakes. It is a find for which most antiquarians search their entire lives."

The rustling of skirts swelled through to the corridor, and Gibb placed his hand on his cabin's latch, pretending to be coming out. "Ah, ladies, you have impeccable timing," he said when their door opened.

"Good morning, captain," said Maribel as she strode past.

Isabella stopped in front of him, her face turning scarlet. "It is a fine morning, sir."

He gave her a sly wink. "Miss Hatch, will you be stepping ashore with us?"

"I think I'll remain aboard. After our fiasco on the

beach before you arrived, I feel as if I've seen as much of Spain as I care to."

Isabella took his elbow, smiling and still as red as an apple. "It seems there is one particular officer who has also volunteered to supervise the watch."

Gibb chuckled. Everyone aboard knew Gowan had fallen for Maribel, and the pair were all but inseparable. Which was best in his book. It took the crew's scrutiny away from him, though honestly, he didn't care what the men thought about him. However, he would call any man out who voiced an ill word against Isabella.

While the men rowed the skiff to the beach, Gibb sat on the bench beside Isabella with his thigh touching hers, wishing he could reach over and hold her hand. Instead, he moved even closer and shifted his leg so that it touched her thigh to his knee. Of course, when she pushed back, he swallowed a grin.

It wasn't until they had set the men to work and headed off under the pretense of scouting the site that he was able to have her to himself. Once they had crested the hill and were out of sight, he wrapped her in his arms and kissed her. "I've wanted to do that ever since you stepped out of your cabin."

She kissed him back feverishly. "And I've been waiting for you to do so."

"I've been wondering..."

"Hmm?"

"Have you any regrets?"

"Not a one." She started to kiss him but pulled away with a tiny gasp. "And you? Are you regretting having...ah...your way with me?"

He grinned and waggled his eyebrows. "Och, is that what you're calling it now?"

"Well, I suppose I did initiate it, did I not?"

"You came to my door."

"But I hadn't knocked yet." She looked up at him, the sun catching those incredible eyes and bringing out a midnight blue he'd never noticed before. "So, do you?"

"Do I what?" Gibb asked.

She thwacked him on the shoulder. "Harbor any regrets, silly."

"Not a one. Life is too short for regrets." He offered his elbow. "Where to now, m'lady? Where might you think Marcus and Flavia might have had their farm?"

She pointed to a spot in the distance. "If I were a farmer, I'd choose the high ground where there is plenty of undulating pastureland and an unobstructed view of the sea."

"Then shall we?"

"Indeed," she said, again placing her fingers in the crook of his arm.

They'd walked about a mile when Isabella stopped and spread her arms wide. "Look at this magnificent site. And nary a soul lives here."

"But you believe this is the place?"

"I do. I feel it in my bones." She strolled along, turning over a few sizeable stones with her toe. "But I would think there ought to be a brick or a stone with a bit of mortar attached to it—something to reveal that there might be ruins hiding beneath the soil."

Gibb kicked a few boulders, seeing nothing but rock. "Are you certain Marcus didn't write about his house?"

"Well, not the exact location."

He tugged her into his arms and brushed away the strands of hair that had fallen from her chignon. "I'd rather keep my excavations to a more personal nature."

She giggled as she gently pulled away. "What will the men think if they see us?"

"I care not what they think."

Twirling in a circle, she raised her hands above her head as if she were as carefree as a Highland lass. "Do you want to know a secret?"

"What is it?"

"I, too, do not give a fig what anyone thinks of us, not really."

After putting his shovel down, he grasped her hand and led her in a minuet. "You ought to."

"Why? Because I'll be ruined and all of society will treat me as an outcast?" She scoffed as she executed three perfect turns. "I was an outcast before I ever met you."

"Merely a self-proclaimed outcast, however. That's a wee bit different."

Together they sashayed forward. "Then shall we continue to pretend our relationship is purely platonic?"

He released her hand and bowed. "Why not? At least, I see no reason to climb the main mast and shout about it for all to hear."

"Very well, no mast climbing. But I'll not deny my feelings for you."

Gibb gulped. "Agreed. Denial would only make us appear foolish." He picked up his shovel and prodded beneath another rock. "Where shall I start digging, madam? Since I brought along a spade, there's no sense in letting it rest."

"Very well." She pointed to a copse of trees about fifty paces to the north. "Why not start there?"

Gibb took her hand and headed for the spot at a jog. Isabella squealed with laughter, holding her hat to her head. "Are you in a hurry?" she asked.

"Aye. We've a treasure to find."

He was about to speed the pace, but something stabbed the back of his leg. With his next step, burning pain shot up his leg. "Argh!" he cried, dropping the shovel and stumbling forward.

"What is it?" Isabella asked, coming to an abrupt halt. "God no..."

Gibb stooped forward and planted his hands on his knees, blinking to clear his vision. "Not to worry. Give me a moment and I'll be set to rights."

"I do not believe so, captain. You've been bitten by a snake!"

The fearless captain's entire body shuddered. "Och, I have never been able to abide slithering serpents."

ISABELLA DID what she could to help Gibb as he limped back to the men, but the bullheaded Scotsman refused to lean on her. Instead, he used the shovel as a walking stick. And though he pressed his lips tightly together and uttered not a word of complaint, there was no doubt he was in pain. By time they reached the statue of Mars, sweat was dripping from his face and he'd turned as white as the sands beneath their feet.

It seemed to take forever for the men to usher him down to the boat, the captain bellowing orders all the while as if he needed to prove he was still in command. As they rowed the tiny skiff, the wind worked against them, stirring up white caps in the sea and making it laborious for the men to row her to the hull of the *Prosperity*.

While Duncan and Mac held the boatswain's chair, Gibb gnashed his teeth when the winch started hefting him upward. "Dunna let go of the ropes," the lad hollered, worry written across his face.

Isabella gave the cabin boy's shoulders a reassuring hug. "The captain's as strong as any man I know. He'll come though this, mark me."

Duncan leaned into her. "Do ye reckon so? My da wasna so lucky."

She grasped the young man's shoulders and bent down so that her eyes were even with his. "I swear to you this day, I will not allow Captain MacGalloway to succumb to a measly snakebite."

Duncan swiped a hand across his face, obviously trying not to cry. "You promise?"

"I do," she said, praying to God she was right. "But I'll need your help."

"You will?" he asked, his voice hopeful.

"As soon as you touch your feet to the deck, fetch Cookie. He might have some sort of remedy for snakebites. Then I want you to find Maribel and tell her I need my medicine basket. Once you've done all of that, I'll require a ewer of warm water brought to the captain's cabin—and a bit of whisky. Can you fetch both of those things for me?"

"Aye, missus. I'll have them for ye faster than you can tie a cat's paw knot."

They hoisted Isabella aboard next. She nearly burst her spleen when she arrived on deck to find Gibb holding on to the rail, bent forward in agony while engaging in conversation with the sailors who had remained on watch. Angry enough to breathe fire through her nose, she pushed her way through the group. "Your captain has been bitten by a snake and needs urgent care!"

Gibb glanced her way, his eyes red and drooping.

"Not to worry. A few tots of whisky and I'll be dancing a reel."

Deciding his reply wasn't worth acknowledging, she pointed to Mr. MacLean and Mr. Lyall. "Accompany him to his chamber...please." At their gaping expressions, she added, "I believe he keeps a flask within —he can have a nip there."

Archie took Gibb by the arm, but he yanked it away with a scowl that wasn't nearly as effective as usual. "I can manage on my own. I'll be inspecting the watch within an hour, mark me."

Duncan arrived on board, and Isabella shook her finger. "You have your instructions."

"Aye, madam. I'll fetch Cookie first, I reckon."

She gave the boy a nod as she hastened after the captain. Isabella didn't know much about poisonous snakebites. They had adders in England, and they were venomous, painful bites, but not deadly. What about in Spain? What ought she expect from a viper on the continent?

*I pray we are too far north for a cobra bite.* She thought back—the asp hadn't flared its neck like the Egyptian drawings she'd seen in history books.

Maribel met them as they proceeded aft. "Goodness, you've returned far earlier than I expected."

Pulling her along, Isabella lowered her voice and quickly explained the incident. "I'll need my medicine basket. Duncan has instructions to find you, and you bring it to me. The poor lad is terribly worried. I would be ever so grateful if you would console him."

"I'll fetch your basket straight away. Then Gowan and I will have a word with Duncan. I shall tell the lad the captain is in good hands with you as his healer."

"God willing, and let us pray the snake wasn't too terribly venomous." Isabella made the sign of the cross, then patted Maribel's shoulder. "Thank you, dearest."

Once in the cabin, rather than sit, Gibb strode to the windows and looked out over the sea. "I reckon a storm is brewing."

Mr. MacLeod moved beside him, clasping his hands behind his back and rocking on his heels as if it were Sunday morn and their fearless captain wasn't about to succumb to the venom spreading through his blood and fall on his face. "Agreed."

Since no one else seemed willing to take matters in hand, Isabella marched across the floor, planted her hands on her hips, and tapped her toe. "Excuse me, but am I the only person who understands how serious a snakebite can be? By your sweaty mien, Captain, it is clear to me that the viper obviously was poisonous. You need to lie down."

He looked at her from head to toe as if she'd suddenly sprouted horns. "It is the middle of the day. I dunna take to my rack when the sun is still ablaze."

She stepped toward him, throwing back her shoulders. "And you most likely have not suffered such an injury before. From what I have read on the topic of snakebites, you will doubtlessly grow sicker as the poison spreads."

Gibb shuddered. "I detest the slithering varlets!"

A knock came at the door. "Your medicine bundle, Mrs. Schuyler," said Maribel, popping inside.

Isabella hastened to retrieve the basket full of healing herbs and bandages just as Cookie arrived with a pail covered with a lid and a wooden box carried under his arm that looked as if it had been splattered with blood. "The lad said the cap'n is in a bad way."

"I'll nay allow a wee snake to best me. 'Tis just a

scratch," Gibb groused, in the midst of pouring himself a dram of whisky.

Isabella set her basket on the dining table and pulled out a chair. "Would you please at least sit down?"

"I reckon you ought to listen to the lady," Mr. MacLean agreed. "Ought we weigh anchor and set sail for home?"

Gibb stumbled as he crossed the floor and managed to land in his chair while half the whisky sloshed out of his glass. "No, no, no! We're not going anywhere. There's the statue of Mars to unearth—and who kens what other antiquities might be buried there?"

"Do you really think we'll find something more?" asked Mr. Lyall.

"Out!" Isabella shouted, thrusting her finger toward the door. "Everyone except Cookie leave this chamber at once."

When finally she and the cook were left alone with the captain, he sipped his drink and gave her a frown. "I'm no' going to lie down."

Cookie set his things down and rubbed his meaty hands on his apron. "Where's the pain, sir?"

"I'm feeling no pain whatsoever."

"And I'm Blackbeard's ghost." The cook shoved up his sleeves. "You're whiter than the linens on the table and are sweating like a man who's played a game of shinty in the hot sun. Tell me where the bloody bite is located or I'll send for the crew to pin ye down and hold ye fast until I find it meself."

Isabella grinned as she stood a bit taller.

"God's stones." Gibb rolled his eyes. "Right calf, just above the ankle." As Isabella kneeled to remove his boot, the captain held up a palm to stop her. "I can do it myself."

"Of course you can."

"What did the snake look like?" asked Cookie.

"I only got a glimpse of it, but he had a brownish tinge with spots," she replied, cringing as Gibb rolled down his sock. The wound was swollen, a red circle with two holes that had bruising all around. "Do you know what kind of snake it might have been?"

The cook stooped to examine the wound. "A bloody poisonous one—mayhap an adder of sorts."

Isabella moved to her basket and started sorting through her vials of herbs and essences. "We'll need to make a poultice to draw out the venom."

Cookie removed the lid from his pail and pulled out two leeches. "This pair ought to do the job."

"Not bloody leeches!" grumbled the captain, wiping his brow with the back of his sleeve. "Damnation, it is hot in here."

Cookie paid him no mind and put the two bloodsuckers on either side of the wound, bringing a wince from the patient. "They're tried and true, Cap'n. The best thing I ken for snakebites."

Though Isabella had never used leeches, she'd read about their use by physicians through the ages, and by the size of them, she imagined they'd draw out the poison for certain. She also set to mixing a poultice with a small mortar and pestle. "I have some violets and whey for fever," she said.

Gibb's face had turned green. "I'm not about to succumb to fever."

"Are you nauseated?" she asked, hastening to the washstand and fetching the bowl.

"I'm ready to fend off an army of Napoleon's—"

Thank goodness she didn't listen, arriving at Gibb's side with the bowl just in time for him to take it from her and lose whatever remained of his breakfast.

"Bless it, woman, you needn't linger and endure this misery," the man barked between heaves.

Cookie gave her a nudge. "We'd best give him some dwale."

"I beg your pardon?" she whispered.

With his two-fingered hand, the cook held up a small bottle. "This is pure magician's tonic, handed down through my family for centuries. Came from a cleric who worked under the Bishop of St. Andrews. The cap'n will be sleeping like a bairn within an hour, mark me."

"Stop speaking as if I canna hear you. I tell ye now, I'll be making the rounds within the hour. I—"

The cook removed the bowl from the captain's grasp and shoved a spoon of dwale into his mouth.

"Ppfh!" Gibb spat. "What the blazes is in that ghastly concoction?"

"A wee bit of lettuce, vinegar, bryony root, and bile." Cookie cupped his hand over his mouth and leaned toward Isabella. "Dunna tell him about the opium, henbane, and hemlock."

"What?" she whispered. "You'll kill him!"

The cook slipped the bowl into the corridor and closed the door. "This contains only small quantities of the latter. Trust me. I make the brew meself."

Isabella returned to her mortar and pestle, mixing with vigor. "Dear Lord in heaven," she mumbled. "Please let no harm come to our captain."

"Amen," Cookie replied. "What's in your poultice, lassie?"

She swirled the goo. "Honey, vinegar, and feverfew."

"Ye ought to add a bit of gunpowder and the yellow of an egg. It'll draw out the poison for certain."

"I'm afraid that the *Lady's Journal of Home Remedies* makes no mention of gunpowder."

"That's because whoever wrote that book most likely spent their days in a drawing room and never set foot on a battlefield."

"But gunpowder seems so...so...so..."

"Cookie kens what 'e's on aboot," Gibb slurred, his head lolling.

"As soon as those leeches fall off, I'll make certain he's in his rack afore I go." The cook tossed a bit of black powder into her poultice and then dug in his blood-covered box, pulled out an egg and a bowl, and proceeded to separate the egg and add a yolk, then topped it off with a splash of whisky.

Isabella sighed. Perhaps she ought to listen to Cookie. After all, he'd tended wounded soldiers, and, as far as she knew, they'd managed to heal. When compared to her book-learned healing arts, she hadn't much to argue with. At least she'd tolerate the gunpowder and egg this once, but if Gibb showed any signs of infection, she vowed to never let the cook inside the captain's cabin again.

# 27

Cookie's dwale was as potent as Isabella had feared. Gibb slept like the dead in an unrousable slumber. Though he most likely needed the sleep, he had told her that he rarely ever slept more than a few hours every night.

While he remained ill, she vowed to stay by his side, especially now that he didn't have a bevy of men lined up to play healer. Cookie had been ready to sit up with the captain during the night, as had Mr. MacLean and Duncan. But on that she remained unmovable, insisting that he had been bitten when they were out searching for Marcus' home, and thus she was responsible. Her excuse may have been a bit weak, but she couldn't face those men and tell them she was madly in love with the captain and would be cast into utter melancholy if he were to perish...and the only person she trusted to see to his care was herself.

As the night progressed, his skin grew warm to the touch and Isabella maintained a ritual of applying cool cloths. Every so often she checked the captain's wound. The redness and swelling had spread, making one calf nearly double the size of the other. She carefully removed the bandage and cleaned it with a vinegar and water solution, as directed by the *Lady's Journal of Home Remedies.* She opted to apply the honey poultice without the gunpowder this time, and she didn't have an egg even if she wanted to use one, which she did not.

Perhaps Cookie's remedies were tried and true, but Isabella didn't know that for certain, and when she pulled Duncan aside to ask the lad what he'd witnessed aboard ship, the lad confided that some things worked and other things didn't seem to be effective.

She kept herself busy for the most part, but sometime after the clock struck three, her strength waned. She pulled a chair over and sat by the bed, running her fingers through Gibb's hair. "I know you were right. You'll be dancing a reel in no time. Perhaps not by morning, but I'll wager a man like you will be up and about well before anyone else in your circumstances would have been."

Of course, the captain didn't respond. He lay on his back, his arms folded atop the bedclothes, looking peaceful.

"You know..." she ventured, since he most definitely could not hear her. "I've given it some thought and did not lie to you when I said that I have no regrets.

"Of course, I would prefer to have fallen in love with a man who wanted to marry me, but I'll take what I can." She grazed her teeth over her lip. Undoubtedly, it would be convenient if Gibb wished to marry her. But she couldn't deny that before she'd met the captain—and before her father arranged her marriage—she had embraced spinsterhood.

Now that she had lain with Gibb, she was in grave danger of conceiving a child. Somehow the words "grave danger" didn't frighten her in the slightest. Warmth spread across her skin.

"I suppose if I were to get with child by you, I might return to Georgia. The estate there is quite remote—a good place for a woman to hide her condition whilst in confinement." She leaned forward and kissed his forehead. "Not to worry, I shall not burden you with any responsibility. Besides, I have waited a very long time to fall in love, and I am now wealthy enough to manage my affairs in any way I please."

Her imagination ran the gamut as she pictured herself with a babe in arms. A week ago, she wouldn't have dreamed such a thing. But, as she considered it, she realized that could become a mother on her own terms—as long as she kept the child a secret. And she was well aware there were dozens, if not hundreds, of secrets roaming about England.

~

GIBB COULDN'T QUITE OPEN his eyes for the mounds of wool that seemed to be packed inside his skull. He shifted his legs and grunted as hot, searing pain darted from his ankle all the way to his ballocks.

*Bloody hellfire and brimstone, have I been shot?*

He flexed his toes, only to be met with another blast of pain. And then he remembered the snakebite.

A cloth was removed from his forehead, bringing with it a cool waft of air and followed by a cooler cloth.

"Are you awake?" a woman whispered. A soft hand touched his cheek. "Your fever seems to have subsided."

"Isabella?" he asked, partially opening his eyes and squinting against the pounding in his head.

"I am here. How do you feel?"

"As if I've been bludgeoned by one of Cookie's remedies."

"I believe the concoction he calls dwale ought to be outlawed. I had to feel for your pulse several times last eve." She doused the cloth in the bowl and wrung it out. "I imagine the wound will ail you for some time. 'Tis very swollen."

She was most likely right, but he would never admit to it.

"Are you thirsty?"

He nodded, his head clearing a wee bit. "Parched." He watched her skirts flutter as she moved to the table and poured from a ewer. "What is the time?"

"'Tis nearly half past ten."

Gibb pushed up onto his elbows, the motion bringing on a bout of relentless pounding. "Bloody hell, why did ye not wake me?"

"I'm afraid doing so would have been impossible. You were under the effects of Cookie's dwale, remember?" She handed him the cup. "Drink."

"What is it?"

"Water."

"Not ale?"

"No, not yet."

Gibb grumbled under his breath, but he guzzled the water as if he'd been stranded in the desert for days. "I was thirstier than I thought." He returned the cup. "What do you recommend for an ache of the head?"

"I've made you a tea—willow bark for your head and feverfew to help with the swelling in your leg."

"Verra well," he said, swinging his legs over the side of the bed, only to have to balance himself by pushing his palms into the mattress. He'd be fine. He just needed a moment to clear his head. "Bring the brew out to the deck, if you would please."

Isabella turned with a mug in hand. "Exactly what do you think you are doing?"

"Taking command of my ship, of course."

"Mr. MacLean has already done your rounds. He has also taken the men ashore to work on the excavation." She set the mug on the table and prodded his shoulder with the tip of her finger. "You are to remain abed and recover from nearly succumbing to a snakebite."

"Och, I nearly succumbed to Cookie's dwale, is all."

Truth be told, it was good to know that Archie had taken charge. After all, the quartermaster was second-in-command. And though Gibb would usually don his kilt and head for the helm no matter how poorly he felt, he let Isabella push him back to bed, but not without capturing that prodding finger and giving the back of her hand a kiss. "Verra well. With a healer as bonny as you in my bed, I reckon a holiday is permissible."

Her smile faded as she tried to pull her hand away. "I am not in your bed, sir."

He tugged her onto his lap. "Well, that's a calamity that must be remedied."

"Gibb!" she said, but he silenced her with a kiss, which she accepted with a lovely sigh. "What about your leg? It is awfully swollen."

"Then we'd best stay abed, had we not?"

She thrust her finger into his chest. "*You* are to stay in bed."

He took the offending finger and kissed it. "I'll not listen to another word until you agree to stay in this bed with me."

She reached for the mug. "Will you promise to be a good patient if I agree?"

He took the tea and guzzled it. "I'm at your command."

"And you're truly feeling well enough to..." She glanced to the mattress. "You know."

"There's nothing in all of Christendom with more healing powers than making love." He nuzzled into her neck. "See? I'm already ten times better than I was when I first opened my eyes."

"Well then, I'll bolt the door."

AFTER TURNING THE LOCK, Isabella slowly sauntered toward the man who sat on the bed wearing only a shirt, his legs and feet bare. She wasn't entirely certain that she ought to lie with Gibb, but if doing so would give him the rest he needed, then she could not argue against it. "You must promise that you will not overtax yourself."

One corner of his mouth turned up, as if he'd never taxed himself in all his days, and he beckoned her to him. "You have my word."

"And you'll not try to walk if it pains you too much?"

He patted the mattress. "Clearly I'm no' walking, lass."

As she stepped between his knees, she smoothed her hands over his shoulders. "I believe there's nothing in the *Lady's Journal of Home Remedies* about the healing powers of affection."

Gibb slid his hands around her waist and gripped her buttocks, tugging her against his erect member. "Then it must have been written by an old crone."

With his hands, he rendered her powerless to turn away. "Perhaps." Melting into his arms, she closed her eyes and savored him. And when he captured her mouth, she went boneless, scarcely able to support her weight.

He pressed one hand into the small of her back while untying the laces of her day dress and easing the gown from her shoulders. "I want to see you bare."

Isabella shuddered as she tugged his shirt over his head. The insides of her thighs quivered while her remaining pieces of clothing dropped to the floor. When all that remained were her stockings and garters, he grinned, slowly lowering himself to his knees. "This is my favorite part."

She threaded her fingers through his thick, tawny hair. "But you should be abed, sir."

"In a moment, when you are there with me." He brushed his thumb through the curls at her apex. "But first I must sample the most intoxicating scent in all the world." He tugged one garter bow. "And I can breathe in your fragrance whilst I unmask the most perfect, shapeliest legs I've ever seen in all my days."

Isabella tugged up on his shoulders, but he caught her fingers and kissed them. "One more garter, *mo leannan*."

As he removed the second stocking, he drew in a deep breath, then took her hands, slowly stood, and raked his gaze along her naked body. "Do you have your journal?"

"Yes. It is on your writing table."

"Read to me the passage you uncovered. The sensual one that you did not want me to read aloud." Isabella bent to retrieve her shift, but he caught her by the arm. "I want to savor your beauty. Release your hairpins and fetch it, will you, please?"

Isabella let her hair down and then slowly crossed the floor. Never in all her days had she walked across a room completely nude, her tresses sweeping across her buttocks. It was so very erotic knowing his eyes were focused on her—to know that she possessed the power to ignite his passion.

She picked up the journal and turned to the passage.

"Bring it here, lass," he said, sliding onto the bed. "I want you beside me."

Though the shy person inside her yearned to dash across the floor, slip under the bedclothes, and pull them up to her chin, she did not. Holding her head high, she went to him, swaying her hips and pushing her hair behind her shoulders. And her brazenness didn't go unnoticed. Desire flooded through her, as she was ever so aware of his watching her every move —his eyes dark, his lips parted, welcoming her as she slid next to him.

Isabella cleared her throat and read aloud. "*My hand is my only solace, but as I stroke myself in the dark hours of night and release my seed, I am only left with a void in my heart. Nothing will ever replace you or the love I feel for you. I love you when you're walking through the gardens. I love you when you are in the fields. I adore you when you are in my bed with your legs around my back as I thrust deep inside you. That's where I want to be—inside you and only you forever.*"

As she closed the journal, she didn't look Gibb in the eye, even though the heat from his smoldering gaze was enough to set her flesh afire.

"Inside you...that is where I wish to be," he whispered, his voice deep and full of want, igniting a ravening fire deep inside her.

Unable to resist touching him, Isabella set the

book aside and slipped her hand over the mat of blond curls on his chest, swirling her fingers down to the trail of hair running from his navel to the tight curls above his swollen manhood.

But she didn't touch it—not yet. Leaning back, she placed a finger in the center of his chest as she drew in a hiss. "I want to ravish you."

He growled—a low, feral moan that told her how much he liked her idea.

She shifted her finger to his navel, then kissed him there, swirling her tongue inside the tight button.

Again, he let loose a savage moan—a sound that thrummed through her body as if he'd touched her between the legs. "I'll come undone if you keep teasing me like that."

Drawing out the moment, she slowly moved her tongue lower and chuckled. "I do not believe Captain Gibb MacGalloway ever completely loses control," she said breathlessly.

When she wrapped her fingers around his manhood, his eyes rolled back and his knees flexed. "My God."

She could scarcely inhale as she smoothed her hand along the velvety shaft. "Can I kiss it as you did to me?"

Gibb's thighs shuddered as he looked into her eyes. "Would you?"

Isabella grinned as she licked him and watched his euphoric reaction.

"Ye ken ye dunna need to take me into your mouth," he whispered, rubbing a hand across her back.

"But I want to." Isabella stroked him as she imagined Marcus did to himself. "It is so soft and beautiful."

*Take him into my mouth.* Oh, yes, she must taste all of him. Tentatively, she slid her lips over him.

"Mm," Gibb moaned, his hips swirling, his movement like a bellows to the flame in her belly while she took him deeper. "Aye, lass, that feels nearly as good as being inside you."

Emboldened by his encouragement, Isabella swirled her tongue around and around, suckling him as he had done to her. His breathing grew labored, his moans more frequent, as he shuddered in concert with her licks, his every sound making the desire deep inside her ratchet upward.

Gibb urged her upward. "I can wait no longer. I must be inside you."

"But you'll overtax yourself."

"Never."

Isabella chewed the corner of her lip. "Is it possible for me to be on top?" she asked.

"Yes. You on top, you from behind, you beneath, you standing against the wall. I want you in any position you desire. I am yours to command."

Isabella loved his idea. She had taken charge of her life, but here in bed she had never dreamed that she would be able to take charge of a man—and not just any man. The fearless captain of the *Prosperity* slid down the mattress and lay prostrate for her.

"Though the wall sounds delightfully scandalous, given your leg, I am quite certain that position is presently out of the question. In my opinion, you will be far less taxed if we make love with me on top." She slid over him and, rocking her hips, rubbed her wetness along his length. "Show me," she managed to say while he slid his thumb over her sex and then slid a finger inside.

"Och, lass, you are ripe for me." Grasping her hips,

Gibb shifted his member to her entrance. "Are ye certain ye want this?"

Frantic for him, she responded by grasping his shoulders and lowering herself over him until he filled her. Looking him in the eyes, she rocked her hips. "I am."

Gibb thrust deeper, the ecstasy written on his face while together they rode the wave of passion. As her need mounted, Isabella dropped forward, rocking her hips while he commanded the tempo, gripping her buttocks.

Ripples of unfettered desire quaked through her body while, faster and faster, she thrust her hips in a frenzied motion.

"I'm coming," he said, bucking into her, sinking so deep that she cried out with the most thrilling passion she'd ever felt in her life. It took but one more thrust of her hips, and her world shattered into ripples of euphoria.

Perspiring as if she had run a race, Isabella collapsed atop his chest.

Gibb softly swirled his hands around her bottom and up her back. "I kent ye were a wildcat the day I found you reading on the park bench."

Isabella chuckled but said nothing as she nuzzled into his neck. Yes, she'd thought him a rake at the time. What did she think of him now? A bit of a rogue, for certain, but so much more. A kindhearted man who would make a good father if he gave marriage a chance.

She sighed and kissed him, still convinced that if she conceived, she would go to Lockhart and birth her babe. No, she wouldn't shackle him with the responsibility of a child.

# 28

They managed to spend three glorious days in each other's arms. For the first time in his life, Gibb was happy to let Archie head out every morning, taking the crew ashore for the excavation of the statue of Mars. Once they were gone, Isabella locked the door to his cabin, and they spent every moment exploring each other. He loved learning what made her squirm, what made her purr, and what sent her over the edge of ecstasy.

Of course, every moment wasn't entirely filled with passion. This morning, Isabella changed the dressing on his leg, as she did daily. It was also a novelty for Gibb to lie still and enjoy her ministrations as he did now, lying on his stomach, his arms surrounding his pillow.

"I do believe the swelling has gone down," she said, applying her poultice.

"I'm glad of it." Gibb glanced back and watched as she wound a fresh bandage over the wound. "I believe it is time for us to take a stroll about the deck."

Her hands paused for a moment before she nodded. "Very well. I'll fetch my pelisse."

"Is there a chill?" he asked, looking toward the windows at the overcast skies.

"A bit—it is awfully windy as well. At least we are not in England. There is often snow in West Sussex on the first day of December."

"Aye, and Scotland is worse. Especially in the mountains up at the lodge. Martin and I once were snowed in up there for an entire winter."

"Oh my. Was that before he inherited the title?"

"Aye—when we were lads. Missed a term at university, we did."

After Isabella slipped away to fetch her pelisse, Gibb donned his clothes then took a few strides across the floor to test his injured leg. The movement made him grunt with the sting, but there was no chance he'd let the lassie know how much it still hurt.

He met her in the corridor and offered his elbow. "Have I told you how lovely you look in violet?"

She patted her hand atop the woolen pelisse and graced him with a lovely smile. "I do?"

"Aye."

"Thank you."

Together they walked to the helm, though there was no one manning it, since they were at anchor. Gibb pulled out his spyglass. "I'd like to see the men's progress on the excavation."

"I understand they have moved a great many pounds of dirt."

Gibb found the men in his sights, though it was impossible to see the statue's detail from the deck. He handed her the glass. "I think we ought to conduct an inspection on the morrow."

"You mean to go ashore?" she asked, peering through the glass.

"Aye."

"Is it not too soon?"

"I am walking, am I not? Do not coddle me."

Isabella folded the spyglass and returned it. "I wouldn't dream of it—however, you're not fooling me. I can tell you are in pain."

"It isna all that bad. Besides, I'm no longer in danger of succumbing to the viper's poison. The sooner I resume my duties, the better."

"Beg your pardon, Cap'n," said Gowan, leading Maribel by the hand. "Would ye have a moment for a word?"

Gibb stowed the spyglass in the cupboard behind the helm. "What is on your mind, Mr. Erskine?"

The boatswain cast an enraptured glance toward Isabella's companion. "Well, I've asked Miss Hatch to marry me, and I was wondering if you would be willing to preside over our vows."

Maribel glowed with happiness. "After you've recovered, of course."

Gibb glanced to Isabella, who had turned positively ashen. "It would be an honor," he said, feeling like a damned heel. He should have proposed to the lass before they stepped out. But he couldn't undo what was already done, so he moved his foot forward and gestured to his injured leg. "If I'm well enough to walk the deck, I'm well enough to hold a prayer book. What say you about the morrow?"

As the two lovers exchanged glances, Isabella nudged Gibb's arm. "Is there not a requirement to wait?"

"Not on my ship, nor is there in Scotland."

"Of course, how silly of me—the stories of Gretna Green and all." She smiled at Maribel, though her eyes reflected sadness. "Dearest, my peach silk will be ideal with your coloring, and if you are to be married on the morrow, we must make haste to ensure everything is perfect."

"Then it is settled," Gibb said, scratching his head. Perhaps they should have spent another day locked in his cabin. "I'll pay a visit to Cookie and order something fitting for a celebration."

The two women left as Gowan bowed. "Thank you, sir."

Gibb reaffirmed his congratulations and headed aft. He should have asked the lass to marry him before he bedded her—that was the honorable thing to do, but no, he had put it off for no logical reason he could think of at the moment. Bless it, how was he going to dig himself out of this muddle?

~

AFTER PUSHING ASIDE her own heartbreak, Isabella put on a happy smile and took Maribel into her cabin to ensure everything would be perfect for her dear companion's wedding. She'd never seen the maid so incredibly happy and was glad to be able to provide her with a lovely gown and a silk flower bouquet she pieced together from a few of her bonnets. Isabella even went so far as to offer Gowan employment as her butler once they returned to England, a post that he gratefully accepted.

Only when the lovebirds left her cabin and she was alone did she allow the melancholy to surge forth. She dropped onto her bed and sobbed until sleep mercifully took her disappointment away.

The next day, Isabella stood as witness during the wedding ceremony, but throughout the service she refused to look at Gibb. It wasn't easy to pretend to be happy and gay as she faced the raw truth that the man of her dreams had never once discussed marriage. Yes, she was fully aware of his desire to remain unwed and his outrageous conviction that marriage would only bring him misery. Moreover, she could not deny having made plans to return to Georgia if she were to conceive because of his stubborn abhorrence of the institution of holy matrimony. But seeing the happiness on Gowan and Maribel's faces as they stared into each other's eyes and pledged eternal love was more than Isabella could bear.

Thank heavens the ceremony didn't last long, and in no time a cask of whisky was opened and the music began with the fiddle, drum, and spoons playing, reminding her of a happier time—a time before she'd arrived in Georgia; a time when marrying Gibb MacGalloway wasn't even a possibility.

Since there were only two women aboard, both Maribel and Isabella were kept busy, dancing with what seemed like every sailor on the ship—except for the one she most wanted to dance with. Isabella felt Gibb's eyes on her like boring orbs. She felt as if he could see through her blue muslin gown, her shift, and her stays, drilling straight to her heart. From the few glimpses she'd stolen, he hadn't shifted his gaze away from her, though he hadn't smiled.

Neither had he asked her to dance.

After the crew bade goodnight to the newlyweds and the deck grew quiet, Isabella stood near the bowsprit and stared out to sea. Even though they had found the statue of Mars, it was time to go home. She didn't want to stay here any longer. No matter how much she loved sharing Gibb MacGalloway's bed, she forbade herself from going near his cabin ever again.

She heard his footsteps approach, a bit of a limp tapping the timbers behind.

Isabella should have known he'd come up there. She had hoped he would, but hoped he would not all the same. Their affair had been monumental, and she did not want to forget, but it was time to end it.

"I thought I'd find you here," he said in his alluring Scottish brogue as he moved beside her.

"The wedding was lovely."

Gibb leaned his elbows on the rail. "It was."

"You'll have to find a new boatswain now. Gowan has agreed to be my butler."

"He told me."

"Are you upset that I made him an offer of employment?"

"Nay—he's good at his job, mind you, but he'll be happier if he can lie in his wife's arms every night."

Those words were like a knife thrust into Isabella's heart, and she did her best not to cough out a sob, though a tear streamed down her face.

Gibb took her hand, those rough pads holding her so securely that when she tried to draw away, he didn't let her.

"I have an apology to make."

She wiped away the dratted tear. "Oh?"

"I should have asked you to marry me before we became intimate, and it was my folly not to have done so."

She knew why he had not. Furthermore, she had recounted all his reasons over and over in her mind enough times to drive herself to the brink of madness.

Gibb kneeled and gazed up at her, his face too handsome for words. But she was finished with allowing herself to be ambushed by his beauty. Blast it all, why did she have to be so teary-eyed?

"I must make amends," he said, drawing his hands over his heart. "You are the most engaging woman I have ever met. You are bonny and smart. You care so very much for those around you, and I cannot see myself living without you. Marry me."

Isabella's heart squeezed to the size of a walnut. After Gowan so gallantly proposed to Maribel, did the captain now feel compelled to take pity on her? "H-how can y-you say that when you've told me you are certain you'd be miserable if you ever took a wife?"

"I was a fool, and I dinna ken you as well at the time. Besides, it was my responsibility to take you to America."

Isabella blinked and swiped the tears from her eyes. Never once during all their time together had he mentioned the word love.

*No.*

No, no, no! His proposal did not feel genuine.

"I am sorry, but I cannot marry you because you are already married. You told me your only love is the sea, and I will not share your love with anyone or anything."

Gibb dropped her hand and stood. "Why? Is it because Gowan proposed to Maribel? Am I too late?"

"You don't understand."

He reached for her, but she slipped away from his grasp. "Help me to understand."

Isabella wrung her hands and paced, trying to collect her thoughts. Finally, she faced Gibb and thew out her arms. "You will abandon me. You may not mean to, but you will, and I cannot bear it."

Gibb opened his mouth, but she silenced him by raising her hand. For the first time in all her days, Isabella needed to express her deepest fears—lay them bare to be stomped upon. "My father abandoned me more than once. He was always off fighting some war and never home when I needed him. Moreover, my mother died bringing me into the world, and was not there to give me the love I craved. I married Mr. Schuyler, and we'd barely made it out of the church when he dropped dead. So, yes. I want to be loved for once in my life!"

A deep valley formed between the captain's eyebrows, as it oft did when he contemplated a quandary. "You think I dunna care for you?"

All Isabella managed was a sad shake of her head. "Clearly, you do not understand, and I doubt you ever will."

She was unable to remain there for another minute, and tears flooded her eyes as she ran to her cabin and locked the door. How dare Gibb MacGalloway ask her to marry him out of guilt? His proposal might have been full of pretty prose, but he'd never once uttered the words "I love you," and until he did, he would always love the sea more than he loved her. Now that she had fallen utterly in love with him, she would never be able to share him.

## 29

Gibb attempted to drown himself in a flagon of whisky, but even that didn't take the pain away. Isabella thought he didn't understand?

He understood all too well.

It tore his heart out when the woman had admitted to fearing the one thing that he never wanted to do—abandon her. Taking a wife was something a man must consider with great forethought. However, once he recited his vows, it was his duty to protect her before all else.

*Damnation, I wasn't supposed to fall in love.*

Before the sun rose, he lowered the skiff and rowed himself to the shore, took up his spade, and began digging like a madman.

Why the devil did he hurt so badly? He would endure a thousand snakebites to relieve the miserable aching of his heart. He'd gladly face a pit of snakes only to hear Isabella say she loved him. To feel her in his arms to hold her now and forever more.

*But she thinks I would abandon her.*

*Would I?*

He'd lost so many good men in battle and couldn't

save them. Dear God, what if he lost Isabella? He wouldn't be able to live with himself.

Gibb shoved his spade into the dirt and hit a rock. With violent hacks, he pounded the earth from side to side, gnashing his teeth. His life had always been the sea, and he'd sworn he had no room in his heart for anyone.

Except Duncan. He would die to protect that lad.

When the spade ricocheted against the stone, making his arms rattle clear to his bones, he stopped, panting, leaning his forehead against the wall of the hole. *I would die for Isabella in a heartbeat.*

Gibb had spent his days insulating himself from the happiness of family because he was terrified of losing another person he loved.

And he loved Isabella with every fiber of his being.

With his next blink, an enormous weight lifted from his shoulders, as if he'd suddenly unearthed the reason for his everlasting torment. The reason he rarely slept. His reason to continue living.

It took all his strength to heft the boulder out of the pit, his breath arresting in his chest at something else he had unearthed, a sand-encrusted, cherubic face. With his fingers, he brushed away a bit more dirt, revealing the cherub's pudgy form. It appeared to be cast in lead.

"Why did ye not wait for us, Cap'n?" Archie's voice boomed from above while his face appeared, his hair dripping wet.

Still dazed, Gibb regarded the faces of his men peering into the hole, all dripping with water.

"Did you swim ashore?"

"Aye, on account ye took the skiff."

"Forgive me." Gibb climbed up the ramp the men

had built for easy entry into the excavation. "I had a great deal on my mind."

Duncan dashed past him and clawed at the dirt. "Look what the cap'n unearthed!"

"What did you find?" asked Archie.

Gibb watched as the lad brushed the relief with his fingertips. "I'm not certain, but the design is of ancient Rome for certain."

An hour or so later, the captain and his men had unearthed a lead box about the size of a medieval money chest.

"Put it in the boat, lads."

"Are ye no' going to open it?" asked Archie.

"I think we ought to give that honor to Mrs. Schuyler."

~

THE BOOK in Isabella's fingers slipped when an urgent pounding rattled her cabin door. "Bella!" Gibb boomed, throwing open the door. "We've unearthed a box!"

"A box? Is it Roman?"

"Aye, hewn from lead. It is covered with Roman cherubs wielding whips and bows, whilst riding in chariots pulled by oxen, lions, and wild boars."

Setting aside the book, Isabella quickly stood and brushed out her skirts.

Gibb took her hand and tugged. "The men are hoisting it onto the deck."

"Carefully, I pray."

"Aye, and they have orders not to pry it open until you give your approval."

Isabella snatched her journal and a pencil from

the table, then hastened to follow the captain out the door. "Let us not delay!"

As they stepped out into the sunlight, the first thing that caught her eye was an ornate dark grey box not more than four hands wide and three hands tall. It was secured by ropes on all sides and suspended over the deck by the ship's winch. "Is it heavy?" she asked.

"Aye. That beauty took six men to pull out of the hole at Mars' feet."

"You've already reached the pedestal of his statue?"

He tugged her into the circle of men while Mr. Lyall took charge of the lowering of the chest. "We have."

Duncan was the first to smooth his fingers over the ornate pattern. "Can we open it now, Mrs. Schuyler?"

"I'd like to survey it first."

Gibb pulled the lad away. "Everyone stand back. Give the lady ample room for her inspection."

Isabella opened her journal to an empty page and made rough sketches as she walked around all four sides, stopping to take note of every aspect, from the molded lead to the joins to the places where the frieze had broken away. "It is in surprisingly good condition."

"I canna wait to see what's inside," said Duncan, earning a stern glare from the captain.

Though she wanted to draw the entire box in detail, she took one look at the expectant expressions on every face and closed her journal. "There must be a man at each corner working to remove the lid. Also, when you set it down, do so as if it were the most fragile item you had ever handled in all your days."

Though Duncan was the first to step forward,

Gibb ushered the lad aside and appointed four sturdy seamen to the task.

Isabella held her breath as the lifted the lid off the box, which very well might be a tiny coffin.

"Cor," Duncan said, his voice filled with awe as the lot of them stared down at a complete tablet embedded in what appeared to be a cache of silver Roman coins.

When the boy took a coin and rubbed it between his fingers, the captain pulled him away. "Mrs. Schuyler, please advise how you would like to proceed. This is your find. We will follow your wishes."

Isabella had been around the crew long enough to know their expectations, and she wasn't about to disappoint them, especially since they were the ones who had carried out the work of unearthing this priceless relic. She looked across the anxious faces and smiled. "Of course, I would like the opportunity to inventory the contents of this chest. As you are aware, these tablets are priceless to me—and this one is in pristine condition. Afterward, as the hardworking crew of the *Prosperity*, I will leave it up to your captain to equitably divide the silver among you all." To their sighs of relief, she raised her voice and continued, "Thank you ever so much for your tenacious labor. Each and every one of you deserves to be rewarded!"

When she met Gibb's gaze, he wasn't just smiling; there was something in his expression that she hadn't seen before—something she couldn't put a finger on, but it brought such a surge of longing from the depths of her soul that she could scarcely breathe.

The howls of glee from the crew faded from her consciousness as, completely motionless, they stood across the chest from each other. It was as if Marcus and Flavia were there weaving their destinities together in a tangled plait. And though Isabella tried to tell herself she was being foolish, she could not block her feelings for this man.

Archie touched her arm, and she startled. "Beg your pardon, madam, but I thought you'd want this afore we tote the wee box into your cabin."

She took the tablet, immediately recognizing the handwriting. "Thank you."

"Would you entertain a little help on the translation?" asked Gibb, moving beside her.

Smiling, she inclined her head toward the cabins. "Perhaps one last time."

~

GIBB AND ISABELLA sat side by side at the tiny writing table, deciphering the contents of the pristine wooden tablet. When they were finished, Isabella placed her pointer finger atop her journal and read aloud:

*Flavia, my wife,*

*My heart is overflowing with my love for you. After nine years of wallowing in the fires of hell, you never lost hope in my return. You welcomed me home with open arms, and my heart overflowed with abundant love as I fell into them. Together we have aged, but the years have made us stronger and more resolute. Because of you, Titus has grown into a fine man—a man of whom I am proud. I will love you until I draw my last breath. You are the stars and the sun. You are my reason for living.*

*Your devoted husband,*

*Marcus*

Gibb marveled at how well preserved this tablet was. "I canna believe he made it home alive, and after all those years as a gladiator."

"It is a miracle." Isabella pushed the journal toward him. "Read the translation from the other side."

Gibb cleared his throat. "Verra well."

*My sweet Marcus,*

*I never once gave up hope for your return because I knew you had more strength and honor than that of all the men in the empire combined. You were always my love. You claimed my heart when I had seen but twelve summers, and now I weep the tears of a bereft widow. By the gods, I miss you so very much. I leave this gift to Mars with a prayer for your safe journey through the underworld. Wait for me, darling. I will be with you soon.*

*My love and adoration,*

*Flavia*

Isabella wiped a tear from her eye, her darling nose a wee bit red. "'Tis a happy but bittersweet ending."

"I reckon it is a verra happy ending, lass. Marcus returned home to his lover's arms—a woman whose memory helped him survive and overcome unbearable odds."

As she nodded, he dropped to his knee once again, praying for the words to come. "Isabella, my love, I dunna ever again want to be separated from you. I ken I've said I'm married to the sea, but you must know that when the *Prosperity* sailed away from Savannah, I felt like a part of me died. I pined for you, and I want to you to know that I love you more than the sea, my ship, or anything of this earth. Wherever you are is my home, and I'll say it again, I never want to be parted from you." Gibb's throat started to close, and he kissed the back of her hand, swallowing. "I love you. I have always loved you, and if you want me to give up the sea, then I shall do so gladly. Please, please, please, reconsider my offer and agree to be my wife."

"You love me?" she asked, her voice trembling.

Gibb stood, pulling her with him and wrapping her in his arms. "I love you, and if you want me to climb up to the crow's nest and shout it to all of Spain, I shall do so at once."

She placed her cool fingers on his cheek, her eyes full of wonderment. "That will not be necessary. But are you sure?"

"That I want to marry you?"

Slowly, she nodded.

"Aye, more than anything."

A radiant smile spread across her lovely lips. "Then my answer is yes."

# 30

Throughout the entire cruise from Spain to the Firth of Forth, Isabella and Gibb spent their nights making passionate love and idled away the afternoons planning their future. By their calculations, when they amassed their fortunes, they not only could expand the fleet without the duke's money, but they could purchase a grand Scottish estate. They decided that Isabella would take on the responsibility of finding the perfect house near the waterfront in Leith, while Gibb set to adding two more ships to the fleet—one to ferry cotton and whisky to the continent and one named the *Captain's Lady* for their own private use.

Gibb had warned Isabella that as soon as they moored in the Firth of Forth, it would take but a day before his brother received word, and their presence at Newhailes would be requested.

Of course, he hadn't exaggerated. Together they took the skiff to the beach at the rear of the estate and were met by Gibb's family, who had all congregated in the park, even James, the heir to the Dunscaby dukedom who was one year of age.

Gibb wasted no time explaining how Isabella was

widowed, how they had found each other in Spain, and announced their betrothal. He had also predicted that the news would be met with overwhelming exuberance, and he was right, of course. The dowager duchess was elated to have a wedding to plan. But most unexpectedly, Martin, the duke, immediately wrote to the prince regent, who bestowed a knighthood upon Gibb for valor while in the service of king and country. On Christmas Eve, the regent's letter arrived, apologizing for not knighting him sooner and requesting his presence in London at his earliest convenience, which Gibb decided would definitely not be before they took their vows.

The holiday came and went in a whirlwind. Despite the protests from the dowager duchess, they managed to keep the ceremony small, inviting only close family—and the crew of the *Prosperity*, of course. Isabella also decided it was time to make amends with her father, at least on her terms. She wrote a long letter explaining how she had been widowed. She left out the details of her expedition to Spain and conveniently forgot to mention the treasure they found, as well as the fortune she had inherited. To her joy, Papa did travel to Scotland for the wedding and gave her away in the ceremony that took place in St. Peter's Church near Newhailes, but Gibb insisted that the reception be in the ballroom of the enormous home on the estate Isabella had found overlooking the Port of Leith.

Their new manor was a six-mile carriage ride from the church, and the duke gladly supplied the carriages to ferry all the guests across town. However, the bride and groom led the way in a carriage of their own, happy to be in each other's arms.

"Did you show Duncan his bedchamber?" she asked, kissing her husband's earlobe.

"I did, though he said he'd rather step in as first mate aboard one of our ships."

"Our ships? I like how you say that. Did you tell the lad that he will assume the post of first mate when we take the *Captain's Lady* to London for your official knighting?"

"He'll come along, of course, and step in as first mate if he'd like. But as far as any seafaring goes, I'd rather have him pay attention to his studies."

"He will. Thane tells me the boy is doing quite nicely, and ought to have no problem being accepted to university when the time comes."

"Good, good. If Duncan stays the course, he'll be a captain in no time."

"Just keep reminding him of his potential—that will keep his nose in his books." She gave him a wink. "Besides, I'd like our ward to be here when his brothers and sisters arrive."

Gibb took her cheeks between his warm palms. "Are you—?"

"With child?" she asked.

Gazing into Isabella's eyes, her husband excitedly nodded.

"I don't think so." She nuzzled against his hand. "At least not yet. Are you disappointed?"

"Never. But I am overjoyed at the thought of all the hours we will spend abed conceiving our children." He gently leaned his forehead against hers. "Today you made me the happiest man in all of Christendom, and I dunna believe I'll ever again be disappointed."

He kissed her. So many emotions were imparted by his lips, Isabella was at a loss to name them all, so she settled with love. Never in all her days had she dreamed that she might actually love a man as much as she loved Gibb MacGalloway. "Have you thought about your title? Will you stay with Lord Gibb, or take on Sir Gibb, or still staunchly insist on Captain MacGalloway?"

"Well, *Lady MacGalloway*, considering we have plans for dozens of voyages to uncover ancient relics, I think *captain* suits me most."

"I do as well."

All too soon, the carriage rolled to a stop, and after they alighted, Gibb swept Isabella into his arms.

She threw back her head, her laugh rolling with joy. "What are you doing?"

"Carrying my bride across the threshold. Now close your eyes. I have a surprise for you, lass."

Since Gowan and Maribel had attended the wedding, a lone footman opened the door.

"Are your eyes still closed?" Gibb asked.

When she affirmed it, he carried her into the grand entrance hall, its floor gleaming with white and black checked marble.

"The guests will be arriving soon," Isabella said. "We must form a welcoming queue."

"This willna take but a moment." Gibb's shoes tapped as he crossed diagonally and stopped. "You may open them now."

"My word," she said, her breath catching as her husband set her on her feet. "The statue of Mars! However did you manage to bring him here?"

"After I purchased the *Lady Bella*, Archie took her out on a maiden voyage to Platja de la Devesa, where he finished the excavation."

"Truly?" She ran her fingers over the cool marble. "Did they unearth anything else? More tablets, perchance?"

"Nay, all that they uncovered was the statue leaning against the pillar, as we see it here."

"I still cannot believe something this beautiful was lost to the sands."

"I suppose it happens, just as the villa was lost on your father's estate."

The sound of approaching carriages reminded Isabella that they had a grand celebration to host. "We'd best take our places—is Duncan in the first carriage?"

"Aye, as are the duke and duchess, my mother, and your father. They'll all be joining our receiving line."

Isabella rose and kissed her husband's lips. "I'd have it no other way."

"And then we shall dance."

She squeezed his hand. "I'm a horrible dancer."

"I've always disagreed with you on that." He kissed her again while footsteps resounded outside. "In my arms you will always be as graceful as a swan and as bonny as a sunset on the open sea. I love you now and forever more."

"And I you, Captain."

# AUTHOR'S NOTE

Thank you for reading *The Captain's Heiress*! I have had a great deal of fun writing the first three MacGalloway books and plan to continue to create the stories for this fun Scottish family. Though the characters and places are entirely fictional, I did use the Newhailes property in Musselburgh, Scotland as one of the duke's favorites, and thus many scenes are set there throughout the series. I visited Newhailes with my daughter in 2019. The house was closed at the time because of renovations, but I was able to arrange a tour with the National Trust for Scotland and will be forever grateful to them for allowing me inside.

Another item of note is the town of Lockhart, which I found on an old map of Georgia gold deposits. There was a mine near the village at the time, which did produce small deposits of gold and silver, though it was reported to have flooded frequently. After the Savannah River was dammed in 1951, Lockhart as well as the mine was swallowed up by Clarks Hill Lake just north of Augusta.

I did consult several maps both contemporary and historical when Gibb and Isabella traveled to Spain. Platja de la Garrofera and Platja de la Devesa exist today, however, the statue of Mars and the Roman *ludus* in West Sussex were from my imagination. Also of note: I got the idea for the wooden Roman tablets from those excavated in Vindolanda (Northern England) which the soldiers used to communicate between forts along Hadrian's wall.

The potent elixir of dwale as well as Cookie's snakebite cure of gunpower and egg yolk were items I happened upon through my research (including Isabella's more predictable poultice of honey, vinegar, and feverfew). Also in this story, I frequently mention ship's biscuits, which were the most common fare for sailors throughout the tall ship era and were often referred to as hard tack. I found this recipe to share:

*4 parts flour*
*1 part water*
*Salt to taste*

*Make a dough and roll on a floured surface to ½ inch in thickness. Cut into 2½ x 3 inch squares. Place each square on a baking sheet and poke with a fork. Bake at 250 degrees for an hour until lightly browned.*

*These biscuits are hard like American crackers. Sailors often soaked ship's biscuits in water, coffee, stew, and more.*

P.S. Don't forget the weevils!

Best wishes,

Amy

# THE MACGALLOWAY FAMILY TREE

To view a larger version of this, click here.

# ALSO BY AMY JARECKI

**The MacGalloways**

A Duke by Scot

Her Unconventional Earl

The Captain's Heiress

**The King's Outlaws**

Highland Warlord

Highland Raider

Highland Beast

**Highland Defender**

The Valiant Highlander

The Fearless Highlander

The Highlander's Iron Will

**Highland Force:**

Captured by the Pirate Laird

The Highland Henchman

Beauty and the Barbarian

Return of the Highland Laird

**Guardian of Scotland**

Rise of a Legend

In the Kingdom's Name

The Time Traveler's Destiny

**Highland Dynasty**

Knight in Highland Armor

A Highland Knight's Desire

A Highland Knight to Remember

Highland Knight of Rapture

Highland Knight of Dreams

**Devilish Dukes**

The Duke's Fallen Angel

The Duke's Untamed Desire

**ICE**

Hunt for Evil

Body Shot

Mach One

**Celtic Fire**

Rescued by the Celtic Warrior

Deceived by the Celtic Spy

**Lords of the Highlands series:**

The Highland Duke

The Highland Commander

The Highland Guardian

The Highland Chieftain

The Highland Renegade

The Highland Earl

The Highland Rogue

The Highland Laird

The Chihuahua Affair

Virtue: A Cruise Dancer Romance

Boy Man Chief

Time Warriors

# ABOUT THE AUTHOR

Known for her action-packed, passionate historical romances, Amy Jarecki has received reader and critical praise throughout her writing career. She won the prestigious 2018 RT Reviewers' Choice award for *The Highland Duke* and the 2016 RONE award from InD'tale Magazine for Best Time Travel for her novel *Rise of a Legend*. In addition, she hit Amazon's Top 100 Best-seller List, the Apple, Barnes & Noble, and Bookscan Bestseller lists, in addition to earning the designation as an Amazon All Star Author. Readers also chose her Scottish historical romance, *A Highland Knight's Desire,* as the winning title through Amazon's Kindle Scout Program. Amy holds an MBA from Heriot-Watt University in Edinburgh, Scotland and now resides in Southwest Utah with her husband where she writes immersive historical romances. Learn more on Amy's website. Or sign up to receive Amy's newsletter.

CPSIA information can be obtained
at www.ICGtesting.com
Printed in the USA
LVHW092339220422
717010LV00009B/110

9 781648 391989